HA.

MAGITECH LEGAC БООК 2

CHRIS FOX

CHRIS FOX WRITES LLC

*For Kurt, Paul, Lasse & the rest of the Magitech RPG
development crew.*

THE MAGITECH CHRONICLES

Buckle up, because you're about to enter *The Magitech Chronicles*. If you like *Hatchling*, we have a complete seven-book prequel series with an ending already available.

We're also working on a pen & paper RPG and the Kickstarter went live right around the same time this book came out. You can learn more at magitechchronicles.com or our Magitech Chronicles World Anvil page.

We've got maps, lore, character sheets, and a free set of rules you can use to generate your own character.

I hope you enjoy!

-Chris

PREVIOUSLY ON

You know that annoying feeling when you pick up a sequel and have to make that monumental decision? How well do you remember the previous book in the series? Do you dive right in or do a reread?

I always tell myself I'm going to do the reread, but I can never wait and so I jump right into the latest book. Sometimes I can't always remember what happened, so my solution for my own books is to write a Previously On, delivered just like the recap before most of our favorite TV shows.

Here's what happened in Dying World, told from Jerek's perspective.

Last time on Magitech Legacy...

. . .

Hey there again, uh...you. So, I'm supposed to recap my amazing adventures. Here's the TL;DR version.

My planet blew up, and I got off. Along the way I picked up my dad, my best friend Briff, and a local cybered-up pawn broker named Arcan. He brought along some muscle...a girl named Rava who turned out to be my sister.

I took control of a Great Ship in orbit called the *World of Xal*, run by Guardian, my new magical assistant, apparently. We used the *Word* to save my alma mater. Did I spell that right? What language is that even? Not ancient draconic, though it's close.

Anyway, I saved 17,000 students, plus Highspire, the pyramid where we all attended lectures. They're all in the level 14 cargo bay. The end.

How about we try a longer version that makes me sound much, much cooler? As you're picturing me, try to imagine the sexiest man you've ever met, and that he tripped and fell into a bucket of awesome.

The long version...

. . .

The story began with me picking a magical lock to an armory door, deep inside a derelict dreadnought from the war that marooned my people on the planet Kemet.

It had been locked for ten millennia, and I was hired to solve problems just like that. Most relic hunters fail. Their O_2 runs dry, or they run into lurkers, or their planet tumbles into the sun.

Not me. If I'm good at anything it's staying alive, and I excel at creative solutions. I used flame reading to peer into the past to get the door code, and inside found an armory full of ancient magitech weaponry.

I invoked the mercenaries armament clause, which means I get to keep what I can physically carry, if I can use it. So I put on a suit of the Heka Aten spellarmor, despite being what you might generously call a guy with a slight frame. And by slight I mean hadn't ever held anything heavier than a game controller.

Spoilers, that armor changed my life. I still don't understand the magic, but it accelerated my muscle growth, and quite literally overnight I went from zero to... well, average at least. I can see muscles when I flex in the mirror. But I'm getting ahead of myself.

So I lugged this armor back to my ship, but that ship, the *Remora*, was jacked by lurkers. Let me explain. Lurkers are space pirates. That's not what I grew up believing, mind you. Our holos paint them as canabalistic monsters who will eat your sister and drain your atmo before stripping your ship.

The bastards murdered my crew and my captain, and then brought our ship back to the LZ to steal the loot I'd unlocked for them. That pissed me off pretty badly, as you might imagine. That anger made me push myself and I snuck aboard one of the landing struts before they took off. Heroically snuck, I mean.

How did I breathe, you might ask? Well that's where I started learning how special the armor I'd taken was. I prayed for a helmet, because this armor didn't have one. The armor answered...it literally grew me a helmet, and even fellow eye-twitchy grammar police will agree it was literally.

That helmet had atmo...and I was able to fuel it with my *dream* magic. I survived the trip back to Kemet, and snuck away when the lurkers landed. I carefully reconnoitored. Reconnited? Screw it. Scouted. I carefully scouted the landing site and used my legendarily awesome spellpistol Ariela to take out, like, six guards as I escaped into the surrounding foothills.

The armor made running easy, and I trotted my delighted ass all the way back to civilization. I still had problems, but I was alive. That was the last moment of blissful ignorance, of childhood, that I will ever experience.

As I was cruising home on our tram system the armor casually informed me that a large comet had been thrown at our planet by someone with divine levels of *void* magic. That comet destabilized Kemet's orbit, and the planet began tumbling into the sun.

If you were me, just some average archeologist long on talk and short on experience, still paying off student loans and living at home with your father, how might you react to this information? Who would you tell?

For me the only real option was my mother, who was dating the minister of our world. She was the first girlfriend, basically. Before that, my mother was the headmistress of the Academy, our most prestigious magitech university. She worked there for four years, and the woman who worked there both before and after her was an implacable force of nature named Visala. We'll get to her later.

I took the tram home, and received my father's unwavering support as I rested and prepared to greet the new day with a smile. No. I'm lying. It was a tram wreck. My dad was quite rightly pissed, because I'd taken out a bond. I'd agreed to pay it back from my haul.

Thankfully, I still had the armor, and could in theory sell it to the same guy I'd taken the bond from. Trouble was…I knew how important the armor was. I couldn't just give it up. Arcan needed money though, so I made a choice that will forever haunt me. I sold him Ariela, the spellpistol my father had given me when I graduated. She'd been in the family for a lot of generations, and she was more than just a gun. She was family.

I thought I'd be able to get the money, and buy her

back. Now I'll never have that chance. Again...getting ahead of myself.

First I called my mom to tell her what I'd learned. She already knew about our world coming apart and seemed alarmed that I did too. She told me that if I could reach her she could get me onto a ship before our world disintegrated.

The quakes worsened as I took the tram to her office, and I saw a pillar of rock, buildings, and people ripped out of a neighboring city, then flung up into orbit. That event rippled outward, and caught the tram I was riding. I was hurled into space, but thanks to the armor, I survived and clawed my way back down into orbit.

I raced home to tell my father what was going on. We grabbed my best friend Briff, a dragon hatchling, who was about to be evicted from his dorm at the academy where he'd been squatting for months undetected. Briff spent all his time playing Arena...our biggest sport. It's both a video game and a real life game, and both are amazing fun.

Right up until you learn that your world is tumbling into the sun.

Briff, myself, Arcan, his daughter Rava, and my father all headed back to the place where the lurkers had parked the *Remora*. I was gambling that they hadn't had time to move it, and turns out I was right.

I took out almost all the defenders singlehandedly, including their leader. I said something witty like...

depths, I can't remember. I'm sure it was awesome. Everyone was impressed.

But! There's always a but. I was heroically injured during the fight. My knee was messed up pretty bad, and I woke up in a lot of pain. It turns out there were two people in the brig, both lurkers.

Vee, a no-nonsense artificer with auburn hair, an incredible smile, and a traffic-stopping ass, and her brother Kurz, a quiet soulcatcher...one of their culture's dedicated. Vee used her *life* magic to heal my wounds, making her even hotter in my book.

So we added her and her brother to the crew, and I have no regrets. I am occasionally creeped out at her casual murder vibe, but hey, everyone has flaws. I don't judge.

Anyway, we piloted the *Remora* off Kemet and into orbit. This whole time there was a detail I left out. The armor had been telling me things and supplying me with information, like where the lurkers were when I heroically took them all out.

Well, it turns out the Guardian *was* the ship I'd taken the armor from. And it told me that if I could take the ship back from the Inurans that maybe I could use it to save people on our world.

The who now? So, let's talk about the Inurans. When people say Inurans they really mean the Inuran Consortium, the premier magitech artificers in the sector. And the richest people anywhere. And the people who threw the comet at our planet. &^%$ers.

So, we landed on the *Word of Xal*, and we took it back from those smug bastards. We took them out, and I flushed them like corrupted atmo. It cost us though. We lost Arcan, and he had Ariela on him when he went. They're both a part of the *Word* now, and always will be. I don't know if that's comforting or terrifying.

Anyway, the ship was ours, so I used it to save the Academy I mentioned earlier, along with about seventeen thousand kids. And headmistress Visala, who didn't love me as a student, and loves me even less as the captain of the *Word of Xal*.

Did I mention that part? I had to go through a bunch of badass trials. Real *pew pew* snarky comment FTW kind of stuff. I pulled it off, and saved the things I most loved. I didn't do it alone.

My crew and I are a team now. But we've got a whole new set of problems, which you're about to hear all about.

I left out one tiny detail, which will be very relevant. Remember Visala? She isn't human. I don't know what she is, but she can regenerate instantly, and doesn't appear to age.

Dun dun dun.

INTERLUDE I

Xal'Aran, demon prince and Hound of Xal, rose from his throne along the brow's calcified ridge, inside the deity's massive cranial cavity and carved from the god's bleached bone. He withdrew Narlifex from his scabbard, and rested the falchion's curved blade along his shoulder as he peered down at the purple star blazing below him.

The Mind of Xal pulsed in thought, as it often did. A dreaming mind? Or a god operating on planes of existence Xal'Aran couldn't even conceive?

What does it matter? Narlifex pulsed into his mind. *Our father lives. We did that. He may do with that life as he wills.*

"I don't accept that," he growled back as he strode to the edge of the cliff overlooking the cranial cavity. It hadn't been so very long ago when he'd been Aran, war mage in the Confederate Marines. "I am no one's pawn, nor will I ever agree to turn a horde of rampaging demons on the sector."

Is that what you believe father will someday ask of us? the blade pulsed thoughtfully. Narlifex was growing in intelligence, but the blade was young and still learning the nuances of politics. A morass Aran was all too familiar with.

"Malila already lobbies for it." Aran lowered Narlifex from his shoulder and stared at the blade, the cracks along the upper third still visible along the dark metal. Those were scars the blade had chosen to keep. Useful scars. "She knows we could overwhelm the Confederacy."

"And why don't we?" came a soft feminine voice from the barest hint of shadow that lay beside the throne. The shadow lengthened and grew, then became a purple-skinned woman who was nearly of a height with Xal'Aran.

Xal'Nara wore a form-fitting suit of advanced spellarmor, the last vestige of her time among Ternus's training programs. She hadn't yet donned her helmet, and he still found her new appearance troubling.

A pair of small horns had sprouted from Nara's temples, identical to Malila's. He didn't need to share her bed to see the growing tail either, or the budding wings. Nara was transforming into whatever species her predecessor had been.

Even her weapon, the legendary rifle Shakti, fit the

demon side more than human. The weapon's long black barrel had ended god and mortal alike, and had recently slain Nara's tormentor, a god they'd not thought possible to kill. Aran didn't even like thinking Talifax's name, as if the mere memory could empower the deity. Perhaps it could.

"Are you even listening?" Nara chided as she gave him a playful swat on the shoulder with her free hand. She tucked her ponytail inside her armor, then slid the helmet on with a hiss.

"You asked why I don't rise up and conquer the sector." Aran knew that every other demon prince, excepting Kazon, wanted him to do exactly that. But he also knew that way lay ruin. "The Pantheon was at their strongest when they worked together. They built the Vagrant Fleet, and brought knowledge and life to the galaxy. Every time a single god tries to conquer, they are overwhelmed by every other god, because those gods know their very survival is at stake. If gods know that there's a chance you can become their ally, they are much less likely to launch genocidal invasions."

"Possibly," Nara allowed, turning that mirrored faceplate in his direction. "If we attempt to unify the sector we'd probably succeed. Voria would never allow it. Frit might see reason. Ternus could be cowed with a surgical strike against their leadership."

"And what about Yanthara?" Xal'Aran raised an eyebrow, and offered an amused smirk. "Are you really so eager to be on the other side of a spellcannon from Crewes? He'll side with Voria. So will Bord and Kez."

Nara tensed at the last mention. He'd scored a hit there.

"This isn't just about politics for you," Nara whispered, a hint of the woman he'd first met lurking in that haunted gaze. "This is about what we end up sacrificing."

"Some prices shouldn't be paid." Aran folded his arms, and stared down at the Mind of Xal, once more wondering what the ancient deity was doing. "I believe—"

Xal'Aran trailed off as the Mind seized him. It wasn't the first time his ability as a Hound of Xal had activated unbidden. Any time a significant being tasted of Xal's magic he felt it, but this...this was on another level.

"What is it?" Nara pressed as she moved to join him at the bony cliff. Below them rank upon demonic rank of foot soldiers had begun their morning drills, their brutish calls echoing up the canyons as they flung spells at each other.

"I don't know." Aran peered into the radiance that was Xal's mind, the utterly massive pool of *void* magic pulsing wildly, as it never had before. "Xal feels something. A renewal of an ancient connection. The best way I can put it is that Xal feels as if a long lost limb were suddenly reattached."

Aran closed his eyes, and felt his way along the tendril of *void* linking him to all beings that had ever tasted Xal. This new consciousness was ancient, and far older than he. Older than the *Spellship*, or Shaya.

"It is a vessel," Aran muttered aloud. "The *Word of Xal*. He is powerful and ancient, and awake for the first time in many, many millennia."

Nara stiffened, then wrapped one hand around Shakti's stock, and placed the other along the weapon's barrel. "How do you want to handle this?"

Her tension bled into Aran as well. They both knew why. If Malila got her hands on a powerful enough vessel, then she could invade the Confederacy with or without Aran's help. They needed to get there first.

"Find the *Word of Xal*, and this Captain Jerek," Aran commanded. "And do it quickly. Malila is also a hound. She felt this too. If we do not get there before her she could trigger a sector-wide war."

"Frit's flame readers will already know about it too." Nara shifted uncomfortably, and Aran didn't need to see her face to know how conflicted she was. "I don't want to fight her."

"If you get there first it won't come to that." Aran rested a hand on her shoulder, then pulled her into a fierce hug. "If she arrives first...the very last thing Frit wants is another war. Get there and investigate, and we'll see where we go from there."

"I love you," Nara murmured. She raised a delicate hand to caress his cheek, which drew a smile.

"I love you too." He shook his head and offered a self-deprecating laugh. "We don't make very good demons, do we?"

"Don't we?" Nara purred wickedly. "We get to decide what being a demon means."

And that was the real heart of it. In Xal's day being a demon had meant being a brutal killer, but it had also meant being a dutiful scholar. That latter part had been lost, though they were working to restore it.

"Goddess-speed," he offered, but Nara was already gone.

Aran turned back to the Mind of Xal, and to the hundreds of demonic legions practicing below him. Already they were the finest ground force the sector had ever seen.

If it came to war the sector would be ashes before this was done.

1

The first time I sat down in the *Remora's* captain's chair might have been the proudest moment of my life. The aged drakeskin leather had been bolted around an ancient metal base that had likely graced hundreds of captains before me. It was almost like joining some sort of distinguished brotherhood, in my head at least.

My squad and I had done the impossible. We'd gotten off Kemet, hours before it came apart. We'd woken a Great Ship, and used that ship to save the heart of our culture, along with our best and brightest students.

It had been a pretty good day.

There were costs, of course, and our pilot's haunted face bore the marks. Rava's sunken eyes spoke of long nights, mostly spent with Briff playing Arena as a way to distract herself from her father's fate.

Well, foster father, as it turned out. Arcan had raised her, but Rava and I shared a father.

My dad sat on his hoverchair directly behind Rava, critiquing every motion of the controls. He was trying to force knowledge into her like he'd be dead in an hour, which always worried me given how lethal our line of work was.

"Rava, take us around the remains of that cruiser, then kill thrusters," I ordered as I forced myself to relax into the cracked leather.

Who knew how ancient it was? Millennia old? Older? Drakeskin didn't really age in a controlled climate. If I ever had a minute maybe I'd scry back and look.

My sister's deft touch guided the tiny *Remora* around the looming cruiser, its rusted out hulk long since picked clean by generations of scavs and relic hunters. We came to rest in the vessel's shadow, and our spin perfectly matched theirs, effectively cloaking us from passive scans.

I tapped the comm button on the chair's right arm. "Vee, we need you on the bridge, please."

The viewscreen showed our target, an utterly massive pyramid that had clearly inspired those we'd erected on Kemet. The silvery surface was broken with what appeared to be magical circuitry, and a trickle of light emitted from both the tips and all along the base.

Most of the ship appeared dormant, though here and there sections of runes were still active. Easily a third of the ship, I'd wager. Did it have atmo?

Boots thumped up the catwalk leading into the bridge and Vee emerged a moment later, a grease smudge on one cheek and a pair of goggles on her forehead. Her auburn ponytail was tucked into her environmental armor, which she'd started wearing the moment we'd left the *Word of Xal*. There was no sign of the helmet.

She took one glance at the screen, then gave a knowing nod.

"That's the *Flame of Knowledge*," Vee said as she moved to stand next to my chair, on the tier above the pilot and navigation consoles. "I know little of its current situation. We don't go there. There is no edict, but enough lurkers vanished that the rest of us avoid the hulk. Every five or ten years someone will decide to try their luck. They don't come back."

I nodded patiently, though she'd given me almost exactly the same speech just before we'd taken off.

"Right now I'm more interested in your engineering knowledge." I nodded at the Great Ship, which was even larger than the *Word*. "Is the bridge more likely to be at the tip, or in the very center of the ship, do you think?"

Unfortunately, the Guardian's repository of data lacked schematics for the other Great Ships, which had apparently guarded such information closely during the reign of the dragonflights.

Vee opened her mouth to reply, but the viewscreen rippled, and a familiar blue Q appeared to signify an incoming connection. A moment later the screen shifted to show Minister Ramachan's familiar face, seated behind her familiar Shayawood desk on her flagship, the *Lance of Seket*.

My mother stood behind her, arms folded in clear support. An ambush then. I'd expected a parting message, but hadn't been sure what they'd ask for. They'd given in a little too easily to all my demands for supplies, and for a charter that would allow me to explore the Great Ships unimpeded by any surviving authorities.

"Minister." I offered a warm smile. "Now isn't a great time. We're in lurker patrolled space, and there could be...other players out here as well. What can we do for you?"

I thought I managed very captain-ish, though neither woman seemed impressed. Maybe I needed a beard.

The minister leaned in toward the screen, and fixed me with her 'I'm in charge' stare. "Jerek, your mother assures me that you are the real deal. You can get things done, and the *Word* wasn't a mere fluke. I'm going to be straight with you. The Inurans have us right where they want us. We survived, but the bill is coming due. When their trade moon arrives they'll expect nineteen billion credits in commerce. If we can't provide that within seven days we forfeit the Great Ships as collateral. As the deal was signed before you salvaged the *Word*...we'd legally have to turn him over as well."

That punched me squarely in the gut, and I rose shakily to my feet. That amount of money was...unthinkable. I glanced back up at the screen. "Who could even afford that kind of credits even if we had something to sell them?"

"It's possible," my mother interjected, her icy eyes and joyless expression a testament to how serious the situation was, "that the Inurans themselves might be willing to buy a salvaged Great Ship, though it is far more likely they'll refuse to buy it, then collect them all. If we could get word to Shaya or the Krox, or even the demons of Xal, then perhaps we could find a buyer. That's our problem. Your problem is finding something we can sell."

"I can do that." I nodded, approaching the screen. It was go time, and I had done my homework. "The *Flame of Knowledge* was a galactic library. They deposited all their knowledge there, and scholars from all over the galaxy— and apparently beyond—came to study with the goddess who ruled it. Her name has been erased from history. Magically erased, if the Guardian's account is accurate. If that library still exists...well, I don't know if it will fetch nineteen billion credits, but it's got to be worth a lot."

"Let's hope it's enough. I expect daily reports, though I must warn you there is a chance the Inurans will be magically jamming all missives, in addition to blocking quantum. It wouldn't be the first time they isolated prey." The minister finally relaxed, if only a hair. It was as if speaking the truth aloud freed her somehow. Her shoulders squared under that business suit. "Maker watch over you, Jerek. We're counting on you."

The communication died before I could reply, and the screen resumed the view of the *Flame of Knowledge*, its pyramidal structure slowly rotating in an internal spin that drew hundreds of ancient hulks into her orbit.

"Rava, take us in slow," I instructed. My sister—it was still weird thinking of her that way—still seemed down, but I'd already seen that activity helped keep her mind off things. I had just the thing. "If we encounter any resistance you have permission to use all twelve missiles in the first salvo. End it."

That drew a grin from her. Progress! Rava drummed her fingers along the console as we slowly drifted out from under the cruiser we were using for cover. Our spin made us appear derelict, just another ancient corvette drifting among hundreds of others.

"Good job, kid," my dad growled, the admission making me blink a few times. Damn. My father gave out compliments like he only had three left and they were all spoken for by someone better than your sorry ass.

Those three words meant the sector, and I hoped my sister knew it. She'd earned it.

Our battered hull was right at home, and any passive scans would turn up nothing. Active scans or magical scans were an entirely separate matter.

"Vee," I asked quietly as we passed a gutted destroyer. "Do the lurkers possess much *fire* magic? Do we have to worry about scans?"

She shook her head, and replied in a bare whisper.

"*Fire* is rare. *Air* is common. *Dream* and *life* less so, though it wasn't always so. *Life* used to be the most common of all. We do not possess much in the way of divination magic, though we have repaired many active scanners that could still pierce our defenses."

I returned to the captain's chair and sat heavily. The Heka Aten armor made me feel like a real relic hunter, but real relic hunters died every day. Yesterday's heroics don't buy today any favors.

That was clever. I should write that down, and find a way to work it into conversation with Vee.

The *Remora* drifted closer to the *Flame*, and no lurkers jumped out as we passed a battleship whose main cannon was largely intact. Enough so that I tensed when we passed in front of the barrel, which was larger than our ship.

"Evasive maneuvers!" Rava barked, shattering the silence. She slammed the controls forward, and both feet worked the pedals with a grace I could scarcely believe. She made my father look like an awkward amateur, and he was one of the best.

I scanned the viewscreen, but there was no enemy vessel. No sudden lurker attack.

There was, however, an adult Wyrm that dwarfed the *Remora*, with shining white scales. Her chest suddenly expanded as she sucked in a breath despite the impossibility of such a thing in a vacuum.

Wyrms weren't bothered by little things like physics.

The Wyrm breathed, and a cloud of liquid white plasma washed over the *Remora*'s outer hull. A horrid metallic pinging began as the vile star-stuff ate through the outer layer, and continued through the bulkhead connecting to the bridge.

I slammed a fist down on the comm button. "Prepare for explosive decompression! Briff, get to the aft cannon. Now!" He'd be the only one able to survive the lack of atmo.

I glanced up in time to see a tiny hole sizzle into existence almost exactly above my head. The terrible scream of oxygen rushing through the gap overpowered my yells.

It couldn't get worse, right? Oh, yeah, it could.

A draconic claw the size of a spellrifle punched through the hull, and a slitted eye maneuvered itself over the hole. "Give me the armor, boy, or I will take it from your corpse."

2

I sat in the eye of a terrible maelstrom, atmosphere and the screams of my companions sucked through the hole in the bulkhead. An adult Wyrm lurked on the other side of that hole, and was ready to tear this ship, and me, apart for my Heka Aten armor.

Instinct took over.

Both hands came up and I balled them into fists, then channeled the first spell that leapt to mind. It was the same spell I'd used on Vee when we'd first encountered each other. The spell that I'd trained myself to use when threatened.

I cast the most powerful dream bolt I could, and as the purplish magic flowed from my fist toward that slitted eye, there was just enough time to wish I'd used a void bolt instead. Wyrms were highly resistant to magic, in their adult forms at least.

The magic splashed into the eye and the face disappeared.

My father was already moving. He'd retrieved the patch kit from the wall, and zoomed his hoverchair up to the hole the Wyrm had made. The ragged tear was maybe half a meter across, just shallow enough that the rubberized patch snapped into place over the hole, instantly ending the flow of oxygen.

"Rava, get some distance and hit that thing with everything we have," I panted, my voice visible in the frigid air left in the wake of exposure to the void. I pressed the comm button again. "Briff, you in position?"

"Green!" he rumbled back through the speakers in the chair.

I sagged gratefully into my chair. We could breathe. Literally. "Get a line on that Wyrm, and light her up with everything you've got."

"Missiles away, Captain," Rava barked, all professionalism as her hair floated in the sudden near vacuum. Ice crystals puffed in her breath.

"They're not going to do squat to a critter like that," my father panted. He punched one more clamp into place to set the seal. "We've also lost the crawl space and ducts, and our armor is paper on the top. She knows it too."

"I'm aware," I snapped, then hit the comm button again. "Kurz, are you secure? You have anything that can annoy an adult Wyrm long enough for us to get some distance? Can you throw a ghost at it?"

"Green, Captain," crackled back over the comm, Kurz's cultured voice a marked contrast to his sister. "There is little I can do without a spell matrix or a direct line of sight."

"Understood. Get up to the bridge. If she comes back it will be here," I ordered, then fixed my attention on the viewscreen.

The rear left portion showed the aft camera, which displayed a cloud of finned missiles streaking toward the Wyrm's glittering white form. Her claw came up, and she began to sketch glowing sigils. *Life, water, life.*

"Dammit," I snarled. "She's erecting a ward."

Sure enough a latticework of sigils swirled around her, and formed a cocoon of magic just before the missiles struck. Explosion after explosion wreathed the ward, but while they discolored the magic they did not pierce it.

"Briff!" I roared. "Hit her with the gauss cannon."

"Can do, sir!" Briff roared back.

A streak of white shot from the cannon affixed to the *Remora*'s rear. The hunk of iron punched through the discolored wards, and slammed into the Wyrm's chest.

The blow didn't do much damage beyond tearing a few scales loose, but the sudden momentum hurled the Wyrm into a derelict freighter, which shattered into debris on impact.

"Get us to the *Flame*, Rava!" My hands tightened on the arm of my chair. I felt so powerless. I wished we had a spellcannon, or a matrix, or some way for me to use the little training I had.

The Wyrm spun behind us as we picked up speed. She stopped, then reversed course in our direction. We had a lead, but she was much, much faster than our little corvette. If only we had that spell matrix. Now that I had *void* magic I could probably increase the vessel's top speed by an order of magnitude.

"Keep firing, Briff," I ordered, as I struggled to maintain my calm. "Rava, find us a place to land. I don't care where. Whatever we can reach quickly. This is definitely going to be a race."

The *Remora* rumbled as the gauss rifle kicked again. This time the Wyrm dodged out of the way, though doing so slowed her. At the same time, since we were firing from the aft cannon, it increased our own momentum.

The pyramidal Great Ship dominated the viewscreen now, and it grew ever larger as we closed. The sight of that behemoth smothered conversation in a way even the Wyrm couldn't.

"Estimated time to docking?" I demanded from Rava.

"Uh," she managed as she checked a readout next to the throttle. "Something like twenty-five seconds?"

"Jer," my father asked. "What are we going to do if the dragon follows us inside?"

"We're going to kill it," I delivered with as much confidence as I was able. "Right now we can't fight, because we have no spelldrive or spellcannon. Inside the *Flame* we can debark, and attack as a group. We just need to get into a situation where we can bring numbers to bear. Even a Wyrm will fall back if we make her."

I didn't have any of the confidence I was trying to peddle, but my father nodded, and turned his attention back to the viewscreen.

"Jerek? You watching this?" Briff's voice crackled over the speakers.

I realized he was talking about the Wyrm, who'd come to a complete stop. She was sketching again. *Air, air, air.*

"Oh, crap. Brace yourselves!" I hurriedly buckled my harness, then willed the Heka Aten's helmet to slither over my face.

Just in time.

A bolt of blue-white lightning crackled across the space between the Wyrm and our engines. It happened so quickly that beyond an afterimage I wasn't even certain I'd seen the spell.

The bolt slammed into our engines, which detonated spectacularly. I heard the thruster sheer off the hull, and winced when a fat cloud of dark black smoke rolled onto the bridge from engineering.

"Get those suits sealed!" I roared through my suit's speakers. Oxygen was likely to be an issue shortly, whether or not the dragon tore the hull apart.

The *Flame* grew ever larger on the viewscreen, but we could also see the Wyrm rapidly narrowing the gap. I seized the arms of the chair again as the *Remora* closed with the Great Ship.

"Come on," I murmured. "Just a little bit more."

The gauss cannon kicked again, and a white streak zipped by the Wyrm, forcing her to slow for a moment.

She gave a shriek that somehow echoed through the void, then dove at us with lethal ferocity promised by those fangs.

"Brace yourselves!" Rava yelled.

The *Remora* shot into a cargo bay, and skittered across the rusty deck as we tumbled through stacks of ancient crates. Sparks exploded from Rava's console, and the lights went out as the ship tilted wildly.

There was a moment of weightlessness, then the *Remora* came crashing down on her side. Something broke internally along the keel, and a fresh wave of smoke billowed out of the oxygen scrubbers as the ship finally came to rest.

A giant crack ran through the viewscreen, and I hung limply from my restraints as I struggled to turn enough to see the part that still worked.

"Sound off," I managed weakly, my voice loud in the helmet as I fought for breath.

"Green!" Briff's voice crackled through one speaker.

"Green," Vee said, though she held her head with a groan.

There was no answer from either my father or Rava. I twisted around and caught sight of both. My father lay against the wall, a rivulet of blood running down his forehead.

Rava was slumped against the controls, her eyes closed but no visible sign of injury. At least she was breathing.

"Green," Kurz's voice whispered over the comm from the same speaker Briff's had come from. "There is a hole in the aft cargo wall. May I suggest we rendezvous here, and quickly. Were I the Wyrm, that is where I'd attack."

I unbuckled my harness and tumbled from the chair. I'd fully expected to crash face first into the floor, and surprised myself by landing on my feet. Thank you, armor.

I reached up and pressed the comm button on the chair. "Good plan, Kurz. We're on our way." I released the button and turned to Vee, who had a welt on her temple the size of my knuckle, but nothing worse to show. "Can you get Rava and my father up? Bring them to the cargo hold as soon as you can."

She nodded, so I climbed into the corridor, which was a lot harder to traverse at a ninety-degree angle. Given that, and the odds that we'd soon be fighting a Wyrm, I willed a bit of *void* from my chest into the armor.

The icy magic slid into the armor, which sensed my need and used it to warp the gravity around me. I drifted off the deck, now able to fly through sheer will. Pretty damned amazing, and one depths of a perk for being captain of the *Word*.

By the time I reached the cargo hold, Kurz had set up opposite a two-meter tear in the outer hull. He'd taken up cover behind two of the crates full of food bars that the minister had been willing to part with.

I took cover behind a pair of crates opposite him, and set up my own firing lane with both fists cupped together. I could use my pistol, but from what I could tell the armor packed a greater punch so it seemed like there was no point. I missed Ariela.

Something heavy landed just outside the cargo hold, a titanic boom echoing through the cargo bay. It was followed by a rustling...of wings.

3

I cannot express the terror I experienced in that moment. My team was on the bridge, and an adult Wyrm was approaching my position. The tritanium hull wouldn't even slow her down, and no spell I could cast would do more than annoy her.

"No one has to die, boy," an ancient feminine voice rumbled, the subsonics making my teeth itch. "Come out, and turn over the armor. I will let you live, and if you are very lucky you will manage to repair your ship, and find a way back to the *Word of Xal*. You will have a chance. You are resourceful. Make use of it. If you do not come out, then you have none. I will kill you and your crew. You have no idea how important that armor is to the Maker's children."

I filed that away for later, assuming I survived this.

Vee might have some thoughts on the Maker's children, as she used the deity's name all the time.

I flipped on the suit's external speakers, and mustered my confidence. "The suit won't do you any good, unless you're able to take the trials. The minister has the core and the bridge under lockdown. The armor is worthless. If you come in here we will defend ourselves. I'm sure you're powerful, but so are we. We will go down swinging."

There was probably more I could or should say, but that was the best I could come up with.

Kurz surprised me by approaching the tear in the hull and yelling at the top of his lungs. "You do not speak for the Maker's children, Wyrm. I don't know who you are, but we have kept the faith, and I will use the Maker's own strength against you if you attack. I possess miracles that he has granted me, and I will wield them in his name."

An idle part of my mind, the part that wasn't occupied by thoughts of being eaten, noted that Kurz wasn't that devout. Vee was, but not him. Then it hit me. He must be playing for time. Kurz didn't have any such miracles.

"A fledgling soulcatcher?" The dragon huffed a snort, and light flashed outside the tear in the hull. The plasma jetting from her nostrils, no doubt. It would cook a man instantly. "You would presume to lecture me about the Maker, because you have a covenant with a ship he built? Inura is my grandfather, little human. His blood flows in my veins. Soon, yours will flow in my stomach."

The bad pun reassured me. At least I wasn't the only one bad at trash talking.

"Wait," I yelled, then hesitated as I tried to figure out where I was going with this. I moved closer to the hole, and peered out at the Wyrm, who was staring right back at me. "Let's say I turn over the armor. What do you plan to do with it? What is it the Maker's children want? Because as I understand it the Inuran Consortium are also his children, and they literally blew up my planet. So I'm kind of short on trust. You get it, right?"

Then I ducked back behind cover, though the Wyrm hadn't made any threatening gestures.

"You are a good deal better at negotiation than I'd have expected given your poor marks." The Wyrm took a step closer, and the deck thundered under her clawed foot. "Perhaps you can see reason. I am willing to trade information, if that will convince you to save your own life and the lives of your crew. The Consortium are an abomination, and they will pay for their many crimes. That armor is how we repay them. I can wake the *Word of Xal*, and I can take up—"

The hesitation was brief, but it was enough. There was only one thing being captain of the *Word* would allow you to take up. Ardaki. The legendary staff that the Guardian insisted I must keep secret at any cost.

"—I can take up my spellblade, and avenge my children and my brothers." The Wyrm's voice quavered, with fury or grief, or perhaps both. "I will find them and flay them, and I will create a new core of Outriders, ones who will eclipse their forebears of old. Ones who will remain loyal and steadfast, no matter what is asked of them."

In that instant I finally put together the obvious. I remembered Visala trying to take the staff, and her hand dissolving. She'd shaken it off like a sunburn. She was in control of the academy...which were probably these Outriders she was talking about. She'd even mentioned my poor marks.

"The staff rejected you," I yelled back, knowing that would provoke a reaction, whether I was right or wrong. I glanced behind me, but there was still no sign of Vee or the others. "The *Word of Xal* will as well. I don't require the armor to maintain my connection. Even if you pass the trials I will still be captain. You'll never get the staff."

That last line was a test. I needed confirmation she was who I thought she was. Confirm it she did.

"So you're saying I must kill you." The Wyrm actually managed contrite, though that didn't make me feel any better. I'd pretty much demanded she kill me. I'm brilliant—what can I say? The Wyrm took a thundering step closer. "It's a pity. You have vastly exceeded my expectations given your complete lack of ambition during your senior year. When I take the *Word of Xal* I will command a monument to Inura be created, and I may even mention you on the plaque."

"Kurz," I hissed as I approached the soulcatcher. "Can any of your souls delay her?"

"I don't know," the bearded lurker replied. I could see his face through his faceplate, which wasn't reassuring as it spoke to how thin the ferroglass was. "I will try."

He didn't ask what I'd be doing, which was great as it freed me up to actually do it. I raised a trembling finger and sketched a blazing purple *dream* sigil in the air. It pulled the magic directly from my chest, and a glowing symbol hovered there, waiting.

I'm not very good at hardcasting, but sometimes it's the only way to deliver a spell. In this instance I was casting an illusion, one of the few *dream* could manage without the aid of *air*.

I added another *dream* sigil, and the two fused together to create a high-pitched sound, one that would irritate most living creatures. The irritating shriek echoed out of the *Remora*, into the cargo hold, and then into the corridors branching out from it.

"Was that some sort of sonic attack?" came Visala's amused voice.

At the same instant Kurz lobbed a fist-sized vial filled with a vibrant green gas through the hole. It shattered at the Wyrm's feet, and the cloud quickly rose, then flowed into the Wyrm's ears, nose, and mouth.

Visala gave an annoyed snort, then shook her head. Her eyes closed, and her gums rose up in a snarl, exposing a sea of razored fangs that would make short work of my armor and my very delicate parts.

"A possession? Really?" The Wyrm straightened and

her eyes opened. "That might work on a hatchling, but even a young adult would shrug off such a—"

She trailed off suddenly, though it took me a moment to realize why. A scuttling sound echoed in the darkness, and I realized it was coming from the corridors leading off from the cargo hold.

Every corridor at once. A veritable army of creatures was approaching, skittering through the darkness as they neared the cargo hold. My phantom sound had worked.

I don't know that anyone could have been prepared for the monsters that emerged. Hideous, misshapen lizards scuttled out of the corridors. They had scales, like a drake, but far, far too many limbs. Eight bulbous eyes stared out of a face more at home on a spider than a dragon.

Magic pulsed from the creatures, and gave each an orange glow from all eight terrible orbs. *Fire* magic. It resonated with the magic in my chest, and I knew a sort of kinship I'd only ever felt with other fire mages like my father.

Each drake-thing carried a staff in two of its hands, and every last staff emanated magic, though they varied in form. The first ranks of drake-things spread out, then lobbed a volley of spells from their staves, all aimed at Visala.

Her claw came up, and she cast a ward exactly as she had against the missiles. White wards sprang up in a globe around her, just in time to intercept the fire bolts.

The spells slammed into the ward, which quickly discolored, then began to fade, and finally broke apart. The last few bolts hit Visala, though they did little more than earn a pained grunt.

Visala's answer was much more effective.

The Wyrm inhaled a deep breath, her chest distending, and then she unleashed a wave of gold-white plasma, just as she had at us. The heat washed into the *Remora*'s hold, and I could feel it even through the Heka Aten.

Her magical star-mass enveloped the first few ranks of drake-things, and each offered a shrill inhuman shriek as it was consumed. When the Wyrm's terrible breath passed, only their staves remained, though not all the magical weapons had survived. A few were lumps of gold or silver, melting into pools on the deck.

Many, many more of the drakes flowed into the cargo hold, and sent another wave of fire bolts. This time Visala was too slow with her ward, and fell back with a mighty flap of her wings as she offered a deafening roar that shook the hold.

The spells assailed her like a swarm of wasps, painful though certainly not lethal. Visala erected another ward, then kicked off the deck and leapt toward the blue membrane as an enthusiastic wave of fire bolts discolored, then breached her ward.

The spells continued to pepper her flanks until she disappeared through the membrane and back into space.

"What is that ground bound phrase you use in your

media so much," Kurz asked as he turned a wry smile in my direction. "Out of the frying pan, into the fire?"

"Let's hope the natives are friendly," I prayed aloud. "Enemy of my enemy and all that."

4

I forced a series of calming breaths as I stared out at the approaching army of drake-things. The deck was littered with their charred corpses. Dozens of the things had just been killed.

Would they blame us? Would that even matter? Maybe. Maybe not. Either way it was my responsibility to take the risk. I heard Vee approaching behind me, and the knot in my shoulders eased when I heard the whir of my father's hoverchair behind her. She'd gotten him up.

Rava moved silently behind them, as always. There was no sign of the wound, nor the knot on Vee's lovely face. It really was nice having a *life* mage on board.

"I'm going to go out there," I explained, partly to convince myself. "I'll try to communicate. If I fail and they gun me down, try to stay quiet. If they attack...well, this is only going to end one way."

Then I bravely urinated in my armor. Now, to be fair, the armor is designed to be urinated in. It's a complete filtration system that will deal with any bodily waste, so that you can stay in it permanently if so desired.

I didn't want to die. But there was very little chance of survival. I badly longed for the days when someone else stepped out first, but being captain came with a whole load of responsibilities. This was the most basic.

I slapped the button next to the cargo ramp, and the torn door opened a meter before grinding to a halt as the mechanism caught. It was enough for me to shimmy through, and I climbed to my feet on the other side.

"Jerek," Vee called, and I paused to face her. "See if they have a spelldrive we can use. If you can get your hands on one I could definitely get it mounted. I might need you to use *void* magic to levitate it."

I blinked at her, though she couldn't see it from my helmet. She'd already taken for granted that I would go out, face down the spider things, and come back with the means to fix the ship.

"Uh...I'll see what I can do." Then I turned back to the drakes, and walked slowly toward them.

Picking a path through their dead didn't exactly set up the image I was going for, but it was what I had. I raised both my hands, and ordered my helmet to slither off my face.

The stench of charred drake-thing immediately assaulted me, so badly my eyes stung.

"Hey there," I called in galactic standard. "I don't suppose there's any chance you can understand me?" I needed them to speak before I could identify their language.

A cluster of the things came together and began a strange sort of clacking that bore no resemblance to any language I'd heard of. The creatures argued fiercely, shaking their staves at each other as they struggled to reach a consensus.

Eventually all but one subsided, then that one shambled over in my direction. It tapped a black-hafted staff with eight ruby eyes on the ground in front of me, three times. Then it clacked at me in its language.

I raised an apologetic hand, then whispered under my breath to activate my academy ability, the very one Visala had granted me, ironically. "Universas Veritas."

The creature cocked a head, then spoke in the clacking again. Nothing. My body went cold. Out of every scholar the academy had ever produced, over thousands of years, not one had ever encountered this language?

"I can't understand you." I gave an exaggerated shrug that I hoped the creature recognized.

"Vyrmonic veritak?" the creature demanded. It spoke slowly and loudly, as if to a foreigner lost in a bad neighborhood. "Dotok daska?" It raised the eight-eyed staff and pointed out the way Visala had flown. "Vyrmonic veritak?"

The meaning seemed pretty clear. The words themselves were nearly recognizable. They sounded like ancient draconic, but the words had harder consonants. Linguistic drift happened over time, especially in isolated populations, though I'd been taught consonants softened over time. Of course, that was for humans.

Was this dialect something they'd developed here over centuries of isolation? If so, how the depths was I going to communicate?

"She wasn't with us," I finally said, pointing at the membrane where Visala had fled. Then I pointed back at the *Remora*. "Vyrmonic veritak beat the tar out of my ship. She took out our engines. We can't even fly."

A scaled multi-segmented limb more at home on an insect than either man or Wyrm suddenly swung in my direction. I considered dodging, but any hostile act might get me killed. Instead I closed my eyes and waited.

Something grasped at my side, and my spellpistol was yanked out if its holster. I opened my eyes in time to see the drake-thing drop the sleek black fleet tech into a crudely-stitched satchel, then the creature stabbed a limb at the *Remora*.

"Nok Socio Habuisse?" the creature demanded, the words so close to being understandable, but maddeningly different.

I closed my eyes and considered what he'd said. Habuisse meant companions, and that was pretty close to what I'd heard. He'd pointed at the ship. Was he asking if I had friends?

Odds were high they'd search the ship no matter what we did. If I lied, would they kill my crew? Would they kill me?

"Yes," I said, nodding at the *Remora*. "I do have crew." Then I closed my eyes. This thing was intelligent, and spoke something similar to ancient draconic. If I spoke ancient draconic, could it puzzle out what I was saying? One way to find out. I opened my eyes, and gave a low, slow bow. I switched to draconic. "*Do you understand my speech? I do have companions, but we do not need to involve them.*"

The drake-thing blinked at me. Its mandible things clicked, and it turned to speak to the rest of its brood in the unintelligible clacking they'd first used. There were some excited responses, then the drake-things gradually settled down to watch me.

"You...understand...speech?" the creature said, each word sounded out slowly. It studied me with all eight unnerving eyes.

I nodded slowly. "I understand. I speak old draconic."

"Where...you...from?" the creature chittered. My skin crawled, though I tried to keep it from my expression.

"From the planet Kemet," I explained. "Deep in the system, after a great battle, my people took refuge. Now our world is gone. My people survive on the *Word of Xal*, another Great Ship, like this one."

It was a lot and I knew it, but the mandibles wiggled in what I took for thought. The creature was highly intelligent, a scholar of some sort if the staff was any indication.

"Who...draaaagon?" The creature waved its staff at the membrane that Visala had disappeared to.

"I've never seen the Wyrm before." I kept my tone carefully neutral. It wasn't a lie. Hopefully he chalked anything odd up to communicating in a strange language. "She attacked our ship. She must have been after something we were carrying." Also the truth.

"Why you come...here?" The thing's head cocked at a sharp right angle with the last word, an angle that would have snapped my neck.

Oh, crap.

I came to rob you blind wasn't exactly the way to open a dialogue. I considered the situation, and framed it in a way that didn't paint us as thieves.

"The Inuran Consortium, powerful magitech artificers, are coming to claim the Great Ships. They will come here, and kill all of you." All true. I folded my arms. "I'm hoping to form alliances, and learn who our neighbors are. And, I'm not going to lie, we're trying to raise the money to pay off the Consortium, or stop them through force."

The drake turned without a word and shambled over to its companions. It went on for a while, and the drake who'd spoken to me seemed to be on the losing side.

They were pondering our fate, and if I was right it didn't look good for us. Sometimes I hate being right.

The creature turned back. It snapped up its staff in two clawed appendages, and *fire* magic lanced down the ebony length, until a fire bolt discharged from the tip and streaked into my unprotected face.

5

Flame boiled over my face, into my nostrils, my eyes, and even my ears. The spell was hideously powerful, the magnitude increased beyond what I could manage had I been casting it. I don't know why the relative strength of the mage shooting me in the face mattered at that precise moment, but my mind is a strange place.

The clarity of pain drove the idle thoughts out as I lost vision in both eyes and clattered to the deck. I knew I'd only have a heartbeat to act. Any longer and the drake-thing might hit me again, and I wasn't sure I could survive another spell.

I reached for the *void* in my chest, and poured the magic into the suit. I activated a spell I'd never used, but knew from hours of Arena. I blinked.

Blinking is a short range teleport that will carry

through the Umbral Depths. My already seared skin was instantly covered by frost, and had my eyes not been closed I'd have lost them.

Then I reappeared with a shivering gasp, inside the *Remora*'s cargo bay. I could hear movement around me, and voices, but none of it penetrated the pain, or the darkness. I was blind.

"It's all right, Jerek," Vee murmured into my ear. "Relax into my arms. Breathe. Focus on that and only that."

I did as she asked, and relaxed back against her chest, though I couldn't stop the series of pained grunts bubbling out of me. Every part of my face, neck, and scalp screamed for attention.

An icy white heat flowed into my neck as Vee cradled me to her breast. The soothing light continued up my face and head, until the pain receded to a manageable level.

I finally allowed my eyes to flutter open, terrified that the darkness would still be there. Vee's concerned face stared down at me, those enormous blue eyes drinking in the whole world.

"Jer, what happened out there?" My father zoomed up, his scowl visible over Vee's shoulder.

Vee leaned away and rose quickly to her feet, though I thought I caught a flush in her cheeks. Wishful thinking?

"Prep for combat," I groaned as I forced myself into a sitting position. Regaining my feet took far more effort than I'd expected, but I did it. "The natives are definitely not friendly. I don't know if they blame us for the...oh, my god, my eyebrows?" I patted my scalp. "My hair! It's all gone."

"Focus, Jer!" my dad snapped.

"Right." I ordered my helmet to slither over my face, and waited the three seconds for the HUD to light. Once it had, I peered through the still open doorway I'd left.

Dozens of drake-things were scuttling closer, and staves snapped up when they spied me. I ducked back into cover just in time to avoid a dozen fire bolts, which heated the wall behind me to an angry orange as the metal distended and I ran.

"Fall back into the mess," I ordered, and led the way. I darted from cover, and more fire bolts hit the wall as I rolled past them to safety in the corridor.

The ship's odd angle made movement difficult, but once I'd cleared the drake's line of fire I was able to take my time.

Vee came next, and then Kurz. My father whirred past another few bolts, then Briff made his run.

He took a shot to the wing, which prompted a startled yelp, but the hatchling leapt to safety with a tremendous push from his tail.

"Oww." He rubbed at his wing, though there was no visible damage to the scales. "Now what, Jer?"

"They're going to have to come into the *Remora*'s cargo

hold if they want us," I pointed out. "We're going to do what my dad taught me."

My dad barked a harsh laugh. "You're going to set up a kill zone. Love it." He glided to the side of the corridor and drew his spellpistol, which he cradled with both hands.

I took up a position on the opposite side of the corridor, and the rest of the team did the same. Only Briff was visible, standing in the middle of the corridor with his spellcannon.

The first drake-thing scuttled into the hold, and thankfully its thorax made getting inside difficult. The creature took long moments to clear the hole in the hull, and when it did a pair of awful wings buzzed over its shoulders.

"Fire!" I roared, then poured *void* into both fists. The magic converged into my very first void bolt, and the dark magic lanced into one of the creature's legs, which dissolved wherever the hungry magic touched it.

The creature collapsed, just in time for a volley of spells and bullets to converge on it. Rava's pistol shot took it in the largest eye, and the head rocked back as the creature issued a final pained screech, then collapsed to the deck.

The body was wedged firmly in the hole.

"That might have bought us a moment." I ducked back into cover, and kept both eyes on the doorway. "They're going to have to figure out a way inside. The best

we can do is make them pay for every step. Unless I want
to do something crazy."

"Crazier then this?" Briff asked as he stabbed a clawed
finger at the drake-thing's corpse. "What do you have in
mind, Jer?"

"The Wyrm wants the armor," I pointed out, and
tapped my chest. "If I send her a missive and offer to give
her the armor, then I'll bet dust to scales that she'll come
back and take out these drakes. All we have to do is
survive long enough for her to take care of the bugs."

"What if she loses?" Rava asked. "She took off in an
awful hurry before."

"Good point," I allowed, then rested my head against
the bulkhead. My kingdom for a nap. "Still, every one of
those things she roasts is one we don't have to fight. It will
buy us time at the very least. I'm going to give it a try."

I ordered my helmet to cover my face, then willed *fire*
magic to flow into the HUD. The Heka Aten sensed my
need, and a little red page icon appeared and began to
flash as the missive connected.

INTERLUDE II

Visala lurked in Wyrm form outside the blue membrane leading back into the *Flame of Knowledge*'s cargo hold. She clung to the Great Ship's truly ancient hull, her claws firmly set into the feathersteel.

The prudent thing to do was flee. Not from the swarm of arachnidrakes, a creature she'd not seen in countless millennia. She could incinerate the drakes easily enough with any number of spells. They were young, and easily killed.

No, she'd felt something far, far more powerful. For an instant, just an instant, she'd sensed immense *void* magic. There had been no Fissure, either. She'd have detected that. The deity who'd arrived must be a true god, one who'd mastered translocation.

That terrified her.

Which deity knew about this system? She'd thought this place safe, far from the important happenings. Learning about the survival of the Great Ships had been a shock, and she supposed that it had only been a matter of time before gods began circling like carrion-hawks.

"Excuse me," came a pleasant voice from a meter behind her. "Do you have a moment to answer some questions?"

Visala tensed, and slowly craned her scaled neck around to peer at the speaker's tiny form, no larger than a mortal. She was an Ifrit, her skin smoldering with the magical fire that was the hallmark of her kind. And, like all her kind, she was beautiful, but a common beauty, identical to every other Ifrit. If rumors were true they'd been created using one of the old pattern inducers. What was one doing here?

She suppressed her natural instinct to attack, or even to cajole. What if this was the god who had arrived?

"I may," Visala allowed. She dipped her head respectfully, though it was larger than the Ifrit. "First I would ask your name, and your purpose here."

"My name is Frit," the fire-girl explained. She offered a respectful nod, her hair swimming in the void like tiny flame-eels. "I am the mistress of the Krox, and a war goddess. I've come here because I saw a vision of a Great Ship of flame. One with hidden secrets within. This ship, I think."

Visala's mouth dried, and her forked tongue rolled

about as she sought to make more saliva. She was conversing with a god; of that there could be no doubt. Gods came in all shapes and sizes, and this one had masked her ability. That meant she could be weak, but if so would she really have risked being so brazen?

Even were that not the case there was the matter of the *void* god. That meant at least two had arrived. She did not like how crowded the field was becoming. She was a demigod in her own right, but she was no war god and would prefer to avoid combat unless it came to it.

"Very well," Visala allowed. "I will answer your questions, Frit of the Krox."

"Have you seen any other gods here?" The Ifrit wrung magma hands. "Particularly *void* or *life* gods? I'd prefer to avoid the latter, and speak to the former."

"I did sense a great amount of *void*." Visala peered through the membrane. The arachnidrakes had begun to swarm around the *Remora*, though they hadn't found a way inside the cruiser yet. She turned back to this Frit. "I did not see anything. Whoever, or whatever it was, cloaked itself quickly."

A smile bloomed on the Ifrit's beautiful face. "Thank you. In return I'll offer you a bit of advice. Stay far away from—"

A buzzing gathered before Visala as a missive spell spun into existence. She allowed the connection, and was mildly surprised to realize the spell had been cast by Jerek.

"Uh, hey there, headmistress." Jerek smiled weakly at her. "We're in a bit of trouble. You want the armor? I'm willing to deal, but it has to be quick."

"Tell him," Frit ordered, her voice suddenly weighing more than a million suns, "that you were about to leave, but that an ally will assist him."

"Ahh, of course." Visala nodded at Frit, then turned to the missive. "You will have help against the arachnidrakes, Jerek, and we'll speak of the price later. For now, I must return to the *Word*."

She killed the missive, but the Ifrit had already glided through the membrane. At first Visala assumed that she'd been talking about herself when she said an ally would help, but her slitted eyes widened when a void bolt streaked from the shadows behind the *Remora* and disintegrated a drake.

For an instant, just an instant, Visala had glimpsed a weapon she recognized. Shakti, an artifact used by the most treacherous of Xal's demonic get. Her grandfather had trusted Xal, but Visala had never been able to stomach demons. Any demon.

What were they doing here?

It didn't really matter. There wasn't anything she could to do stop either of these gods. The best thing she could do was retreat, and attempt to fortify her position aboard the *Word*.

The boy was on his own.

6

I had no idea what Visala meant about an ally coming, but I wasn't really in a position to question her. Hopefully she wasn't lying. At the very least I had a name for the ship's natives.

Another arachnidrake forced its way into the cargo hold, and shoved aside the corpse of its brethren. A volley of spells and bullets welcomed the creature, but this one was better prepared.

The air around the arachnidrake thickened like molasses, and the bullets stopped before touching the creature's scarlet scales, glittering wetly like blood. The spells detonated against an invisible ward that sprang into view when tested.

My hand shot up and I began sketching sigils. *Void, void, void.* I didn't cast a void bolt this time. Instead, I plucked one of the fragmentation grenades the minister had so graciously given from my belt, and popped the pin with my free hand.

I finished the spell, and willed it to target the grenade. The small black sphere disappeared from my hand, and appeared directly underneath the drake's thorax. The resulting explosion coated the inside of its ward with a slick oily residue, which churned my stomach. Eww.

Without the mage to sustain it the ward quickly dissipated, and there was a squishy plop as the remains coated the cargo hold's floor and wall.

Vrroof. Vrrrooof.

I cocked my head as I realized the distant sound was coming from outside the *Remora*, from inside the *Flame of Knowledge*. Whatever it was...the magical signature touched a memory I couldn't quite recall. Those were spells being cast. *Void* spells, like the one I'd just used.

"Do any of you feel that?" I called softly through my suit's speakers. "There's someone out there. Looks like Visala may have been as good as her word."

Vrrrrooof. Vroof. Vroof.

"I don't like it." Vee frowned up at the ceiling. "It's powerful, whatever it is. And it won't much like me or Kurz. We're of *life*. It's...of the *void*."

"So am I, and so is the *Word of Xal*," I pointed out, and nodded down at the creature I'd killed with the grenade. "*Void* is a tool, just like *life*. It's just magic. Not morality."

"I'm sorry, I just can't see it that way." Vee shook her head emphatically, and fixed me with a searching look.

"Is that really how you view things? Magic is just magic? What about gods? Do you know what *void* gods have been guilty of? How do you think our people came to this system? Who do you think was hunting us?"

"Sister," Kurz interrupted, his tone soft, but firm. "Now is hardly the time for a theological debate. The captain is right. Magic is a tool. A tool that, in this instance, appears to be used for our benefit." Kurz nodded at the cargo hold door, which he'd positioned himself near.

I moved closer, and risked a look outside. There was no sign of any arachnidrakes, beyond the charred bodies Visala had left. That terrified me, because I didn't think they'd had time to drag away bodies.

The drakes were being ruthlessly culled, one after another, literally removed from existence, their atoms given to the Umbral Depths and whatever dwelt there.

I did spy a few creatures lurking in the corridors leading deeper into the ship, their multifaceted eyes peering at the *Remora*, or at whatever *void* creature had saved us. It sounded as if the spells were coming from directly above us.

"Hello?" I called out through the now wider hole in the *Remora*'s hull. "Hey, there! Thanks for the, ah, assist. Name's Jerek. I was told to expect an ally, but we don't have a whole lot of details."

There were no further spells, but also no answer.

"Jerek?" Vee whispered, which drew my attention to the crew behind me...and the new arrival.

An athletic woman in midnight spellarmor stood between Rava and Briff as if she had every right to be there. She cradled a sniper rifle with a long, thin barrel. Runes ran the length of the weapon, and they glittered with untold power, their complexity far beyond my understanding of the arcane.

"Hey there," the woman's voice echoed cheerfully through the speakers on her suit. "I'm going to take my helmet off, and when I do you might be tempted to say some rude things. Please don't."

She extended a hand and a vertical slit shimmered into existence as she opened a void pocket that appeared to be anchored to her armor. She deposited her rifle into the extra-dimensional space, then reached up with both hands and removed her helmet.

Long, dark hair spilled down the kind of perfect face that would haunt a man long after he'd kissed her. I mean, uh, she was brunette with freckles and I totally wasn't into her.

Also, she was a demon.

Ram's horns curled from her temples, though they were small and appeared newly formed. Her skin was a shade of violet touched with black, though it did nothing to soften her beauty.

A pair of bat-like wings extended over her shoulders, and I noted a tail curled around the feet of her armor. Not exactly the girl next door, though I wish I'd had girls like that next door growing up.

"Maker protect me," Vee whispered, which wouldn't have been a problem, except that her skin began to glow, and a wave of golden magic pulsed outwards.

The instant the light touched the demon-lady her skin began to smolder, and she gritted teeth that would have been at home on any human or Inuran.

"See? This is exactly what I was talking about," the demon woman managed, though the cost in pain was clear. She glared at Vee. "Stop that, or I will stop it for you."

"Vee," I snapped, then willed my helmet to slither off my face. By the time it had, whatever miracle Vee had just performed had ceased, though streams of smoke rose from the demon's skin. "My apologizes. You helped us, and we appreciate that. I haven't caught your name."

The deity glared at Vee for a moment, until Vee glanced away. Only then did she turn to me.

"Nara," she said, then cocked her head as if considering. "Just Nara." She adjusted the leather tie on her ponytail. "I bought us time, but I've seen feral arachnidrakes before. They'll swarm again soon enough, and we need to be gone when they get here."

"You've seen them before?" I raised an eyebrow. I'd read extensively on everything from Shayan to Virkonan lore. No one mentioned anything like this.

"I've seen many things you wouldn't believe." She

replaced her helmet with a hiss. "So what's this about someone telling you to expect me? I'm working alone."

"Ahh...also a long story I guess. We were attacked by a white Wyrm." I peered cautiously out from the cargo hold again, but the eyes in the corridors were gone. "The drakes drove her off, or maybe your arrival did. It would be just like her to try to claim credit for you. So, if she didn't send you, how did you know we were in trouble? And you're here to help, right? I have a feeling that if you aren't we're not going to be more than a light snack for you."

Nara gave a girlish laugh, and shook her helmeted head. "It's amusing to see what people believe about demons. You're supposed to be educated right? An archeologist?"

"That's right." Wow, that came out more defensively than I'd intended.

"Demons," Vee interrupted, her expression thunderous, "are well documented. You bring war and destruction, and corruption. The void can't be trusted. Almost every evil god this sector has ever seen came from the void."

"Oh, you aren't wrong about that," Nara agreed as she retrieved her spellrifle from the void pocket. The pocket snapped soundlessly shut as if it had never existed.

I so needed to learn that spell.

Nara's faceplate went transparent and she met Vee's glare, kilo for kilo. "Nefarius was a terrible goddess, and so was Talifax. I had a hand in putting both down. Xal, on the other hand, was a craftsman and an empire builder. But the void doesn't have a monopoly on corrupt gods. Are you familiar with Krox the deceiver? Don't even get me started on Nebiat."

"I've heard of Krox, but not Nebiat." Unless new gods had been recorded since I'd graduated last semester, which seemed unlikely, then this Nara had been to places and seen things I could only guess at. Who knew how ancient she was. I turned to Vee, then directed the question to Kurz. "Will you please keep an eye on your sister, and make sure she doesn't do anything...rash?"

Kurz paused for a long time, then offered a slight nod. "Of course, Captain. Though I do not think she will do anything now that it is clear we're dealing with an ally."

"So, Nara," I said in an attempt to steer the conversation. "If you weren't sent to help us, what brings you here? I mean, not that I want to look a gift goddess in the mouth, but it seems like an awful coincidence that you arrived precisely when we did."

I climbed out the *Remora*'s door, and back into the *Flame*'s massive cargo bay. Nara followed, then Rava and Briff, my dad, and much later Kurz and Vee. She kept as much distance between her and Nara as possible, and wore a perpetual scowl that did nothing to undermine my attraction.

"That's a delicate question, Jerek." Nara leaned her rifle on her shoulder, then massaged her own neck with her tail. "I was sent to meet with the new captain of the *Word of Xal*. Xal thought his creation lost, and wants to make contact with the current...inhabitants."

"Inhabitants," I countered, "not owners. Are you here to take the ship from us?" I was going to have to give it up anyway, but there was no reason she needed to know that. Though, given what I'd already seen her do, she might already know. She'd clearly researched my past.

"Depths, no." Nara offered another good natured laugh, the kind that made me want to trust her. "We're kind of after the opposite. Other gods are going to come and take the ship, and you're going to need help defending it. We can provide that help, because we have a vested interest in keeping it out of the hands of—"

A hot orange light flared into existence a meter above the deck. I spun to find a literal fire woman. One of the legendary Shayan Ifrit, comprised of flame and magma, with a sea of tiny glowing tendrils of flame for hair. She was beautiful and alien...and looking at Nara like she knew her.

"—Out of the hands of gods like me," the Ifrit growled. She fixed Nara with an imperious stare, one I was grateful not to be on the receiving end of. "You could have sent a missive. We could have worked together."

"We still can. I'm sorry I didn't reach out, but I didn't think I had time." Nara removed her helmet, and offered a cautious smile. "It's good to see you, Frit."

"An Ifrit, named Frit. A literal hot girl." My father,

who'd been quietly hovering behind me until now, snorted a laugh. "Now I have definitely seen it all. The sector is a very strange place. Very pleased to make your acquaintances. I don't suppose you're, ah, in the market... I've got loads of fire resistance so you don't have to worry about—"

"She's taken." Nara's voice had gone suddenly cold, more in keeping with what one would expect from a demon. "And trust me when I say you don't want to meet the hatchling she's dating."

"Wyrm." Frit swelled with pride. "Kaho has undergone his first molting. He's a full Wyrm, and greatly respected on Nebiat."

"I hate that you named your planet that." Nara rolled her eyes.

It was like watching a pair of academy roommates who were catching up after several years apart. Except both were gods. I could feel the strength of them.

"So," I said, risking their wrath, "you said we should get out of here, right, Nara? Before the drakes come back? Maybe the two of you can tell us more about why you're here...while we walk."

"We still need a replacement engine," Vee pointed out as she jerked a thumb at the *Remora*'s battered form. The cruiser had fared better than expected, though she definitely needed time in a dry dock. Not to mention a new engine. And a new cargo bay bulkhead. "If your gods can help us find that I'll put aside my aversion."

"Aversion?" Frit asked, a flaming eyebrow raising in a way that made me very uncomfortable. "Why don't you tell me a little more about this aversion?"

"What she means," Kurz interceded as he stepped in front of his sister, "is that the Maker has specific edicts about dealing with creatures of the void. They aren't without cause. Our planet was, quite literally, destroyed by a *void* goddess named Nefarius, many thousands of years ago. My sister's concession is an honest one. You will receive no trouble from either of us."

Frit seemed like she might respond, but hesitated as something skittered in the corridor. Many somethings. The drakes were returning. From the echoes there had to be hundreds of them. Thousands.

"Time to go," I all but begged. "If either of you have a spell that will help we'd be grateful. If not, then my squad needs to hightail it up another corridor. Now."

7

T aking my next step, the first step away from the *Remora*, was one of the hardest things I'd ever had to do. The *Flame of Knowledge* wasn't like the *Word of Xal*, which had been uninhabited, so far as I could tell.

This Great Ship had an entire developed culture old enough to have evolved their own language. Who knew how much of the ship was occupied? Or by what?

I hurried through the ancient cargo bay, the ceiling disappearing into darkness broken by a few functional lights. My boots crunched oddly as I walked, like I was walking on gravel or sand.

I glanced down to find the deck coated in a coagulated goo that had long since solidified. It reminded me of something an insect would excrete. Were the arachidrakes responsible?

Or something worse.

"Rava, Dad, take point," I ordered as I ventured onto the stuff. It crunched underfoot, and oozed an odor that reminded me of rotten eggs. "Briff, bring up the rear. Vee, Kurz, I want you with me."

Frit and Nara, our odd new benefactors, held back a ways. They conversed in low tones, and I couldn't make out a word of it. Not one. I willed a bit of *fire* into the armor, and activated piercing eyes, a spell I'd learned at the academy, but never had much cause to use until now. It pierced illusions and exposed true natures.

My eyes flared with heat, not enough to be painful, and then the HUD shimmered and showed a projection of an invisible field enveloping Frit and Nara. They'd erected a powerful ward...then cloaked that spell's existence. And I hadn't noticed so much as a single spell being cast.

All sorts of data now scrolled down the screen next to each deity. Projected spells, masteries, vulnerabilities. The suit was building profiles now that I'd identified as the gods worthy of notice.

"Did you do that all on your own?" I murmured, though there was no answer from the armor of course. Not unless I addressed the Guardian directly.

A threat assessment sigil with the number 12 appeared next to Nara. A 34 appeared next to Frit. If that was relative strength, then I knew whose good side I was more worried about staying on. Thankfully both goddesses seemed friendly, though they were still locked in conversation.

"Vee, Kurz," I called in a low voice. Once I had their attention I dropped it even further. "How much do you know about either god? Or gods in general? What do we need to expect? Are we in danger?"

"Extreme danger," Vee shot back immediately as her gaze bored into Nara's back. "They could probably end us with little trouble, but odds are high they wish to make pawns of us. They want something. I'd advise you to find out what it is."

"Kurz?" I asked quietly as I turned to the taller lurker. He still managed unassuming, though now that I knew the power that lay in the vials across his chest I would never underestimate him, or any other soulcatcher, again.

"I concur with my sister." He darted a glance back at the gods, then flicked his gaze back to me. "They are beyond dangerous. Their presence will not go undetected by the denizens of this ship. Anything powerful knows they are here. If they take offense we could get caught in their squabble. It does not end well for mortals who tarry around gods."

I nodded slowly and considered how to extricate ourselves. The gods could be reasoned with, it seemed. I'd start with that.

"Follow Rava," I ordered, and slowed my pace a bit. "I'll speak to them, and see if I can learn why they're here."

"Don't you want me to watch your back?" Vee's eyes narrowed to slits as she watched Nara. "I don't trust her motives."

"My goal is learning those motives," I pointed out, then offered a smile. "I'd like to do that without offending her. Let me see what I can learn. Keep an eye on me, but do it from twenty meters out."

Vee offered a grudging nod, then followed Kurz as he approached Rava and my father at the front of our little caravan. They lurked just outside the corridor leading deeper into the ship, and what little I could see had been coated with the same secretion, with the same rotten stench.

I waited until Nara and Frit approached, then fell in beside them. After consideration I willed my helmet to slither off my face. I wanted them to be able to look me in the eye. The heat rolling off Frit would have caused me to take a step back had I not possessed *fire* magic myself. Hopefully she sensed that kinship.

"Thank you for the rescue back there." I smiled at Nara as the demon-goddess picked a path across the strange sediment. Only then did I notice that her feet never actually touched the deck. No wonder she was so silent. "Now that we're clear we can talk. You said you were looking for the captain of the *Word of Xal*. That's me. How can I help you?"

Frit raised a flaming eyebrow and fixed Nara with a reproving glare. "Yes, Nara, how can he help you?"

"The same way he can help you I imagine." She removed her own helmet, and deposited it in her void pocket next to her rifle. "Aran is hoping to acquire the *Word of Xal,* though he's not trying to displace the crew, or take it away from anyone. He wants an ally, if possible. Now that we know there is at least one other ship, the pantheon will scramble to acquire them. We want a seat at the table, at the very least."

I blinked a few times. We needed money. Badly. Nineteen billion credits badly. I licked my lips, and asked a question that made my heart thunder, and I did it like I was asking the weather, so they didn't sense my desperation. "Were we willing to sell you a functional Great Ship like the *Word of Xal*, what kind of purchase price would you consider fair? We would conduct an auction, of course, but our leadership might be amicable to selling at least one ship. Perhaps all of them."

"Including the *Word*?" Nara asked, her eyes glittering like hard chips of obsidian. "Are you willing to forfeit your bond, and turn over that armor so we can assume control?"

"Yes to the first," I agreed, then shook my head. "No to the second. We have another set of Heka Aten spellarmor. If you need a set our minister would be willing to include it in the purchase price, I'm sure. We'd be looking for something in say, the twenty-five billion credit range. That would scale based on the vessel of course, and some could be, ah, much more expensive."

Both women nodded as if what I'd said was fair and reasonable. Frit spoke first. She licked flaming lips, perfectly shaped to mimic a Shayan. "That can be done, assuming payment can be made through a combination of scales and magical materials."

"Xal can offer much more of the latter," Nara broke in. "Though if need be I imagine we could produce enough scales. We just finalized a trade deal with Virkon."

Mind. Blown. I was brokering a deal between gods.

"It won't be up to me, of course. The minister would be brokering the deal." I wasn't really sure where to take things, so I started up the corridor to buy myself time.

"Of course," the goddesses chorused as they followed me up the corridor. Depths, but this was surreal.

Nara cleared her throat. "Would you mind if we took our leave and withdrew to pursue dealings with this minister?"

"Thank depths. I mean, of course." I offered a low bow. I have no idea why that felt right. Both women eyed me oddly. I straightened. "We should be fine, though we may need repairs for our ship."

"I don't have any such expertise," Frit said, then nodded at Nara. "She doesn't either unless you learned it recently."

"She's right. I don't." Nara pursed her lips and her eyes adopted a faraway look. "I think you'll be fine for now. I will relay your need to the minister. I'd love to help, but both Frit and I need to be very careful here. Everything we do will be scryed and dissected by the Confederacy. Our goal is to avoid a sector-wide war. Direct interference in planetary matters between member factions is a clear violation of the treaty."

The message was clear. We were on our own.

"Thank you again." This time I nodded instead of bowing.

Then, just like that, both women were gone. I could detect no spell use, nor did the armor seem to. Translocation had been described back in my magical theory class, but actually witnessing it...I suddenly felt even smaller than I had.

We were alone on a hostile vessel, and I'd just sent away our best support. Now I needed to find a way to take this ship and keep my people alive in the process.

"Hey, Jerek?" Rava called from up ahead. She'd knelt to inspect a fresh pool of white goo at the base of a wall where the corridor branched. "You need to see this."

I hurried to join her, and knelt beside the strange substance. I had no doubt I was looking at the secretions. A white drip broke the pool near the center, sending a ring of ripples outward.

We all glanced upward, and what we saw will always live in my nightmares.

The white substance dripped from webbing, thick webbing, that had cocooned a large figure. Too large for a human. Just large enough for an arachnidrake. Wings buzzed frantically in the cocoon, but the struggles were already growing weaker.

Thousands upon thousands of tiny black spiders scurried out of the cocoon, moving as one swarm, as if guided by an intelligence. They began to flow down the wall...in our direction.

8

I didn't think. I acted. Both hands came up on instinct, and I poured all the *fire* and all the *void* into my palms that I could. The suit combined them somehow, into voidflame, the most destructive part of both elements.

I was familiar with it, but normally casting voidflame required you to master the greater path of destruction, which I'd had exactly no time to study in the time since I'd gained *void* magic.

My armor didn't seem to care.

A wave of dark flame disintegrated the swarm directly in front of me, and set the webbing aflame. The fire spread quickly, and the spiders skittered back from it.

"Let's move!" I roared, then sprinted up the opposite corridor.

"Where does this lead?" Rava sprinted up, easily overtaking me with her cybered reflexes. Her rifle was cradled easily in both arms, ready to be used, though useless against the spiders.

"Away from the spiders?" I kept running, but risked a glance behind me to make sure everyone was with me.

Briff rumbled along in the rear, his tail swishing behind him as he lumbered up the corridor. There's no way he'd have left anyone behind, and his silhouette comforted me.

I don't know how long we ran. Maybe ten minutes? I didn't think to check my HUD before we'd started, but then I'd been a little busy. I finally halted, long after I could no longer hear the skittering, and began sucking in gigantic lungfuls of stale air. Air that bore an even thicker musk than that we'd detected in the cargo hold.

"Oh, gods," Vee panted as she spun in a slow circle. "We're approaching some sort of nest. We must be. Look at the webbing. It's thicker up along the ceiling."

"But not along the ground," I pointed out, then knelt to show her what I meant. "See this? This corridor must see a lot of traffic, or the spiders would web it. They haven't in a long time, so those webs must not be worth putting up. I don't think you're wrong about us being near some sort of hive. Rava, do you want to range ahead a bit and see if you can find a branching corridor, or a way to another level that isn't crawling?"

Rava gave a nod, then trotted silently off into the darkness. I lost sight of her more quickly than expected, and blinked a few times as the HUD updated her profile. The armor superimposed an outline of a dark metal that coated her entire skeleton, which wasn't unusual for anyone with a cyber harness.

What was unusual was the metrics the armor ascribed to the metal. Magical dampening? Did that make her more resistant to spells? Interesting, and potentially useful information. I'd have to ask her when she got back. I didn't know much about cyberware, or how it functioned.

I turned to the rest of the squad. "Everyone get close, and watch the ground and walls behind us. I want to make sure we detect spiders as far out as possible."

Nods all around, and the group retreated into a compressed knot with all our backs to each other. The dim illumination made every shadow crawl, though when you looked more closely you saw nothing more than a few wayward spiders, nothing like the horde that had followed us.

I tensed when I heard crunching from the direction Rava had come, but eased when my sister came trotting into view, her leathers nearly invisible in the darkness. She came up to our knot, and licked her lips before speaking.

"One corridor is webbed off," she whispered, then darted a glance over her shoulder as if fearing something were behind her. "Something was...aware of me. I can't describe what it was like. But it didn't like me. At all. It wanted me gone. Jerek, what is this place? I thought it was a ship. Why are there spiders, and drakes, and... depths, I don't know what else? It's like we stepped into *Horror Dreadnaught*."

Briff shivered beside me, an odd reaction from a dragon. His wings bunched up close to his back. "I don't like survival games. I don't want to be trapped in one. Jer, how are we going to get off the ship? The *Remora* needs an engine, and we don't know anything about this place."

He wasn't wrong. I didn't have a solution, nor did I have the luxury of time to come up with a plan. We needed to keep moving. Of that I was certain.

"Let's take it one step at a time," I decided aloud. My gaze landed on my father, and I realized I could see the whites of his eyes, like a stallion about to bolt. "This isn't as bad as it appears. This ship is massive. We just need to navigate around the spiders, and find a place where we can catch our breaths. Worst case scenario I could always missive Nara or Frit, but I don't know if they'll come, or if we even want them to. Let's solve this on our own, if we can."

Rava gave a confident nod, and the tension bled from her. She even smiled, and in that moment I saw my father in her. "All right then, I'll get back on point."

We moved out in silence. My little speech seemed to have galvanized people, and I have to admit I liked the way Vee and Kurz were looking at me. There was respect there, and maybe something more from Vee.

We prowled up the corridor Rava had explored, and as promised the webbing thickened, though not to any sort of dangerous level. Dozens of tiny spiders moved on the webs, but again they seemed to lack the directed consciousness we'd seen from the swarm that had killed the arachnidrake.

That raised so many questions, but until I had more data there were no answers.

We finally reached a four-way intersection, and the corridor to our right was completely barred with webbing. Spiders scuttled in and out of the mass, but there was barely enough room for the small ones. At least nothing large could come out of that corridor.

That left three directions to choose from. I nodded at Rava to go straight, and she trotted silently up that corridor. The rest of us followed, and after about a hundred meters the webbing began to thin.

We reached another corridor, where the webbing was thicker. Rava turned to me, and I shook my head no. It wasn't worth risking. We backtracked, and tried another corridor.

The process was exhausting, but two hours later we still hadn't run into a serious threat, and must have covered several kilometers of ground.

"Jerek," Briff called suddenly.

I paused and turned. It wasn't hard to guess what had drawn his attention. We'd passed a narrow doorway shrouded in darkness. Briff disappeared inside.

"Rava, Dad, follow Briff," I ordered. "Vee, Kurz, watch the door please."

We sprang into motion, and I followed my team inside. The doorway spilled into a wide room about thirty meters across. It was broken up by floating tables, with a number of unfamiliar apparatuses on them. Some sort of workshop?

Shelving ran along the back wall, and when I saw what they were covered with I began to salivate. "Those are knowledge scales!"

I sprinted across the room, and skidded to a halt at the base of the closest shelf. There were easily fifty scales on this shelf alone. Priceless, and filled to the brim with ancient knowledge.

"We. Are. RICH!" my father yelled as he pumped a fist in the air. "Every library on Kemet—"

"Kemet no longer exists," Kurz broke in, smothering the mood. I glanced back to find the soulcatcher standing in the doorway. I guess technically he was guarding it, though really that fell on his sister, who still stood outside.

"The money is nice, but it's about more than that," I pointed out. "This is about finding a way off the ship. This room is some sort of workshop. These knowledge scales are probably some sort of reference library for whoever worked here. If we explore them we can learn more about the ship. That may tell us where we can locate an engine, and since this place is on the way back to the *Remora* we'll only take what we want to carry, and come back for the rest."

My father gave a grudging nod, but still zoomed to the far shelf and began pocketing scales. I couldn't blame him. We'd lived in poverty ever since Mom had left, and this was enough wealth to retire on any world in the sector. Maybe for all of us.

Only then did I realize that there was precisely one person in my squad who understood the significance, and I'd asked him to stand guard. "Briff, would you mind trading places with Kurz so he can help me look through these scales?"

"Of course, Jer." He seemed relieved, and squeezed his bulk through the narrow doorway to stand with Vee.

That left me as an untended kid in a candy store. I love knowledge, and there was every possibility these things had been sitting here for ten millennia or more. Who knew what glimpses into the past they would offer?

I approached the shelf and looked for any sort of identifying marks that might tell me which scales were grouped and why. There was nothing.

"Wait," I murmured to myself. "What about the armor?" I grinned. "Guardian, can you hear me?"

Nothing. I waited a few more moments to be sure, but there was no response.

Okay, not the end of the world. I fed a bit of *fire* to the armor and asked it to categorize the scales, just to see what it would make of them.

Each scale adopted a bar directly underneath it, most of those bars nearly filled, though a few were closer to the halfway mark. Was that their capacity for storage?

I reached for the scale on the far left. There was no reason to expect that whoever'd made these organized them the same way we did on Kemet, but in the absence of anything else to try I figured it was worth a shot.

The moment my gauntlet brushed the scale it flared to life, and an illusion of a disembodied female Wyrm head appeared over it. "Ego sum Thekmet. Quomoo protest his mihi ministrant?"

"Oh, thank the Maker." I relaxed, just a hair. Finally something going our way. The language was ancient draconic. Pure, and unaltered, and easy for me to converse in. "*Okay, Thekmet, can you give me a catalog of your relevant contents?*"

The Wyrm's eyes flashed, and lines of scrolling text appeared in the air all around it. They were grouped into dozens of topics. Most seemed centered around a single topic, with an icon to represent the contents.

"You've found something far more interesting than I have." Kurz's voice startled me, and I spun to find him staring at the illusion my knowledge scale had conjured. "I believe we are looking at a resource map."

I blinked a few times as I turned back to the map and tried to find what he meant. It wasn't until I spotted a familiar icon, one corresponding to the Catalyst we called Sanctuary. I looked closely at the other icons, and realized they must all be Catalysts. That was what Kurz meant. Magical resources.

"And this room...." I spun to the tables, filled with apparatuses I didn't recognize. Golden tools in all shapes and sizes, even a boomerang, of all things. "This is an artificing chamber. Magic items were made here. And this *is* a research library...." I spun back to Thekmet. "Can you display the location of every Catalyst in the galaxy?"

A map popped up, and hundreds of dots flared to life all over the Milky Way.

"Well, shit," my father muttered, gaping at the map. "I don't know if that's worth nineteen billion credits, but I bet that will fetch a pretty penny."

I grinned back at Thekmet. Who knew what else the room contained?

9

I rubbed at my eyes, then leaned back against the wall. I'd been sitting for hours, long after the rest of the squad had gone to sleep. The current knowledge scale detailed the geopolitical climate of the day. It broke down the galaxy by the dragonflights that dominated that area, and if it was accurate, then our sector used to be primarily *air, earth,* and *water* Wyrms. That part tracked, as they were more common on Kemet, though all eight were represented.

What had happened to the dragonflights, and why? That part was maddening, because all the knowledge these scales contained took place before the battle that had marooned my ancestors here. There wasn't even a clue as to what had driven them here, and from what I could see there wasn't a force in the galaxy that could have challenged them.

So what had happened? If I could have reached the Guardian, I bet he'd have had a lot to say about it, and now I actually had some context to understand his perspective.

"Are you still at it?" Vee's whisper was quiet, but it made me jump, and the knowledge scale clattered to the floor with a metallic ring, extinguishing the illusion it had been displaying.

Vee moved to join me against the wall, and slid down next to me, her shoulder touching mine. "If you don't sleep, you won't be able to lead us. Exhausted minds make mistakes."

Her scent penetrated the mind fog, and I blinked away all the extraneous thoughts. "You're right. I wish I could say I was up because I can't sleep, but to be honest...nothing like this has been discovered. Ever, to my knowledge. This data doesn't exist in our sector. Not even Shaya or Ternus have it, or Virkon, or any of the others."

"That's a good thing, yes? The treasure map is ours and ours alone." She stifled a yawn with one hand that made the gauntlet on her environmental armor creak. It was ancient, but she seemed to love it.

"Definitely a good thing." I looked up at the ceiling as a distraction. "The question is...nineteen billion credits good? I don't think so. This might make us rich personally, if we can find someone to sell it to who won't kill us and take it. I don't think it solves our problem though. We need something bigger."

"Huh, huh." The words came from Rava's bedroll, a couple meters away. I'd thought she'd been asleep. Rava rolled over with a mischievous smile. "I bet you want to give her—yeah, I got nothing involving 'bigger'. I'm more interested in the 'we get rich' part. This archive. These scales. Can we hold them back and sell them as a crew?"

"That's the plan," I gave back immediately, without thinking. These people were my crew. My family. "If we can make it back to the *Word of Xal*, or all the way to Shaya, then we could probably get rich. I don't like abandoning the fleet though."

"It's not our choice yet," Vee pointed out. She rested a hand on my shoulder. "We have one task. Find a priceless treasure. If we happen upon a spelldrive, or a way to fix the *Remora*, all the better. If not, then you will find another way. That is why you are captain. No one else can, Jerek."

Rava's snort made it clear what she thought of that, which was probably a good thing as otherwise Vee was going to inflate my ego to unmanageable levels.

"I did learn a bit about this ship." I nodded at the numbers rune-etched onto the wall. "Draconic numbers give the range as part of the number. If you have, say, the number 7, out of, say, nine total numbers, it will be spelled 7 of 9. We're on the 409th level...out of twelve hundred."

"Clever." Vee offered a smile that made me wish we were alone. She tucked her ponytail into her armor, then plucked her helmet from against the wall. "We make for the center of the ship then?"

"That seems the best plan." I glanced at the others to find Kurz sleepily packing his bedroll, and Briff standing with a yawn and a stretch of his battle-scarred wings. They made him even more intimidating, though he seemed to have no idea, of course. "If I'm oriented correctly we want to move down the corridor to the left. That will take us to a main access tunnel, which leads to the elevators on this level. From there if we can find a functioning lift maybe we can maneuver down to the six-hundredth level and have a look around."

We fell into formation with Rava sleepily taking point. No one mentioned breakfast, which with Briff was never a good sign. They all knew how little rations we had. They'd have been right to blame me for not asking them to grab the food bars as we left, though in my defense we'd been in a bit of a hurry.

"Jerek," Rava called, a bit louder than I'd have liked.

She stood about ten meters ahead, at a T junction. Two of the three corridors were walled off with webbing. The last was completely bereft of webs or spiders. I crept up to join her, and studied the one available corridor. It led the exact opposite direction.

I faced the way we needed to go, and studied the webbing. A knot of frustration had been growing for a while now, and it had begun to pulse into true anger. We were being herded.

"We're going this way." I nodded at the corridor on the right. "Just let me make a hole first."

This was my chance to show off, and I took full advantage. I poured *fire* into my fists, then added a layer of *void*. I amped the magnitude as high as I could, then flung my spell at the webbing.

A cone of purple-tinged flame boiled into the corridor. Everything it touched burst with a tiny pop, the remains consumed by the *void* a moment later. When the spell cleared, the first fifteen meters of the corridor were cleared.

There'd been a chance that the entire corridor was webbed, but that seemed like a waste of spider-power, if I were the head arachnid. Thankfully it wasn't. There was some webbing beyond, thick ropy strands, but they ran along the ceilings and the right wall.

"Briff, you're up." I nodded back to the hatchling. "Take point. If it crawls I want it incinerated with that plasma thing you do."

"Jer," Briff hissed in a wounded whisper. "You know about my...inability."

"That was years ago," I countered, then nodded up the corridor. "This is your chance to redeem yourself. You're not a second year asked to fill in for a fourth year. You're a badass Wyrm who's part of a badass squad. Handle it. I know you can."

Briff straightened. Then he gave one of those too-toothy grins. "You're right, Captain." He bounded up the corridor, then paused before the first large cluster of webbing.

A swarm of dark spiders flowed from what must be some sort of nest in the wall. Hundreds of fat black spiders with angry red markings swarmed toward the hatchling.

"You got this, man." Rava moved to stand just behind the hatchling. "I'm not even a little worried."

"I am." Briff's eyes widened, and he glanced between Rava's leather-clad form and the spiders.

Then his chest swelled like a bellows, and his neck elongated a good half meter. His whole body contracted, and then expelled a ball of gold-white plasma that splattered into the mass of spiders.

Hundreds died with tiny inhuman shrieks, and the rest spun as one, racing back into the crack in the wall where their nest lay.

Briff turned and offered us a smile. "Looks like it's clear."

I trotted up and clapped my friend on the wing. "Great work. Keep moving, bud. Rava, pick off anything that gets past him. When you run out of grenades let me know and you can have mine."

We pushed up the corridor with Briff roasting swarms, and Rava picking off stragglers with enthusiastically hurled grenades. She only had to use two by the time the corridor spilled into a larger room.

That room was swathed in patches of webbing, but only in the occasional corner. Most of the floor space was covered by pulsing egg sacs of varying sizes. The largest towered over our heads, and nearly brushed the shadowed ceiling.

"Huh," Briff commented. "At least we found the elevators."

He was right. Four sets of double doors stood on the opposite side of the room...beyond the eggs.

10

I raised both hands defensively before me, though none of the egg sacs had done anything more than pulse disgustingly. The squad tensed all around me, and Briff stepped ahead of us protectively, which made me love the hatchling even more.

"We're making for those elevators," I decided into the comm. Everyone had their helmets on. Depths, I might never take mine off again. "Briff, make a path. Don't hit any egg sacs unless you see a—"

I trailed off and froze, one foot still in the air, about to follow Briff into the egg chamber. Three of the large eggs had begun to tremble violently, their entire mass quivering...as if something inside were suddenly seeking a way out.

Just like that the eggs exploded, and began disgorging a tide of spiders.

"No!" Kurz shrieked, a full octave higher than the usual. "Get them off me! Get them off. Veeeee!" He dropped to the ground, and began swatting at himself, though I saw no spiders on him.

Vee dropped to her brother's side, then looked up at me through her faceplate. "He'll be all right, but I need a minute to get him stable."

"We'll buy you time." I moved protectively to join Rava and Briff in the line they'd formed at the edge of the room.

My father floated up next to me with his pistol cradled in both hands, and his tired eyes fixed resolutely on the closest egg. "This is gonna get ugly. There's too many to shoot with anything but *fire* magic. Jer, means you and I are gonna have to shoulder the load here."

The eggs erupted simultaneously, and each disgorged a tide of black and red spiders, larger than those we'd seen, about the size of a hand. They didn't attack. Quite the opposite. Every spider scuttled toward the center of the room, away from us, and swarmed into a pile of spiders that nearly touched the ceiling.

Those spiders began to...arrange themselves.

"By the depths," I whispered. "What are we seeing?"

"Got me." Rava holstered her pistol, and withdrew a grenade from her belt. "Kill it with fire?"

"No," I ordered as I raised an arm to forestall her. "These things aren't threatening us like the others. Everyone line up a shot and be ready to nuke them, but don't until they do something threatening. Something is happening here."

"Whyyyyyyy," hissed a voice from the pile of spiders. The sound had issued from...was that a mouth? The spiders had become a crude face, with eight eyes and a spider-like mouth. "Whyyy do youuu kill offspring? Why burn Web? We saaaawww you kill feral drakes. Ally? Or foeee? Tommmb robbers, maybe. Why youuuu commme?"

Kurz's faceplate snapped open with a hiss, and he vomited noisily all over the deck, his entire body shaking as Vee cradled him.

"How do you speak galactic common?" I wondered aloud. Maybe not the best response, but more time wouldn't have let me craft a better one. I took a step into the room.

"I seee muuuch," the spider face hissed. "I seee Kemet. I seee Inurans. I seee you. *Word of Xal.* Whyyy you commme?"

"The Inurans threaten us all," I pointed out. I took another step. No reaction. I nodded at the squad to follow, and they filed in after me. I turned back to the spider face. "We're here to find something valuable. If we can't, then the Inurans will steal this ship and all the others."

"Nooooo," the spider wailed, and the shrieking went far beyond this chamber. Every spider, in every part of the ship, cried out all at once. "The flame must be protected."

"The flame?" I asked, unclear what it was trying to protect. "Is that an artifact?"

"Flame allll around us. We serve flame. Flame serves Neith."

"Did that make any sense to you?" Rava whispered as she stepped up to join me.

"Maybe," I whispered back. "So the *Flame* is this ship, then?"

"Yesss." The spider face worked, and the eight eyes blinked in a most unnerving way. "Whaaat you seeek?"

"Knowledge." I took another step, until I stood within the shadow of the thing. Stupid maybe, but if I didn't extend trust there was no way I was going to receive it. Just because this thing looked alien didn't mean it couldn't be an ally. "I've already found some. The records of the galaxy as it was are valuable, but I need more. I need something valuable enough to pay off the people coming for the Great Ships."

"Webbb of divinity. You seeek Webbb," the spider face quivered with...pleasure? Hard to know. "Webbb seees alll. Weee protect Webbb from ferals, and frommm Ciiin-dra's clutch. Archiiive old and vaaaluable."

There was a lot to unpack there, and I wasn't sure how much time this thing was going to give me to do it.

"Yes, we seek the Web." I assumed it must be some sort of divination device, which meant there were probably knowledge scales there. Lots of knowledge scales. That was my best hope at finding something valuable.

"You seeek knowledge. Goood. Thisss goood." The thing quivered in pleasure again. "Briiing knowledge baaack to gaaalaxy."

The face burst into a thousand disgusting spiders, all flowing past my feet, and into the hallway behind me. I froze, as did everyone else.

Everyone but Kurz.

"Noooooo!!!" He shot to his feet as the swarm approached him, and reached for one of his vials.

The last vial had wiped out nearly a hundred Inurans. I couldn't let this happen.

My gauntlets came up and I reached for the *dream* in my chest. It came easily and eagerly, a purple-pink bolt that sizzled through the intervening space and slammed into Kurz's forehead.

I didn't wait to see if the spell worked. I hit him again. He blinked sleepily, then collapsed to the deck just before the spiders reached him.

They swarmed around him, every last one careful not to touch him as they flowed past into the corridor.

"Thank you," Vee called hoarsely as she knelt next to her brother, seemingly oblivious to the spiders. "I don't know what he would have done. He's terrified of them. One got trapped in his suit when we were kids. It bit him dozens of times."

"I can't say I blame him," I pointed out. "Briff, can you

carry him? Looks like we've got permission to use the elevators."

Briff nodded, then lumbered over to retrieve the soul-catcher. He scooped Kurz gently, and cradled him in his arms as the squad moved single file toward the elevators. Despite having permission I couldn't outrun the terror.

The room positively writhed as we worked our way through. Finally, a lifetime later, we reached the lifts. Each door was three meters tall and two wide, and the closest one slid open at my approach.

Inside lay a pristine floor, untouched by webs, though the metal itself had eroded in places. We stepped inside, and the tension finally abated a hair when the doors slid closed.

The controls next to the door were in ancient draconic, and easily understandable as numbers. Unlike a traditional lift, though, this one moved in three dimensions and could deposit us in a number of locations. It included a helpful cutaway of the ship, complete with "you are here" in draconic.

"What do you think she meant by Cindra's clutch?" Vee pressed her shoulder against mine, and eyed me sidelong.

"Clutch can only be two things, and we aren't lucky enough for it to be snakes. She meant an adult Wyrm and its offspring. One I'm guessing is a lot older, and more powerful, than Visala. Let's just hope we can reach the bridge without running into her."

INTERLUDE III

Jolene's smile deepened as a Fissure split the black, the cracks veining for thousands of kilometers, far larger than any Fissure had a right to be. It opened upon the Umbral Depths, feared by god and mortal alike, though necessary for rapid interstellar trade.

The Consortium's greatest triumph, one that allowed them to survive as a culture long after Nefarius had obliterated their fabled homeworld, lurked on the other side of the titanic crack in reality. The Trade Moons were portable homeworlds, all three constantly on the move, and never in the same system. Ever.

Bringing one here had taxed even her influence, but the deal she had signed with the minister of Kemet had made it more than worth the risk.

An enormous silver sphere, easily equal to Kemet's

surviving moons, slid through the Fissure, and back into
the light. For an instant Jolene glimpsed something slith-
ering behind the moon in the darkness, a tentacled mass
nearly as large as the moon itself.

The creature thought better of the light, and
vanished back into the depths. The Fissure snapped
shut, and the moon slowly drifted toward the Vagrant
Fleet.

Jolene tapped an icon on her desktop, and waited for
her underling to answer.

"Yes, Matron?" came a meek voice. She couldn't even
tell the gender, it was so soft. So timid. Was this the best
of what she had left?

"Hail the moon, and inform them that I have
requested the board's presence on my flagship." It galled
her to ask them to do anything. She'd handpicked each of
them, lickspittles and servants all. And she had so many
levers on each of them.

Yet somehow they'd collectively found a spine, and
now they wanted to defy her. She didn't doubt that they
craved her failure here. If she was unable to secure the
Great Ships, or at least the *Word of Xal*, then they would
hang her with this.

They'd attempt to anyway. She may not be a god of
the same divinity she'd possessed before, but she was still
a powerful archmage, one of few in the sector. Few had
troubled themselves to acquire all eight aspects of magic.
The Blood of Nefarius had given her the last aspect, and

unlocked the greater paths of summoning and destruction.

The *Word of Xal* would dramatically enhance both, making it ideal for her new flagship. She had to take it first, of course, but that was merely a formality. Bortel had ten legions of crack mercenaries, and the *Word* was crewed by children.

Technically she couldn't attack just yet, as the Kemetians weren't in default of the contract.

Her intercom flashed, and Jolene darted an agitated hand down to stab the offending icon.

"Matron?" the genderless assistant whined. "The council has refused your invitation. They are holding for a conference missive. Shall I complete the spell?"

"Do it." She leaned back in her hovercouch, and adopted an imperious pose. This defiance was unacceptable, but letting them see that they were having an effect would only incite greater defiance.

The screen flickered, and a hologram burst to life over the desk. Eight Inuran nobles sat at a horseshoe-shaped table, obviously designed to place her on the defensive.

"Esteemed board members." She inclined her head, but only slightly. "I find it puzzling that you declined my hospitality. I consider each and every one of you...friends."

Several faces paled, though the greater number firmed with resolve. They saw the threat, and didn't waver. That was troubling in the extreme. What had changed? Where had their courage come from? Not a one had the bloodline to unseat her. They could block her, but not remove her, and they knew it.

Not unless she caused catastrophic damage to the Consortium. Even then it would require not only a unanimous vote from the board, but a majority vote from all stockholders. That was something she was well prepared to deal with, especially given that Kazon's stock had reverted to her when he'd been declared dead.

"Can we set the posturing aside?" Uthe said. Her former protege was even more handsome than your average Inuran, not that such things mattered to her. It was his mind that had intrigued her. For a time at least. Uthe leaned forward, his hologram nearly brushing her face. "We all know that you have the means to destroy us...individually. But we also have a responsibility to the Consortium. The shareholders are still our greatest masters. We refused your offer, because we stand as one, and we needed to deliver our ultimatum."

Jolene's eyebrow twitched, but she refused to give them anything more. She smiled prettily. "Do go on."

"If you succeed, and deliver even a single Great Ship, then the board will laud you publicly as a hero. You'll have our total support. You'll have once again earned it." Uthe sat back in his chair, and avoided her gaze as he delivered their threat. "However, if you are unable to procure a ship, as you have promised, then you will be asked to furnish the Kemetian's forfeiture fee, personally.

You will shoulder the cost, even if that means selling your stock to do it."

"Very well," she agreed, as if the matter were of no great concern. "That seems a fair price to ask. I wouldn't expect the Consortium to bear the weight of my failures, had there been one. There hasn't. There won't be. We will have our first Great Ship soon."

"The clause doesn't trigger for another seven solar cycles," Uthe countered. The others were looking to him...a champion then. What a surprising choice, especially given his relative youth. "How will you justify seizing one before then? So long as the Kemetians possess a functioning government and populace they are protected under Confederate law."

"They are only eligible if the Confederacy knows they exist," she snarled. And it was a snarl. Their flinch was delicious. They still feared her. "I will take the ship, and I will document the treachery that made such an action necessary. The Kemetians were going to flee the system with our property. Technically, that means they reneged on the contract, which triggers our possession of the fleet."

"*If* they flee," Uthe pointed out. Several of his supporters nodded at that. Not a one of them met her gaze, though, not even through a hologram.

"When," Jolene pointed out. She narrowed her eyes. They knew what she was saying, and she needed their tacit approval. "I've already received word of their plan."

"And you'll have evidence we can present at a Confederate inquiry?" Uthe demanded. He folded his arms expectantly, apparently gaining confidence.

"Let's say you do unseat me," Jolene ventured, changing battlefields. "Which of you will replace me? Is it you, Uthe? You think your esteemed grandparents will sit well with the Consortium as a whole? They'll never follow a pirate."

Uthe's hands began to tremble, the only sign of his rage. "You are not the last of your bloodline, Jolene. I can't replace you, but we can find someone who could."

"Kazon." She barked a derisive laugh. "My son is a demon, Uthe. Our literal opposite. He was declared dead."

"I didn't say it was your son." Uthe gave a predatory smile. "Your daughter, Voria, might be interested in receiving a quantity of stock, and taking up the position of matron."

"Voria?" Jolene blinked a few times. She couldn't even manage a laugh, though the very idea was beyond ludicrous. "My daughter will never soil her hands with the dirty business of the Consortium. She considers us beneath her, Uthe. You'll never get her to sit as a matron."

"Maybe." Uthe offered a non-committal shrug. "But we can and will make the offer, should you fail us."

Jolene didn't fear Voria doing as they wished, but she did fear her daughter being notified of her actions here. Voria must not be allowed to find out, no matter the cost.

That was why she'd taken such extreme measures. "Then I must not fail. I need your help, Uthe."

"How?" His beautiful face was an impassive mask now, as were the rest of his cabal.

"Jam them. No quantum. No missives. Keep them isolated for seven days, and I will deliver you the first Great Ship."

"Very well." Uthe nodded, as did the others. "It looks like you have our support. We will ensure no word leaves this system. You deliver us the *Word of Xal*."

"I will see it done." She killed the missive. It was time to order Bortel to ready his strike. He'd dislike it, of course. No one enjoyed attacking children. But he'd do it, because his contract demanded it.

11

T he squad's collective gaze bored into my back as the ancient magitech lift whirred to a stop. None of us had any idea what to expect, but they'd take their cues from me. If I were afraid, they would be. Leadership sucks.

The golden doors dissolved into particles like evaporating mist, and exposed my idea of the perfect afterlife. There was no need to fake my enthusiasm.

The single most wondrous library anyone had ever dreamed of stretched into the darkness before us. Knowledge scales lined shelves that climbed all the way to the shadowed ceiling, and there were three full levels. Maybe more that I couldn't see.

"Briff, take a stroll," I ordered. It wasn't easy clamping down my enthusiasm long enough to follow protocol, but I didn't know what lurked in those shadows. There were no webs, but there could be worse things. Even lurkers. "Rava, you're Briff's shadow. Be ready for something to jump him. Vee, get us a light source please. Nice and bright. Dad, cover Kurz and make sure no one stops him from casting."

The squad flowed into the library, with only Vee at my side after the first few steps. She raised her right arm, and her silver bracelet flared. Veins of light flowed from the bracelet into her hand, and coalesced into a ball, which she flung high into the air.

It illuminated most of the first floor, though the globe also made us a beacon for anyone in the library. They definitely knew we were here, if there was a hypothetical they.

"How old is this place?" Vee whispered through her suit's speakers. She paused before a shelf and hefted a scale.

"At least ten thousand years," I ventured as I moved to the same shelf. These were labeled, unlike the ones in the workshop. "I think we're looking at some sort of logs. This one is called *Reevanthara's Accord and the Exodus From the Great Cycle*." I slid that one into the pouch belted to my right thigh. "I wish we had a way to carry more of them."

"I might be able to arrange that," Vee ventured, as if relating a secret she'd been hiding for some time. Her voice went even more quiet. "I am an artificer, as I've mentioned, I think. I can build objects, but I can also create spell anchors. I can't actually cast a void pocket, but if you can learn to do it, or meet someone who can, I can anchor it to anything from that fancy armor to a spellpistol."

"If I still had one," I pointed out with a chuckle. "That's good to know, though. Thank you. I'd kill to have a void pocket."

"Hey, Jer!" Briff called from the middle of the first level, in a voice far too loud for a tomb like this. "I think I found something important."

He pointed toward the ceiling, and I glanced up to see webbing, but not as we'd seen before. This webbing was clean and refined. The spiders flowed in neat, orderly patterns, like pulses of data. The webs themselves resembled circuits.

More, I could feel a unified purpose to it all. The spiders, the Web...they were part of something much larger. A vast and complex system.

"Do not fear," an inhuman voice whispered from the shadows behind the nearest shelf. "I am an ally, or can be if you will listen after what I have done to you."

It took a moment to place the voice, but it came back quickly. It's hard to forget the creature that burnt off your eyebrows. A single arachnidrake lurked behind the shelf, and the staff clutched in too many hands told me I was dealing with the same one.

"Captain?" Rava hissed into the comm, internal only. "You want me to waste this guy?"

"What do you want?" I asked over the speakers. I didn't approach, but neither did I back away. This thing was a threat, but we outnumbered it and it had me curious. "And what happened to your accent?"

"I've used my magic to learn your language," the drake said. It bobbed its head apologetically. "I felt the effort necessary. You do not know how important you are. How important your coming is. You will shift the balance of power. After millennia there will be...change."

"You're talking about a prophecy, aren't you?" Vee demanded. She stepped up to the shelf, and peered through at the drake. "Tell us."

"Time is short." The drake scuttled further into shadow. Something glinted in one of its hands, though I couldn't make it out. "Cindra's clutch will be coming now that the lift has been activated. You must be prepared to flee or wipe out your opponents. Survive and reach the bridge."

The glittering object flashed as it sailed through the intervening space toward me. My hand shot up, and I managed to snag it before it hit the ground.

It was a golden knowledge scale, covered with hundreds of tiny runes. From a *life* Wyrm, most likely. I was about to activate it, but of course we couldn't have that, could we? No time to puzzle stuff out.

"Contact," Rava breathed over the comm. "Second level and headed this way. I think they saw the light."

"Kill the light," I whispered into the comm as I went

internal. "Get into covered positions. They're above us. This could get nasty. Be ready to fall back."

I glanced back at the drake, but it was...gone. Predictable. So depths damned predictable. Not that I blamed it. If it was here alone, then getting caught in a fire fight between two unfriendly groups wasn't conducive to survival.

I was just annoyed that he'd dropped a cryptic hint, and then scuttled off. Why did no one ever offer a straight Q&A session? Just, like...five questions.

"Incoming," my father breathed into the comm.

I glanced around, but it took me a while to spot his hunched form. He'd managed to wriggle onto a shelf, then shimmied between two levels so he had perfect cover, but could still fire at the level above.

Instinct took over. I pulled a bit of *dream* from my chest, and used a chameleon spell to blend into the shelf behind me. I'd still show up on thermascans, but someone called the Clutch of Cindra would use—

I paid for my arrogance in blood. A spellrifle whined ominously far above me, from out of sight.

Indescribable agony flared in my heart. The *fire* and the *void* tore at my very existence as they attempted to create a micro-singularity in my chest.

A detached part of my mind asked how the spell had found me. There'd been no void bolt. No visible spell of any kind. He'd quite literally shot me through the wall. How? The answer terrified me.

The agony abated...I was still alive, though every ragged breath made me wish I weren't. I gritted my teeth, and thanked the depths that I'd acquired *void* resistance when I'd Catalyzed aboard the *Word of Xal*. If I'd not had both that and *fire*...I'd probably be dead.

"Er-radicator," I gasped into the comm. "On the s-second level. Just hit me with an implode."

"I'll get a ward up." Vee rolled between shelves, then crawled the last few meters to the shelf I lay slumped against. "I told you the *void* was insidious. We can't even see that forked-tongue bastard."

Her wrist came up, and the silver bracelet flared. A dome of shimmering white light covered us both. The spell ensured we'd be visible, but also kept us safe. Well, for as long as Vee could maintain the wards anyway.

"Rava?" I whispered into the comm. My voice still shook, despite my best attempts to stop the quaver. I still couldn't take a deep breath. "Make me a dead eradicator, please. Kurz...need you to play spotter. Can you have a spirit l-locate them?"

Then I sagged back, panting like I'd sprinted the last four hundred meters out of an exploding building, despite having only spoken.

"Let me look at that." Vee rested the hand with her bracelet on my armor over the heart. I couldn't see her through the faceplate, not in the dim light of the wards, but I could feel the tension in her. The resolve.

Golden light bubbled from her palm, and into my

armor. The armor seemed to sense where it was needed, and fed the flow directly into my wounded heart. Every muscle eased, all at once. I hadn't realized how clenched I'd been, but the sudden salve eased the residual, grainy pain.

I relaxed, and took a full breath.

Only then did I realize a staccato of fire bolts had been raining on the wards, and that Vee had already replaced them once. Through the discolored magic I could see my father returning fire, quite literally.

His pistol belched balls of flame, and he scored a hit against a dark-scaled hatchling on the second level. The creature carried a spellrifle, but I didn't think it was our eradicator. My father's spell took it in the face, an expert shot that I doubt I could have managed.

I'm sure the creature had *fire* resistance, as I did, but it got to learn the very painful lesson I'd just learned two days ago. Fire bolts to the face hurt anyway, and, in his case, burn away most of your scales.

"The scales are finally balanced," I muttered, then immediately regretted the pun. No one heard, I think, but I could feel the universe judging me.

Vee grunted with effort as she renewed the wards again. "I can't do this for too much longer."

"You won't have to," my sister whispered into the comm. I'd never heard the tone from her before. Not just predatory, but maliciously so. She was savoring the kill.

A high-pitched reptile shriek sounded from the third

level, then was cut off with a wet squishing over the comm. "Target eliminated."

I spotted movement above, and winced when I realized she'd tossed a hatchling's head down to the second level. The grisly head rolled across the main room, and came to rest in a clearing between tables.

The move was sickening. The disrespect unthinkable.

It was also devastatingly effective.

Three enraged hatchlings charged out of cover, and my father peppered them with fire bolts. That slowed them, and Rava took full advantage.

My sister poked over the edge of the railing with a grenade in one hand, and an automatic pistol in the other. She hurled the grenade in the exact center between the three hatchlings, and it detonated, tossing them all in separate directions.

Her pistol snapped up, and she added a second hand to stabilize her grip, then tracked the first hatchling's unintended flight. It all happened so fast that I couldn't track it all. Her pistol coughed once, and the hatchling's wing detached in an explosion of flame and bone.

It sailed out over me and I raised both hands. I couldn't do any flashy destruction spells, but I could dish out one depths of a void bolt. I poured everything I had into the spell, and a thick, dark, negative bolt streaked into the hatchling's chest, directly above the heart.

The spell blew out a half-meter hole, which doubled when it exited on the other side. The hatchling didn't even cry out. Its limp body tumbled into a shelf, then lay still.

Briff leapt into the fray, and landed on the second level. I couldn't see what he was aiming at, but I watched his spellcannon swivel to track it. The barrel filled with the deep blinding white of plasma, then a ball rocketed into his target.

His target shrieked. Then silence.

"Do we have eyes on any hostiles?" I whispered, even as I scanned the shadowed levels above. I couldn't see any movement, not even Rava.

"Negative," my sister's frustrated voice came back a moment later. "One of them got away. You want me to track it down?"

"No." I clutched at the prophecy scale the arachnidrake had given me. "We've got other business to look into. Let's head the opposite direction. Find us a place to hole up. A workshop, or a chapel, or something defensible."

"On it."

12

The circuit-like webs along the ceiling thinned as we made our way to the far side of the library, the area we needed to cross to reach the ship's bridge, if my brief glance in the elevator was accurate.

"Can't believe we're leaving it all behind," my father groused as he whirred past me. His battered spellpistol was cradled in his lap, in both hands, ready for action should he need it. "Billions of credits, and we can't even haul it."

"Someone else's billions of credits," I pointed out, though I felt the knife keenly. "We know where it is if we can get the *Remora* up and running, and I don't see any reason we can't stuff the hold with scales."

That seemed to perk everyone up, except for Kurz, who was doing everything he could to avoid looking at the webs. I couldn't even imagine what being here would be like for someone terrified of spiders.

We hurried across the first floor, with Briff lagging a bit behind to cover us, and Rava scouting. There was no sign of either my new arachnidrake friend or more of Cindra's hatchlings.

Long minutes later we reached the library's far side, with a similar vaulted archway leading up a wide corridor that stretched into the darkness before us. I caught one brief glance of Rava, then she disappeared into the corridor as if she'd been nothing but an illusion.

We moved largely in silence, accompanied by the jingle of packs and Briff's huffing breaths as he lumbered behind us. At least there weren't any spiders.

Perhaps ten minutes after leaving the library Rava broke radio silence. "Captain, I've got something. There's a bunch of rooms, just like the first one we hid in by the ship. The rearmost one looks safest. If we're quiet, should be green."

"Best news we've had all day. We'll be there shortly. Meet us in the doorway."

I picked up the pace to a fast walk, which the squad mirrored. The last hundred meters were agony, as I waited for the inevitable last minute attack that would prevent me from studying the prophecy scale.

Nothing disturbed us. We made it past a pair of door-ways, then another fifty meters up. Rava stood outside the fifth set of doors, with her rifle barrel propped nonchalantly on one shoulder, my father's trademark grin plastered on her face.

"Did I mention," she drawled, "that this room isn't empty?"

I peered past her and blinked. This room resembled the first, which Vee had told us they used for artificing. This room was similar, except that it contained a pair of devices that were recognizable despite being constructed by people long since dust.

"My gods," I whispered. "Is that a forge?"

"What?" Vee's head snapped up, and she pushed past me into the room. "Maker's blessing...."

She stopped in front of a boxy black box precisely one meter across. One side had a logo of a dragon roaring on it, which would be the door. The back side was lined with tubes, which disappeared into another box behind it. Those would be the raw materials.

Vee wrenched off her helmet and pitched it to the ground without a care. She knelt next to the forge and studied the door.

"Can someone explain what we found?" Briff asked from the door, his expression sheepish. "I, uh, don't recognize the box."

"Boxes," Vee corrected. She pointed at the second one against the far wall.

"It's a forge," I explained to Briff even as I approached the forge. "And I'm betting the second box is a foundry."

"Okay, I mean, I know what a forge is." Briff stepped

into the room, and turned one slitted eye on the forge. "What makes these ones special? We've had 3D printing for thousands of years. I mean, it's cool, but they had four forges at the academy."

"It's not the forge that will make it special." I moved to the terminal next to the black box, and noted the complex circuitry flowing into the forge. "Our current forges are all made by a company called F&F. If you want to make something you need a schematic. This ship is ancient, and if this thing was used to make magic items then all the schematics might still be in the memory. In a way, this is more valuable than any number of scales."

"*Might* be more valuable," Vee countered. She knelt next to the terminal as well. "It all depends on what's in memory. I can read ancient draconic, a little anyway. Self taught. It will be faster if you do it though."

I tapped the screen, and brought up the main inter-face, which was divided into types of objects. I blinked at the list. "We can make weapons, armor, communications devices, appliances, and furniture. The last ten schematics used are all weapons."

Only then did I realize what I was feeling from the tubes behind the forge. All eight tubes glowed...with magic.

"Guys?" I let my helmet slither off my face just so I could grin at them. "We might have just found our nine-teen billion credits. This thing can make magic items. Forges were invented by Ternus...for making tech. They work with nanites. If there are versions that make magic items, then they're an Inuran secret. This thing proves that you can make magitech with a forge. The confederacy will pay a fortune for this."

"I hate to be the smoke in the O_2." Vee's excitement dimmed a hair as she spoke, and she retied her ponytail, the auburn hair catching the light from the ceiling. "This thing is stationary. You aren't going to be able to move it, and even if you could we can't carry it. Briff might be able to get the forge, but we have no one to carry the foundry."

A sigh escaped almost of its own accord. I stared hard at the equipment, but she was right. There was no way for us to carry it.

"Vee, you're an artificer. Can you detach the panel with the schematics?" That perked me up some. "Failing that, can you dump the schematics to knowledge scales? I don't care what you have to overwrite. This stuff is vital. Someone could set up a rival to the Inurans if they had access to this."

"It will take some time," she said. Vee moved to the panel, and knelt to inspect it closely. "I can do it though. Can we stay the night? I need to be exempted from watches."

"I want to study this prophecy anyway." I glanced back at the doorway. "Rava, can you patrol south? Dad, you're north. Come back immediately if you make contact. Briff, keep an eye on the door. Kurz, you're with me."

The squad burst into motion, with the soulcatcher moving to sit against the wall near where I was standing.

"You look like you haven't slept," I whispered as I slid down the wall to sit next to him. "Do you want me to cast a sleep spell on you tonight?"

Kurz wrested his hands in the lap of his environmental armor, and didn't look up. He was silent long enough that I almost spoke again, but he finally turned to me. "I would appreciate that, Captain. This place has... unnerved me. I apologize for my weakness."

"That isn't an issue," I whispered back. "You more than pull your weight." I raised my voice. "In fact, that's why I needed you. I want a second pair of eyes."

I withdrew the prophecy scale from my pouch, and stroked the surface with my thumb. Light flared across the scale, and a woman's disembodied head sprang up over the device.

She was pretty, in an impish sort of way, and a river of hair the color of midday sun cascaded down slender shoulders where the illusion ended. The woman's face broke into a dimpled smile. She spoke with a lilting accent not unlike the drifters on Kemet. "Hey there. Name's Patra, soulcatcher of Inura, and you are a good deal less limbed than the last person I spoke to."

"The intelligence is incredible," Kurz whispered as he studied the scale.

"I'm standing right here," Patra protested. She shot

me a wink. "You want to hear about my prophecy, don't you?"

"I do," I admitted. I figured I'd let her show me what she could before I piled on the questions.

"This ship is the key," Patra explained as an illusion sprang up next to her.

Kurz leaned in close and stroked absently at his beard as he studied it. "That's the *Remora*. There can be no doubt."

I also studied the ship, though I came to a different conclusion. "That's the *Remora*, but not as she is. As she was. How old is this illusion?"

"You're joost the kind of mind I was hoping to find." The drifter gave a musical laugh. "I don't know how long has passed, but this was recorded two weeks after the battle that marooned your people in this system. So... however long that's been."

"Ten millennia, give or take," I supplied as I continued to study the ship. I'd known the *Remora* was old, just not how old. "It looks like your version has a spelldrive and a spellcannon. Our has a broken keel and and no engine, much less weapons."

I paused as a loud humming came from behind me. Kurz and I pivoted to see Vee at the forge. She was working at the console, and the forge appeared to be making something, though I couldn't see what. She shot me a smile that definitely got my attention, but Patra spoke again and drew me back to the conversation.

"I don't think that will be a problem." Patra delivered another wink. "All you'll need to do is reach the bridge and use the matrix there. When you're ready I can activate the spell that will imprint the prophecy into your mind."

"I don't suppose you have a text version?" I was fine with the spell, but I wanted to understand what the prophecy wanted, not rely on magic I didn't understand.

"Fine." She rolled her eyes. "The ship is a beacon and will set your course when you sail upon time. You will return the light of the past to the present, and offer the present to the past as recompense. A life restored, a willing life given in balance."

Kurz's face turned down into a rare frown. "That is... maddeningly cryptic."

"Give me the spell version." I hefted a small sigh, and wished things were simpler. If I ever created a prophecy I'd start by saying this is what you need to achieve, and this is how you do it.

A tendril of *dream* swirled up from the scale and parted into twin plumes that forced their way up my nostrils. I gasped and choked as the magic swirled into me, then toppled to the deck.

13

I awakened slowly, by degrees. The room slid into focus and I realized someone had propped me in a corner, out of line of sight of the doorway. The rest of the squad had taken up similar positions behind the forge or in the corners to the right and left of the door.

Only my father was awake, his face awash in the soft glow of the circuitry on the forge's control panel. He watched the doorway, but I could see from the tilt of his head that he was mostly focused on listening.

"Been quiet as a derelict," he whispered with a glance in my direction. "Don't think anyone comes to this part of the ship. After meeting those cinder hatchling things, I can see why."

I rose with a yawn and scratched at my cheek. I was going to need to shave soon, or accept the fuzzy almost-beard my face was threatening to grow.

"Did I miss anything after my forced nap?" I stretched, then rolled my neck.

"Nah." My dad shook his head, and whirred a bit closer, though still out of line of fire from the doorway. "Been meaning to talk to you."

"Uh oh. Am I going to need my helmet for this?" I couldn't help but wince. No good conversation ever started with 'been meaning to talk to you.'

"You might." My dad offered a serious nod. "'Cause you're gonna blush." Dad winked and offered a lighter version of the smile I'd seen on Rava earlier. They looked so much alike. "I just wanted to say...I'm proud of you, son. Your mother and I used to joke about you being the super-kid. Her brains and my reflexes. And that's exactly what we ended up with. You're just starting your career, and you've already done so much. Saved so many people. It's just been a real privilege to ride alongside, and watch my kids grow into adults. Both of 'em."

I smiled at that. The praise was nice, though also awkward. But the kind words for my sister were something I could focus on. I loved that they'd gotten close, especially after Arcan's death. Both of them had needed each other. Still needed each other.

"Thanks, Dad." I knew anything more would only make us both uncomfortable.

A pleasant chime suddenly came from the forge. As if on cue, Vee's sleeping form straightened at the waist into a sitting position. Her hair hung loosely around her shoulders as she blinked sleep from her eyes.

"Izzit done?" she mumbled as she pried open an eye and glanced at the forge's control panel. "It's done!" She leapt to her feet, the excitement overcoming the last vestiges of sleep. "Jerek, wait til you see."

Vee reached for the forge's door, and slid a finger along the top to trigger the latch. The door slid open to reveal a single printed object...a pistol with a thick grip and even thicker barrel. The weapon reminded me of Ariela, though this eldimagus was undeveloped. New, and untouched by external magic.

The primary materials were a silvery metal. Feather-steel maybe? And a darker metal running along the inside of the barrel. The grip was studded with fire rubies, and the sight along the top of the barrel might have been made from air diamonds. This thing was powerful. Or would be one day.

"Did you make that?" I leaned closer to study the bore. "I've never seen the design. What is it?"

"Yes, I made it." Vee's grin threatened to swallow her face, a shocking development for the normally stoic lurker. She took the pistol and offered it to me. "For you. To replace Ariela. I know how much it hurt when...you never said anything, but I still see you reaching for your sidearm."

"Where did you get the schematic?" I turned the pistol over in my hand, impressed with the balance. It fit as snuggly as any weapon ever had, with the selector between explosive ammo and spells lining up perfectly with my thumb.

"I told you. I made it. Call I the Vee Mark VII." She punched me lightly in the arm, which I couldn't really feel through the armor. "Design is a passion. One I'm good at. I've just never had access to a real forge before. I wish we could take this one with us."

Kurz slowly rose to his feet, and began packing his bedroll. He was the only one still using one, as the rest of us had started relying on our armor.

"You know, Captain," Kurz mused with a yawn, as if beginning a new conversation. "There are no gender specific norms around initiating courtship within our culture. The more potent the gift, the more potent the interest, it is said."

Vee's face went scarlet and I suddenly found the pistol very interesting.

"Does she have a name?" I asked in an obvious attempt to change the subject.

I turned the pistol over in my hand, then slid her into the holster on my right thigh that had been home first to Ariela, and then to the nameless black pistol I'd taken from the *Word of Xal*. This pistol felt right in a way that only Ariela ever had.

"That's up to you." Vee cleared her throat, and knelt to retrieve her helmet, which she placed over her head with a hiss. A moment later the faceplate darkened to hide her face. "I'm glad you like her."

"She's amazing." We both knew I wasn't merely talking about the pistol.

"I'm going to be sick," Rava muttered as she rose with a stretch. She hefted her pack over one shoulder, and moved for the door. "At least there's a gun involved. I'd go on a date with a rusty servo if it gave me a weapon like that."

"You and me both, kid." My dad zoomed up next to Rava, and clapped her on the shoulder. "You just let me know if that servo has a sister."

"Eww. Don't make it weird, Dad." Rava shrugged off his hand, but I noted the soft smile as she trotted into the corridor and took point.

The squad followed, and I didn't even have to issue orders. We all knew what to do, and how to do it well.

The corridor was dimly lit, but we'd been in darkness long enough to have mostly adjusted. It was the sounds that made it bad. Every odd ping or groan of a bulkhead made me tense, and once I almost drew my pistol.

Always nothing of course.

"I think my dad was right," I whispered into the comm. "No one comes this way. That's odd. Why would they avoid the bridge? I'm not sure we're going to like the answer."

"Reverence, perhaps," Kurz suggested, which was an angle I'd not considered. "If they see this ship as holy, then perhaps they seek to keep the unworthy from the bridge. That might explain why this Cindra lives elsewhere. Otherwise, why not make a lair of the bridge and maintain control of the ship?"

Briff cleared his throat behind us, not over the comm, but loudly enough that we all turned back. "What? Oh, sorry, just clearing some plasma."

If we hadn't been facing him we might not have seen the approaching eyes in the darkness. There was no clanking, though there should have been. A hatchling stepped into the dim light, only half illuminated as it studied Briff from behind.

I feared that it might raise its spellrifle and shoot my friend in the back, but it made no move to do so. Several more shapes stepped up behind the hatchling, and I had the impression that still more lingered in the shadows.

"Your scales," the creature said in draconic. She was female, I noted. "They are not blue, and not white. I have not seen this shade before. You are a *life* hatchling?"

Briff turned to face the taller hatchling, and backpedaled several paces when he spotted her companions. There were a lot more of them than there were of us. "Umm. Jerek, what should I do?"

"Do you not speak the old tongue?" the hatchling asked. She took a step closer, and I spotted scars across the side of her face, over the dusky scales.

"Pardon, master." I darted forward and offered a low bow. There was no way I'd be able to pull this off. I was going to try anyway. "I am a servant. I carry ancient tongues so that my master does not have to. I can translate, if you wish." I bowed low and waited for a response.

She nodded impatiently, so I turned to Briff and kept my tone servile. "Okay, buddy, she thinks you're the boss, and we're your slaves. I think she has a crush on you. She's asking where you came from."

Briff perked up immediately, and his wings fluffed behind him. "Uh, tell her I'm single. Tell her I really like her rifle, too. That thing is awesome."

"Mighty daughter of Cindra," I began. That sounded right. Or right*ish* anyway. "My master comes from the *Word of Xal*. He is indeed a *life* hatchling. He is most impressed by your weapon."

She puffed up in much the same way Briff had, and if we weren't surrounded by very lethal, and very hostile, dragons then it would have been cute.

"Tell your master," the hatchling explained magnanimously, "that I am called Cinaka. He will journey with us to meet my great-grandmother, the mighty Cindra. How are you called?"

"Uhh," I tried to keep up the act as I turned to Briff. "Looks like she wants to go on a field trip."

"Oh." Briff shifted uncomfortably, and clutched his spellcannon tighter to his chest. "What about you guys?"

I turned back to her. "My master is called Briff. He asks what will be done with his slaves while you are hosting him?"

"I don't care." She waved a clawed hand. "So long as you do not follow us. I understand your master doesn't have our tongue. Tell him that my grandmother can speak all tongues. She will help him understand our language. Your kind are not welcome, though, slaves or no. Grandmother would eat you. Scurry off and hide until I return your master to you."

"Well, looks like you're going to meet Cindra." I glanced back at the squad, then at the hatchlings. "We can't take them all. They came up on us silently, which says they have an illusionist. They've got us dead to rights."

"I don't mind going." Briff perked up a bit. "It doesn't seem like she wants to hurt me."

Part of me screamed that he was being naive, but what choice did we have? I hated this.

"The rest of us will make for the bridge," I explained. "We'll come for you as soon as we're done. Be careful, bud."

"You too, Jer." Briff clapped me on the shoulder, then walked off with the hatchlings into the darkness.

I hoped I wasn't signing his death warrant.

14

Hearts were heavy as we marched up the corridor in the opposite direction from Briff and what might be his captors. No one said anything, though I caught Rava glaring at me. That was fine. If something happened I'd be the correct target for that anger.

Maybe three hundred meters later we ran into a pair of wide double doors. They were the same silvery metal used in the pistol, and were covered in runes from all eight aspects.

"This thing is heavily warded," I muttered, as I moved to inspect the door. "It looks like a simple mechanism. We supply the missing rune, or runes, and the doors open."

I was honestly glad to have a puzzle to occupy my mind. My first instinct was to cheat, as I had when I'd repaired the control pad back on the *Word*. That was my go to for a reason...flame reading worked.

Curiously, though, I didn't need to. My hand rose of its own accord, and I began sketching sigils. A *dream* sigil there. A *fire* sigil there. The prophecy I'd snorted?

The doors rolled into the floor and exposed the bridge we'd come so far to reach. I stepped inside...a mostly empty room.

"Where is everything?" Rava snarled as she followed me in. "This is what we gave up Briff for? There's nothing here."

"Not nothing," I corrected as I approached the real prize. "This is the primary spellmatrix. The control mechanism for the entire ship."

It had the same gold, silver, and bronze rings as the *Word*, in the same configuration, but these were locked to the stabilizing ring, probably by the previous captain. Would it accept another? There didn't appear to be a Guardian, as there had been on the *Word*.

"Do you feel that?" Kurz asked as he finally entered the bridge. "Power. *Fire*. Near infinite *fire*. Over there." He pointed to the far side of the bridge, where an orange glow emanated from the floor.

I carefully approached, and stopped at the edge of a metal ring that overlooked a pool of lava many meters below. The heat pushed me back a step, even with my resistance. I willed the helmet to slither over my face, and waited for the HUD to light.

Metrics scrolled across the screen and showed an immense amount of magical power beneath us. I turned back to the matrix and studied it as well. I could detect the magic coming from the sigils, but not much else.

"I wish this thing came with some sort of scanner," I muttered, and walked back to the matrix.

As I approached, a whirring came from the right shoulder of the armor, and to my delight a device extended and emitted a magical scanning field that inspected the matrix. "Ask and you shall receive, I guess."

Data scrolled across my screen, and one word in particular leapt out at me. Temporal. This matrix was linked to time? If that was the case, then it would explain a bit more about why the prophecy talked so much about the past and the present.

Theoretically, if the specs being displayed were accurate, this thing would allow me to pilot through time in much the same way a ship normally piloted through space.

My scans revealed one other interesting detail. Filaments of spiderweb were attached to the base of the matrix, and tiny spiders flowed in precise patterns, as they had back at the library.

That furthered my guess that the Web was some sort of scrying device, though I still had no idea how it was used. I could make some guesses though. Maybe the Web let you see when you wanted to go, then the matrix took you there?

It seemed like a depths of a guess, but something in the recesses of my subconscious prodded me onward. The lingering spell that I'd snorted, I hoped, and not just a random guess.

"He will bring the light of the past to the present," I whispered.

I hadn't been aware I was speaking aloud until Vee stepped up next to me. "What do you think it is? Or means?"

"I can use that to fulfill whatever this prophecy is." I touched the stabilizing ring. "That's assuming we can unlock it. It could be—"

I trailed off as the rings slowly disengaged from their locks and begin to spin. They'd resize to fit me if I ducked under the stabilizing ring, but there was no way I'd try that without better understanding how this thing worked.

"We can't get Briff back until you finish with that thing, right?" Rava folded both arms, and her leather jacket creaked over her armor.

"Yeah." And that pretty much cinched it. I was going to have to get into that thing. "I need to understand what it wants me to do first."

"What purpose do you think that it intends?" Kurz asked. The soulcatcher approached the matrix, but was careful not to touch it.

"The scale showed me the *Remora*," I mused. There was an answer here. "Bring the light of the past into the present. If I can really travel through time, then maybe this thing wants me to retrieve the ship?"

"Let me see if I'm tracking," my father interjected. He whirred up to the matrix, which he was also careful not to touch. "This thing can take us back in time? If that's the case, then why not go back to before Kemet exploded? We can stop it. Blow up the comet before it threatens our planet. This thing must have an awfully big cannon."

"I'm not sure it works that way." I shook my head slowly, somehow certain I was right. The prophecy again? I didn't know. "That kind of magic requires immense power, and this ship is running on fumes, just like the *Word*. I don't even know if we have enough magic to move the ship. But maybe it's got enough juice to grab a corvette and pull it to us."

Kurz shook his head emphatically. "I am no scholar, but I've studied magic. There is always a cost, one that cannot be paid with mere magic. If you wish to grab that ship, then there must be something to balance the scales."

I rested my hand around the grip of my new pistol. "There's always a cost. If I don't pay it, then we don't get Briff back."

So I ducked inside the matrix.

15

There was a moment of pure magnificence when I was able to appreciate where I was standing and what I was doing. The gold ring spun by overhead, its faint hum a small comfort. Then came the silver, and finally the bronze.

I watched them spin around me, not altogether different than the matrix on the *Word*. The consequences would be different, though. First, I needed to bond to the ship.

I began with *fire*, and tapped it on all three rings. With each press the vessel rumbled, and something answered within me. On the third press we were one. I could see through the *Flame of Knowledge*, and something altogether primal peered back through me.

Madness. That was the single word that described the mind before me, both the ship and its closest servants, all driven to insanity, though by what I couldn't say. A vast ocean of pain and trauma surged through me as we joined.

It trickled down the back of my throat, and whispered into my ear, and promised to scour away my sanity. If I let it.

I had power here, and I fought back. My mind was my own. I focused on that, on the matrix, and the rings around me. In that moment I finally became aware of the sea of infinite possibilities around me.

I understood.

The Web of Divinity stretched in all directions, a vast interconnected flow of branching realities. I could perceive them as a seamless whole, and journey to the one I wished. Or merely peer into them, and study what our galaxy might have been.

The experience was overwhelming in the extreme, and focusing on any one thing caused pain and blurred my vision. There was a sort of undulating tide to the possibilities, one I hadn't yet learned how to ride.

"The light of the past." I closed my eyes, and let the prophecy guide me. A resonant chime sounded in the distance.

When I opened my eyes I could see a glittering object in the distance, though it lay underneath a half score millennia. I saw the *Remora*, not as she was today, but as she'd been in another age, a magnificent magitech vessel with a gleaming hull.

A powerful pulsing came from within the vessel...a sort of beacon. Time beacon? Temporal beacon? Was that what I needed?

I studied the beacon, even as the insanity filled my stomach, and my mind, and my nightmares. There was something else in that sea of possibility.

I spun around and spotted a second beacon. A second *Remora*. This one lay much closer. This was the vessel we'd arrived in. The hull rusted and pitted, and full of rushed patch jobs. It too bore a beacon. The same beacon, cleverly hidden in a bulkhead all those millennia ago.

All I needed to do was swap the two. Bring the original *Remora*, and superimpose it over my own. Simple, right?

Nothing is ever simple.

Jerek? It was Vee's voice, and it bore an edge of panic. *What's happening?*

This is the depths damned vortex of death, my father's gravelly voice came next. *I can hear your thoughts. All of you. I don't like it. A father shouldn't be privy to this kinda nonsense.*

I focused on our reality, and realized that the matrix had pulled from the massive reservoir of *fire* magic beneath the bridge. It was using that magic to fuel whatever ritual I'd been performing, and part of that magic had spilled onto the bridge. Onto my crew. I'd pulled them into the spell, somehow.

Everyone concentrate, I instructed. *I didn't intend for you to be here, but since you are I need your help. That shining star out there is the* Remora *from the past. We need to join the two ships together. Think about the* Remora *as it was, with the temporal beacon, and imagine it down in the hold where we crashed the real ship. Our ship.*

I could feel their compliance, just as they could feel my need. We focused on the original *Remora*, as a group, and together we envisioned it in our own timeline. I don't know that I could have completed the spell on my own, but with my friends the shining beacon seemed to be moving closer to the matrix. Closer to our reality. To our time.

Closer and closer the old *Remora* came, until finally it lay directly on top of the beacon in our own time. We'd done it! Elation surged through our link...for a moment anyway.

Then despair and horror began to leak in as one by one we realized our predicament.

Something is missing, I thought at the others. *Anyone have an idea?*

There is a soul on that ship. I can feel his purity and strength, Kurz thought to us. *We are attempting to bring a person ten millennia into the future. Such things cannot be done without sacrifice. The spell calls for such, or we* will *fail.*

I knew he was right. The prophecy had warned me. I thought it to the squad. *A life restored, a willing life given in balance.*

That seems pretty cut and dried, my father thought, and I could feel his intent. We all could. *I'm tired, guys. I love seeing my kids kick ass, but I don't want to do this anymore. And retirement just isn't for me. You saw how it was, Jer. I was miserable.*

That doesn't mean there isn't some new, better path, I countered. *There's no reason to do this. We don't even know who's on that ship, or if they're worth saving.*

We know they're important, my dad reasoned. *We know that a prophecy exists just so we can bring them back. And we know we don't have a ship, unless we do this. I was supposed to die on Kemet, Jer. You gave me every day since, and a chance to get to know my daughter.*

Rava was silent, but the bond exposed her emotions. The raw pain, layered atop the loss of Arcan, was more than she could bear. But in her mind I also read resignation. She knew dad was right.

They all did. Only I refused to accept it, even though I knew it was the only real answer. *Dad...*

It's my choice. There was a moment of pure elation, and then my father was gone.

Our version of the *Remora* flickered, and vanished, then was replaced by a shining ship I only half recognized.

I released the magic, and collapsed to my knees. The rings above me slowed, and the spell ended. I panted into my armor, and my head lolled to the side in my helmet.

The first thing I saw was Rava. She rose shakily to her

feet, and I blinked when my HUD updated. That couldn't be right. Her chest now contained a seed of *fire* magic.

I glanced at Vee, then Kurz, and their profiles updated to match. Both had also gained *fire*. And me?

I probed within myself mentally. I'd already possessed *fire* magic. Had the ship given me something else? Yes, it had. I could feel a complex spell woven into my very soul, something involving divination, though it wasn't clear to me what it meant.

Normally I'd have expected greater fire magic, which would have increased both my resistance, and my own pool. It's what every mage craved, really. More raw power. But the ship apparently had other plans, and I didn't have any time to investigate.

"Why?!?" Rava shrieked. She beat at her sides with her fists and screamed wordlessly. "I don't understand why it has to be so hard. Why do they have to keep dying? It isn't fair. I just found him..."

In that instant I knew what a terrible person I was. My sister was crying out for our father, who'd just sacrificed his life, and I was worried about the magic I'd gained from a Catalyst?

I ran to Rava, and threw my arms around her. We sank to our knees, and rocked back and forth as we began to cry.

"I worked so hard to keep him alive," I whispered. "I'm sorry. I tried. I did everything I could."

"It isn't your fault." Rava hugged me even more

fiercely. "I'm angry...but not at you, at least not about this. Not even dad. He did it for us. And..."

"...And it was the right call," I finished for her. "I hate that it was."

I shook my head to clear it as something involving the prophecy welled up. It wanted us to go to the *Remora*, but this time I wasn't going to be yanked about like a puppet.

"What now?" Vee asked quietly, her tone subdued. Her attention was focused on her bracelet, which now sported an enormous trio of fire rubies that hadn't been there before.

"Now we get Briff back," I decided aloud. "I learned some things in there. Things that are becoming clear now. I know what the swarm is, and why it's insane. I know who Cindra is, and why she never took the bridge."

The bridge's golden doors began rolling into the floor again. I hadn't realized they'd even closed, but perhaps that had happened when I had gotten into the matrix.

Whatever the reason...once the doors were gone it exposed about a dozen arachnidrakes who were clearly awaiting our arrival as they lounged outside. They were led by the same one with the silver staff, though I didn't have a name for the drake who'd given me the prophecy.

"It seems my trust was well placed," the drake called. He scuttled onto the bridge, and bowed. "We were not formally introduced. I am called Kek. I have brought those who wish to see an end to the strife. Who believe that we can work with our neighbors, and perhaps restore this ship."

I might not have recognized the creature, but the black staff with the eight red eyes was unmistakably the same as the one who'd shot fire bolted me.

I nodded and strode over to Kek without the slightest fear now that the Web had provided a glimpse of his life. That impression still lay in my mind, though it was fading quickly. "I saw you when I was in there. Saw your people. I believe Cindra will see reason, and we're going to need her help to deal with the swarm."

INTERLUDE IV

Minister Ramachan hated that a title had replaced her first name. Her identity as a mother, as a woman, and as a lover had all been sacrificed to that title. Never more so than today.

The hoverchairs in front of her desk were occupied by literal goddesses. On the right sat a woman that Ramachan knew by reputation. Nara, or Xal'Nara as she was now called. The purple-skinned demon had begun as a war hero, then been accused of being a traitor, and finally defected to her true people, proving her detractors correct.

In the other chair sat a woman with a deceptively innocent appearance, despite being crafted from magma and flame. She looked like a Ternus pleasure house model made to fulfill some awful fantasy. Coy. The girl next door. But utterly lethal, even before she'd become a god.

Frit was also known for her treachery against the Confederacy, though she'd since been pardoned, and the Krox had nominally accepted her into the fold, as Ramachan understood it.

The idea of the Confederacy, of Ternus, working with the Krox after having a half dozen of their colonies scorched to the ground seemed preposterous. Yet there it was. Peace, at any cost. And maybe it was the right choice.

Wasn't she about to make a deal with the very same Krox?

"When will you know?" Nara asked quietly. There was an intensity to her that Frit lacked. The knowledge that if you displeased her she could and would disintegrate you. There was no threat, of course. But the demon exuded menace all the same.

"Soon, I hope." The minister blinked as her mind returned to the conversation. "When Jerek passed the trials he said that his experience was nearly instant. They will happen in the mind, I imagine. Whatever the magic they are nearly instant."

She realized sheepishly that she'd just repeated herself. That was a mistake she'd not made since the first year of college, when she'd met Irala. Back when they'd just been roommates. She was rambling.

"If it isn't inappropriate," Frit began, her tone as gentle as her appearance, "perhaps we could discuss specifics? We understand your need for funds, and whether you choose the Krox or the tech demons, we will see that you have the credits to pay the Inurans in time."

"If they play fair, you mean." Ramachan rose from her desk, and nodded at the scry-screen that covered the wall. It currently showed the Vagrant Fleet, and beyond that the Inuran trade moon, nearly as large as the *Word of Xal*. She'd chosen to remain on her flagship, rather than the Great Ship. Her gut said stay here. Be ready to run. Her gut was why she was still alive. "The Inurans are going to make a move. I don't know what it is, but the hammer will fall soon. They'll make an excuse. They'll accuse us of something. Then they'll attack with everything they have. And they have a lot. Unless one of you ladies is interested in disposing of them? We could factor that into the purchase price of a Great Ship."

The door to her office hissed, and a figure in midnight armor strode in. The ropey sinew around the suit's neck slithered away to show Irala's beautiful face, her smile a salve on their awful situation.

"I've done it." Irala approached, and sat heavily on a hovercouch against the wall. "I'm connected to the ship. I'll still need Jerek to turn over command, but I'm listed as an officer and can control most functions."

"Well done, my love." Ramachan beamed a smile, her relief shining in her eyes, but never voiced as tears.

Both Nara and Frit were watching them, their

empathy clear. Even demons had loved ones, she supposed.

"We cannot intervene," Nara said. She looked to Frit, who nodded. "The Confederacy has specific laws, and if we break them there are those who'd use it to fuel war. The Confederacy is still a fragile thing. We need to use proper channels."

"And what are those proper channels?" Ramachan's hand trembled, the rage a living thing. "What am I to tell my people? The barest remnant survives, but the Inurans plan to remedy even that. They plan to take our ship, and your Confederacy won't help. Can't you translocate back to Shaya and fill out whatever form you require?"

"It isn't that simple." Frit offered an empathetic sigh. "And you're right to be angry. This is dragon dung, I agree. But if we don't play the political game everyone loses. You need to contact the Confederacy on your own and ask for help."

"How?" Ramachan cried. A single tear slid down her cheek, bearing the sum of her frustration and rage. "The Inurans are jamming communications. They can and will manufacture an excuse to attack. Illegally. Yet you will stand by and do nothing?"

"We all know what Matron Jolene is capable of, but she hasn't broken any laws yet." Nara rose and shrugged, which at least appeared sincere. "I am terribly sorry. Your world has paid the price for politics that have nothing to do with you. I know exactly what that's like. I know how impossible this feels. Find a way to do it anyway, or your people will pay the price."

The minister closed her eyes. She would not cry. There had to be a way around the Inuran blockade, but she just couldn't see it. They were trapped and blind, with no allies worth a damn, other than Irala.

She shouldn't have expected so much from demons, and whatever the depths Frit was. "I see. Thank you for your time, ladies. Please contact me when you've acquired our asking price, and we'll discuss the terms of delivery. Please make it soon, or you may find there are no ships left to claim."

16

I walked tall as I strode down the corridor, through the library, and into the part of the ship where Cinaka and her hatchlings had taken my best friend. Briff and I hadn't spent much time together lately, and if I'd sent him to his death I'd never forgive myself.

Thankfully, I was guided by my vision in the temporal matrix. Only now did I begin to understand what it had imparted. I'd perceived things the human mind was incapable of processing. A fourth, and possibly fifth dimension. Time and...probability?

What I'd been left with was one perfect moment of clarity. In that moment I'd seen the entire sector, though I hadn't been consciously aware of it. I'd seen the swarm, and Cindra, and the *World of Xal*, where my mother was about to step into the reactor to begin her trials.

I'd seen far more, though. I'd seen Shaya, and Virkon,

and Nebiat, and Colony 3, and Ternus, and...beyond. Some of that was still in my head.

In this case it meant that I understood Cindra, and her children. The hatchlings, and their Wyrm Mother, were honorable. They wouldn't harm Briff, unless he gave them cause.

So I strode down that darkened corridor without fear, and my company followed after me. We were too many to call a squad any longer, at least if I got to count Kek and his people. On the one hand the responsibility terrified me.

On the other people were looking to me with real respect, including Vee. More importantly...I respected myself. I knew what the other path was like. I knew about disappointing myself over and over, and pretending it wouldn't happen again when I knew it would.

Somewhere back on Kemet I'd made a choice to be a different guy. A guy who built and helped, not consumed and burdened. I guess maybe that was what becoming an adult meant. Maybe that was why my dad was proud. I'd finally made the conscious choice to become a man.

Our company flowed down the corridor, and we made no move to hide our presence. They had to know we were coming, and the question remained what they'd do about it. There was a chance they'd attack, but I thought it more likely they'd alert Cindra and ask what she wanted.

Cindra would be curious and unthreatened, if my glimpse of her mind was accurate.

We entered a long corridor that was much wider than the rest. I recognized a killing field when I saw one, and realized this must be why the hatchlings had chosen this place.

One had to cross a hundred meters of open ground in a corridor thirty meters wide, only to reach another choke point on the far side. An enemy force could easily fill the room, where they'd be cut down until their opponents ran out of spells or targets, whichever came first.

"Hey, bro," Rava whispered into the squad's private comm. It was the first time she'd called me that. "Are you sure you want to do this? If we step into this room, they could end us all."

"Point taken," I whispered back. Then I raised my hand and clenched a fist. The column came to a halt, and I activated my external speakers. "I'm going to proceed alone. I expect they'll meet me at the hallway. If they cut me down, then we know I was wrong, and you guys need to hightail it to the *Remora* and get back to the *Word* with as many scales as you can carry."

No one protested, but as I stepped into the wider corridor and began to cross I noticed that Rava, Kurz, and Vee all followed. For a moment, just a moment, I found myself scanning for my father. No. Focus.

I turned back to my destination and walked boldly toward the other end. The rest of the squad fanned out behind me. Only Rava had her weapon out, though her rifle was lowered at least. My hand rested on my new pistol, mostly for comfort.

As expected, we were met at the other end. A pair of unconcerned smoky-grey hatchlings stepped from the point where the hallway narrowed to meet us.

"You are the white-scale's pets?" the male on the right rumbled in ancient draconic. "Why are you with the twisted ones? They are not welcome here, and we will slay them if they approach."

"They won't," I reassured him, then punctuated it with a bow. "I've come to speak to Cindra, about the Web of Divinity, and about this ship. I think she'll want to see me."

The hatchling blinked slitted eyes down at me as he considered the request. He remained silent for long moments, and out of the corner of my eye I could see the squad tensing. This could get ugly if I didn't hurry it along.

"I doubt it, but it's your life," the hatchling finally said. He pointed behind him, up the narrow corridor. "You may go, but only you. The rest of the no-scales must stay here. If there is treachery, then we will devour them all. Is that understood, pet?"

"Understood," I confirmed. Then I switched to internal comms. "Get ready to bolt if you need to. Fall back rather than fight if threatened, unless you have no other choice. I'm going in to get Briff."

I wasn't really sure what to expect as I entered Cindra's lair. I had ideas from holos and books, but no idea about the real thing. I might have glimpsed a moment in time, but it left massive gaps, and this was one of them. I could still be walking to my death.

At least I was doing it alone. The *Remora* would make it back, and if my mother succeeded, then the *Word of Xal* would still have a captain. No one else would be endangered, except Briff.

I quickened my step and was almost trotting by the time I reached the first hatchlings. I emerged into a cavernous hangar dominated by a pair of ancient rusted out turbines. The hatchlings had built their houses in and around the turbines, and had what appeared to be a small marketplace setup around them.

All the walls, and even the ceiling, had been lined with metal spikes. Most of those spikes were empty, but here and there an arachnidrake skull, or a particularly large spider, had been staked out as a trophy.

A few hatchlings glanced in my direction, but none seemed all that interested. They eyed us warily, but in a way that said we were someone else's problem unless we made ourselves one of theirs.

I skirted the edge of the market, and scanned for an area big enough to hold an adult Wyrm. One of Cindra's age would be massive...probably equal to Visala's size, or somewhere close.

The problem was I didn't spot anywhere that a Wyrm

like that could be, or any area like a throne room, or even HQ. This encampment resembled a mercenary swap meet more than it did an organized military force or even a town.

Hatchlings flowed down one of four corridors, including the one I'd entered through. Maybe this place was larger than I'd glimpsed in my vision? I'd been certain she was somewhere in this room.

I wandered around the edge of the market and noticed that as I approached the far side, the level of technology increased. More hatchlings wore armor and carried spellrifles instead of melee weapons.

One hatchling I passed had a cybernetic eye, which whirred in my direction as I hurried past. He lost interest and disappeared into the crowd. I kept glancing behind me, but didn't see him following as I threaded between two rows of canvas tents.

Hatchlings sat on the floor or on hovercouches, each in groups of two or three. They were clustered around holounits, and they were playing...Arena.

"You've got to be..." I trailed off as I realized what I was seeing. They weren't just playing Arena. They were playing *this season's* version of the game. These bastards had been pirating our content. Ah, well, couldn't really blame them as there didn't seem a lot to do on the ship.

I slowed my pace as I passed between the tents. There was no sign of the cybered hatchling, who probably had nothing to do with me. I was more interested in finding...Briff.

The last tent on the right had a giant screen with two players. My best friend and a creature out of my nightmares.

His companion wasn't human, though she could be mistaken for one. In fact, she looked a lot like me. Hairless. Where there should have been skin, though, lay tiny scales of the same shade of grey as the hatchlings. A pair of draconic wings rose from her back, and she had a tail, albeit a small one.

"Jerek?" Briff rose from his hovercouch with a grin. "How did you get here?"

His companion paused the game, and rose to study me. I knew instantly that I was looking at Cindra, though I hadn't a clue about the body she currently wore. Legends said Wyrms could shape change, but the Wyrms on Kemet hadn't been in a hurry to confirm or deny that.

"Long story, bud." I considered telling him about my dad, but that could come later. "The important thing is that I saw the Web of Divinity, and I touched the insanity that's infesting it. I know the cause. I thought Cindra might be interested in hearing more."

Cindra blinked at me. Her face was human, but the eyes were draconic and alien. "No. I am not. You're a fool if you think the Web can be tamed, or the swarm reasoned with. Or even exterminated. They are eternal, and that part of the ship is best avoided."

Well, crap. That seemed final. I couldn't give up though.

"The Web showed me your mind." Maybe telling her wasn't the smartest idea, and I could feel myself taking a step backward out of the stall. "I know you're honorable. I know you served on this vessel before it was marooned here. This is the *Flame of Knowledge*, right? And you remember what the dragonflights were like before? This is your chance to correct the mistakes of the past. To bring your children back to the galactic stage, and help the galaxy grow and learn."

"Nah." Cindra turned back to the game and unpaused it. "You can stay and play if you want, but I've got no interest in your quest. Keep your politics."

17

I stood there in mute protest, wishing that I had a line of attack that would convince this literal dragon-lady that I was worth her time. I glanced at Briff, who'd sheepishly picked up his controller and gone back to playing Arena with Cindra.

A thought tickled the back of my mind. Cindra oozed boredom. She was ten millennia old, and had seen and done everything. The most exciting thing to her was anything new, which is why she was hanging out with Briff.

I wondered what would happen if I took away her toys? I prayed that this didn't backfire spectacularly.

"Hey, Briff, buddy, we're going to head out." I jerked a thumb over my shoulder in the rough direction of the *Remora*. "Our friends and family are counting on us. We have to complete the mission. Are you with us? If you're not and you want to stay, there won't be any hard feelings, man. This place is paradise."

Every once in a while I have a good idea. This was, thankfully, one of those times. Cindra's ears perked, and by the end she was studying me openly. I dangled the adventure before her. Now to see if she'd take the bait. That all depended on Briff's answer.

"I'm green, Jer." He rose with a flap of his wings and tapped the pause on the controller. "Sorry, Cindra. I appreciate the games. You're probably the best scout I've ever seen, and I've played with Rava. You're really good. I hope we get a chance to play again, but I have to go help my friends. What we're doing is important."

Had we been anywhere else I'd have delivered the kind of hug that was perfectly at home in the kind of bromance Briff and I shared. He'd had my back, as always. How could I not love him?

"Thank you for your hospitably, Cindra." I gave her a bow, and offered the praise sincerely. "Enjoy your match. I prefer the stealth kit when I'm playing mage killer. I wish I had your reflexes."

She returned an eye roll, then lounged back on her hovercouch. "You're seriously going to run off, right back into the fray? You're willing to watch your friends fail and die, and turn on each other?"

Briff stopped and turned back to her. "Yeah."

"It's that simple for you?" Cindra raised a row of slightly lighter scales that I took for an eyebrow.

"Yeah," Briff repeated, this time with more confidence, but then seemed to realize more was required. "I like Arena. I mean, I *really* like Arena. But I like making a difference more. The Inurans are bad people. They'll come for you here, someday. If I stay then we'll have to fight them alone. But if I go back I can make sure you never even know that they exist. Jerek will stop them. But he needs me."

"You're right about that." I clapped my friend on the wing. "You're my brother, man. Family. I've got news, when we head back."

"Who?" Briff's wings and tail drooped to the deck, and he wouldn't look me in the eye.

"My father." I licked my lips, and repressed the emotions. Emotions are bullshit, as we've previously discussed. "He chose it. The prophecy showed me what to do, how to finish a spell they started ten millennia ago. But to finish we needed a sacrifice, and he...he just did it."

Briff stepped forward and gathered me into a hug. I was grateful for the helmet. No one saw the tears, which I couldn't have stopped even if I had wanted to.

"I'm sorry, Jer." He hugged me fiercely, which could have been lethal if not for the armor. "You're my family too. That sounds just like your dad. He chose how he went out. I bet he liked that. If you want maybe we can tell stories about him over dinner."

"I'd like that." I pressed gently and he released me. "I think Rava would too."

"Okay, okay," Cindra interrupted. She rose to her feet and fluffed her wings with a disgusted sigh. "I can't not see this all play out. Tell me more. And tell me what you think your 'solution' to the madness infesting this ship might be."

I tempered my expectations. She hadn't agreed to anything yet, but at least she was listening. And I'd had a minute to catch up with my friend.

"When I touched the Web of Divinity," I explained as I sought the best way to articulate what I'd learned, "I saw the swarm. I saw you, as you were on the day of Planetfall. And since. I've spoken with Kemet, the Guardian of my ship."

"Admiral Kemet?" Cindra blinked those slitted eyes at me. "That Kemet?"

"I think so." I had no idea what rank he'd held, but that tracked. "We've brought the *Word of Xal* back online. There's no reason that you can't bring the *Flame of Knowledge* back online. But the Catalyst is untamed. The magic is running wild, which is why the swarm has gone mad, and expanded to be so large. There was always meant to be a buffer there, the same buffer Kemet fills on our ship."

I paused then, to see if she was tracking. Her faux brows knit together in what I took for anger. "So your solution to a madness that, even now, infects the edges of your mind, is to sacrifice me to it? Have you considered the consequences if I fail? Can you imagine what would happen if I went insane? What this ship might become? The horrors it could unleash?"

"Yes, and it terrifies me," I answered quietly, and it did. "Someone, a soulcatcher named Patra, decided that it was worth doing. So much so that she sacrificed her life, and created a prophecy to bring about this whole sequence of events. Our meeting. You have the power to alter the fate of this system, of this fleet."

"No." That was definitely a glare. She folded her arms imperiously, and towered a good hand and a half over me. "I will not risk my life. I will not be a...a buffer to this ship, only to end up slaughtering my children. If you wish to stop the Inurans that Briff told me about, then you have my aid. I will send a dozen of my finest to the hold where your ship waits. As for the *Flame*? She is lost. Leave it be, or it will consume you as it has countless others. Do you think you're the first to try? The hundredth? The hubris. It sickens me. Now go, child. You are lucky your friend interests me. Be well, Briff, and take care of your human. He must require constant looking after."

She turned back to her game. I thought about replying, but sensed that would be a mistake. Instead I turned quietly and slunk away. In this instance I couldn't blame Cindra, nor could I refute what she was saying. What right did I have to ask that she become Guardian?

But if she didn't, then I couldn't safely use the Web. No one could. That terrified me, because when the

Inurans came...what would their experiments create? I couldn't let them be the ones to tame this ship.

How would I prevent it though?

My shoulders were slumped as I trudged back through the bazaar and down the narrow corridor where the pair of hatchlings still had the rest of our squad under guard.

Thankfully, they hadn't devoured my friends as threatened. Instead, someone had broken out a Kem'Hedj board, and Kurz was annihilating one of the hatchlings, his sea of white stones enveloping the black.

The guards rose at our approach, and the one who'd been playing seemed relieved the game had ended. He offered Kurz the briefest of nods. "Well matched."

Kurz returned the nod, and spoke in his usual monotone. "Well matched."

The squad fell in silently around us as we approached Kek and his arachnidrakes. I used the time to think.

In a way, the encounter had been a victory. I had Briff. Cindra had even agreed to send troops to help us fight. So why didn't this feel like a win?

Because Cindra was right. I could feel the madness lurking in the dimmest corners of my mind, hiding from the light of rational thought. Just a shade, but also a warning of what could happen if I continued to use the Web. The shadows would grow.

This ship was dangerous.

If I left it as it was the Inurans would use the Web

without a second thought, and if a pilot went insane they'd simply kill the poor fool and install another.

In their hubris they'd never realize how much damage a pilot could do before they realized how far gone they were. I'd moved a ship from ten millennia in the past into the present, with no training.

What could a pilot who understood this ship do? What could Cindra do? I understood her terror, but I was still convinced I was right. This ship needed a Guardian, or it would never heal.

Kek scuttled closer to meet us as we approached, ending my solitude. He rapped his staff on the deck three times. "Welcome, friend Jerek. Were you successful?"

Had I been?

18

I was conscious of the eyes on me when I answered Kek's question. The squad was watching, as were Kek's companions. It seemed they could all understand us, though they seemed to prefer conversing in their native tongue, which I wished I had the time to study properly.

"We were partially successful," I finally answered, and it seemed to fit. I started walking up the corridor, and waited for Kek to fall in beside me with that awkward shamble of limbs before I spoke again. "Cindra won't oppose us, but she won't consent to becoming Guardian of this ship. I'm convinced that's what it most needs. A mind to tame the swarm and shape it back into the ordered mass the Web was intended to be."

"Hmm," Kek exclaimed. His staff clicked on the deck in time with his lurching gait, and I found a rhythm there

I'd missed before. "What qualities must this Guardian possess? Have you observed one? Did you have them on your world?"

It occurred to me that this ship comprised Kek's entire world, and that unlike the hatchlings he didn't seem aware of the signals Kemet had broadcast. He lived like an ancient scholar in some isolated colony.

"Almost all Catalysts have a Guardian," I explained, as Kemet had explained it to me. "That Guardian serves as a protector, archivist, and even an executioner, depending on need. In the case of this ship they are a kind of steward that keeps it all running. They'd be connected to the Web, and to the swarm. That's why Cindra isn't interested. The swarm is insane, and touching insanity...well, it spreads."

I shivered and glanced at the wall next to me. It crawled with spiders...until I looked it directly. Then the wall was empty, unless you counted pitted rust stains.

"This Guardian," Kek prompted as we continued away from Cindra's territory, the rest of the squad behind us. "They must posses an iron will, yes? A trained will?"

"I'd imagine so. They'd also need to be a powerful *fire* mage, or they'll never survive the union with that core." I wrapped my hand around the grip of my new, as of yet unnamed, pistol, then glanced down in sudden realization. I'd been touched by the core, and so had it.

I drew the pistol and examined the changes as we walked. The metal had taken on a dusky red tint, and I could feel the power within it. The flame, waiting to be discharged. I could also feel a child-like intelligence, the barest beginnings of a mind.

The weapon was more potent than Ariela had been. She'd never developed speech, though occasionally I had empathic impressions from her. This pistol, though, already seemed to possess that much intelligence.

"You really like it?" Vee asked as she moved up on the side opposite Kek.

"It's amazing. Thank you. Again." I holstered her again. "I have a feeling she'll tell me her name when she's ready."

"It seems you are already bonding the weapon," Kek chittered, three of his eyes fixed on my holster, while the rest studied other angles. It was unnerving, but probably gave a massive advantage. How did you sneak up on something with eight eyes? He nodded respectfully to Vee. "You are the artificer who birthed the weapon?"

"I did." Vee's shoulders squared, and she wore her smile openly. "It's the best thing I've designed so far. I never thought I'd see her given form. This ship is amazing. Terrible sometimes, but also amazing."

"Indeed." Kurz's voice came from directly behind us, though I hadn't been aware of the soulcatcher. "There are...terrors. But also wonders. And an incredible wealth of history and lore. The souls in this place are ancient and numerous. I see them everywhere."

His eyes were downcast, and for the first time I

thought I might know why. If the dead were all around me, would I want to look them in the eye? Probably not. I could use *fire* magic to configure my HUD to display the location of souls, but beyond ensuring I never slept again I didn't see the point.

"Friend Jerek," Kek chittered. "I believe that I possess the necessary qualities to be Guardian. I believe that the prophecy was meant to prepare me, and I have devoted much of my life to its study. I will hold the swarm at bay, and contain the insanity. I am powerful, but not so powerful that I might become a threat to the sector as Cindra could. I have an idea to that end."

My hand wrapped around my pistol grip again, more for comfort than anything else. When I'd wanted someone to be Guardian I'd assumed they'd be powerful enough to contain the swarm and heal the ship.

"What's the advantage of you becoming Guardian if you're just going to go insane?" I shook my head. "I don't see the value."

"My people have a concept we practice," Kek explained. "We call it no mind. Perhaps meditation is a better name, though that does not capture it fully. When you practice no mind you gradually empty your cup of concern. Of anger. My peace, it is a salve. When I am used up, then you will simply apply more salve. Eventually the true healing will begin, and a real Guardian will be found. For now, though, I can begin the process. If you will support me in this, friend Jerek, then I will send my people with you in your fight against the Inurans. You will make an ally of this ship."

I hated that I was essentially duct-taping the problem, but I couldn't argue with Kek's logic. A temporary Guardian could begin the healing and manage the swarm. And who knew? Kek might last for years, or even decades, before the cracks began to show. We had no way of knowing.

That wasn't true. We did have a way.

"All right," I agreed. We'd nearly reached the outskirts of the library. "The bridge isn't that far from here. Let's push for it, and see if you can bond the ship."

A rustling like leaves in the autumn wind back at academy rolled through the library around us. It came again, stronger, and there was a word there. A single insidious whisper from a thousand, thousand mouths. "Treaaacherrryyy."

"Uh oh." I yanked my pistol from its holster and cradled it in both hands. It felt so much more natural than firing through the suit. "I suspect we're about to have a lot of company. Anyone with *fire* magic—that's everyone in my squad now—cut a path to the bridge. Briff, focus on larger targets."

"It will be so, friend Jerek." Kek nodded, then turned to chitter a long string of gibberish at his companions. Many nodded, and the arachnidrakes scuttled out to establish a rough perimeter around Kek.

I trotted forward with my pistol ready to bring up. I'd

made it maybe twenty meters when a writhing tide of spiders carpeted the floor before me. They surged forward, far more quickly than I'd thought the swarm could.

My pistol came up and I filled her with *fire*, then added a layer of *void*. That had worked before, and hopefully the pistol would amplify it.

A rolling wave of flame twenty-five meters long jetted into the swarm, and sizzled away spiders, rust, and even the grime on the floor. Only smooth gleaming deck was left...for an instant.

The tide of spiders was endless, and this time they weren't daunted by my spells. They kept coming. But I wasn't alone.

Rava hurled her last grenade deep up the hallway, and it detonated spectacularly. The resulting wave of fire cooked everything within twenty meters, duplicating my spell but with more fanfare and shrapnel.

Vee raised her bracelet and a ball of pure white flame appeared in her hand, she held it there until the next wave of spiders surged, then she tossed it casually into their midst.

The flame was similar to mine, but where I'd infused it with *void* she'd done so with *life*. The flames cooked far hotter, and left an oily residue in their wake.

More spiders clawed their way forward, but each time someone from our ranks answered.

We marched slowly up the corridor, and wound

through the library as wave after wave of spiders approached. They were still small, none larger than a sidearm, but they were unending. The larger ones would be on their way, no doubt, but I hoped if we moved quickly we might reach the bridge before they did.

At least we didn't have to pass the egg room and the elevators again.

"Above us!" Rava shouted.

I got my weapon up, but too late. A large multi-limbed body knocked me to the deck, and more spiders, of all sizes, were landing all around us.

"Nnnnoooooooo!!!" Kurz's hands shot up, and each contained a vial. He crushed both, and twin clouds of toxic green flowed outward in living tendrils. "You will not have us!"

The smoke curled outwards, snaking into the closest spider's mouth, then the next, and the next. All of the spiders who'd landed among us suddenly froze. Their eyes, which burned with inner flame, now reflected the same toxic green.

"Protect us," Kurz demanded. "Kill your brethren. Let none reach us."

The dominated spiders scuttled into the masses gathering to attack us, their limbs and incisors stabbing outward as they devoured their smaller brethren. The largest spider paused, then spit a river of silky white over the corridor. Thousands of smaller spiders were covered, and unable to move.

I raised my pistol, and began emptying spells into the webbing. The flames spread quickly, and the screams of the dying spiders haunt me still.

We sprinted through the library, and our escorts made short work of their more numerous brethren. Here and there one of us added a *fire* spell, but most of us were husbanding resources, as we didn't know when we'd be able to rest next.

Finally we made it through the library and into the far corridor, which led to the bridge. The spiders were thinner there, and I finally holstered my pistol as they fell back before the onslaught of Kurz's enslaved minions.

The arachnidrakes loosed the occasional fireball from the tips of their staves, and with so many of them it appeared each had many spells remaining. I hoped it was enough.

We pressed up the final corridor, and to the sealed golden door. I hurried up and supplied both missing sigils, and waited impatiently as the metal slid into the floor.

The spiders were waiting for us.

19

Weapons came up, but I raised an arm, and my people held their fire. The spiders hadn't advanced. They clogged every visible part of the bridge in writhing mounds.

Kurz emptied his stomach onto the deck, but then straightened and wiped his mouth. "I'm green, Captain."

I turned back to the swarm, and took a single step into the room. As I'd half hoped, the mounds gathered, and the face we'd seen before re-formed. It studied me with all eight of those terrible eyes, each comprised of dozens of smaller spiders.

"Whhyyy," it hissed. "Why do youuu betray us? You said knowwwledge. You said here to helllp."

"I *am* here to help." I slowly pointed at Kek. "He is willing to help, too. Kek wants to merge with the ship. To heal it. To make it like it was. Do you remember what that was like? Before the pain?"

The face writhed in what I took for thought. When it spoke the tone was still accusatory. "You triiick. We kiiilll. None willl leave alllive."

"Guess we're done negotiating." I yanked my sidearm from the holster, and reached for my magic.

We were standing no more than thirty meters from the hole in the floor that led to the lava. I reached deep for the *void*, and then raised my spellpistol and launched a ball of pulsing black energy.

My magic was stronger now, and so was my weapon, which reflected in the size and potency of the magic. The gravity bomb detonated directly over the pit.

Spiders skittered across the floor towards us...at first. Then the gravity well seized them, and one by one they were picked up and sucked into the micro-singularity.

It wasn't powerful enough to kill them, but that was okay. It didn't need to be. A rain of spiders fell from the spell and tumbled into the lava below. Hundreds became thousands, and those few who escaped met with the fury of the rest of the squad.

Within moments we'd cleared out the bridge. I waved everyone inside, then sealed the door. My chest was heaving, but more with elation than fear. We'd done it. Now, theoretically at least, we could finally end this.

"Kek, you can see the lava pool," I panted as I staggered in that direction. "If you're really set to do this, that's where you need to go."

"I am resolved." Kek shuffled forward, and stopped near the edge of the pit. He stared down into the lava, which cast him with a hellish glow. Then he turned back to me. "I do not wish to kill my companion through my actions, however." Kek extended his eight-eyed staff toward me. "Take her. She is called Kithik. She will serve you well, and if not you then another. Do not let her die, friend Jerek."

"I will use her, or find her a better home," I promised as I took Kithik's black haft in my free hand. I still had my pistol drawn, and was reluctant to holster it even though the bridge was secure. "We appreciate what you're doing. The whole ship. The whole fleet. I will find a way to get you help, Kek. Just hold on as long as you can."

"Of course, friend Jerek."

I expected some long speech, or a wave or something. Kek simply leapt, and tumbled down into the lava. He landed on it with a sizzling hiss, then slowly sank beneath the surface. If the lava caused him pain he didn't show it, which boded well in my opinion.

His body disappeared entirely, and I was left standing alone at the edge of the pit. I glanced behind me, but the rest of the squad were all clustered near the door, clearly ready to bolt.

"Hey, bro," Rava called hesitantly. "Is this guy going to be able to keep the spiders off us now? If yes, let's bail.

Yesterday. These things make my skin crawl. Kurz gets me, right?"

"I cannot get off this ship quickly enough." The handsome lurker gave a shiver and closed his eyes for a moment as he mastered himself. "I do not love spiders, though I will never again run from them. In that I suppose this ship has been a test sent by the Maker. We do not always like growth. It is messy and painful, but ultimately what we need."

Rava barked a short laugh. "I'd like to avoid any more pain. Briff, you realize that we're boned, right? The *Remora* switched places. It took our rig. We can't play Arena."

Briff patted his satchel and offered Rava a toothy grin. "Cindra gave me a unit, and it's got the final patch before...the end. We can set it up on the new ship once we get there."

Rava perked up at that. "You are a god."

"Let's move out," I ordered. There was no sense putting this off. If the Guardian thing worked I don't think it mattered where on the ship we were. He'd be able to find us.

Vee tapped the door, which slid silently into the floor and revealed the library once more.

"Oh, crap," I muttered.

Everyone looked at me.

"We're going to have to go down that lift," I pointed

out as I started to walk, "and we're going to have to pass through the egg room again."

"Is there another way?" Vee asked, though she didn't seem terribly concerned by the idea of facing that room.

"There is not." An arachnidrake comprised of pure flame ignited in the hallway before me, and I blinked when I realized it was a perfect replica of Kek. He offered an awkward bow. "It appears I was successful. I have merged with the ship. There is so much...too much...to grasp. And the madness covers everything. Everything I touch. It has festered for so long. The swarm is in so much pain..."

"I pity them," I agreed, "but we need a way off this ship. Can you keep the spiders away from our path back to the ship?"

"I—no." Kek's mandibles quivered. "The swarm will not obey me. I can control the parts of the ship that still work, but the swarm is its own entity. It was conditioned to listen to the ship, but not required. Someone more powerful than I will need to master the swarm. I am sorry, friend Jerek."

"You did wonderfully," I countered. "You gave your life for us, and for the ship. If you can maintain your own sanity while helping to restore the ship, that's all we can ask. I will find you some help, somehow. There has to be someone out there strong enough."

"I believe in you, friend Jerek." The way he bowed said quite the opposite. He thought I was leaving him here to slowly go mad. "Be well, and take care of your ship. Never let it become like the *Flame*."

An urgent skittering sounded in the distance.

"Time to move!" I bellowed. I sprinted toward the lifts at top speed, and prayed that we wouldn't run into anything until we were inside.

We ran full tilt through the near darkness, aided only by the occasional failing light set into the walls. Along the way we passed a fortune in knowledge scales, but no one complained. My father would have, and his absence pressed down on me.

I ached for my dad, as he'd have been incapable of passing without grabbing at least a few. I ran twice as hard.

Eventually I saw the light of the lifts in the distance, and the whole squad redoubled their pace. The surviving arachnidrakes shambled behind us, not as fast, but steady.

We piled into the same car we'd arrived in, and the doors rumbled shut behind us. I studied the lift's console, my chest heaving as I gulped lungfuls of stale air.

Think. Think. How could I get us to the *Remora* safely? The spiders knew our destination, and they'd stop at nothing to kill us.

"Guardian, I know you can't control the swarm," I called into the air, as Kek hadn't entered the lift. "Can you incinerate us a path? Fill the egg room with fire, and the corridors leading back. Scorch this place, so we can get back to the ship safely."

Kek's voice hissed through the speakers in the lift's walls. "It will be so, friend Jerek, but the spiders are many and will return. You must be swift. Run. Run and do not look back or you will be lost."

I tapped the controls to bring us back to the egg room, and forced my breathing to calm as we whirred off in that direction. No one joked. No one bantered. We were exhausted, and justifiably terrified.

"When the doors open," I said in a low tone, "we make a run for it. Do not stop for anything. We make for the cargo hold."

20

T he lift doors slid open to reveal an utter wasteland. I didn't know what Kek had done, but every web and every spider were now ash. "Go!" I bellowed.

We sprinted out of the lift, and back up the corridor we'd taken originally. At first I allowed a cautious optimism to take root, but it was as if the ship were waiting for that.

A distant layered screeching began, and it somehow conveyed the hatred the swarm felt for us. They were coming from everywhere, all over the ship. And they were coming for us.

No one needed to speak or confirm it. We saved our breath for running, and moved as a group. I could have gone faster, and I'm certain Rava could have lapped us all, but no one outpaced Kurz, our slowest member.

Minutes rolled by and the screeching grew louder, and louder, to the point where conversation wasn't possible without out internal comms.

"We've got about four hundred meters left," I panted as I pumped both arms furiously. "Rava, Briff, get in there and tell them we're coming in hot. Vee, get ready to treat wounded."

"And me, Captain?" Kurz choked out as he ran.

"You said this ship is full of souls, right?" I slowed and let Kurz get a slight lead on me. "Wake them up. And make them fight spiders."

Kurz slowed, then stopped, and withdrew a vial from the bottom of his satchel. It was larger than the others, and I hadn't noticed it before because the glass was opaque. There was a glow, either because it was empty or the glass wasn't designed to let light through.

"I will need time, Captain." Kurz reached into a pouch and began setting out ritual supplies next to the bottle.

"I'll give it to you." I turned back to face the corridor, and my stomach roiled.

I could see them now. A rolling tide of spiders from floor to ceiling, one endless tide being thrust through the ship like a limb of the maddened swarm. It wouldn't matter how many spiders I killed. If I had a flamethrower that never ran out of fuel I'd still be overwhelmed, and probably in seconds.

"Don't mind the shaking." I raised my pistol and

studied the corridor. "Suit, identify load bearing bulk-heads in the next forty meters, please."

My HUD added four points between me and the approaching swarm. I hated doing this crap in a hurry.

I carefully aimed my spellpistol at the furthest bulk-head, and unleashed a void bolt, then shifted to cast another at the opposite side. I walked my shots up the corridor, and when I reached the third set of bulkheads the ceiling began to collapse.

I kept firing, this time at the last set of bulkheads, which were no more than ten meters away.

The spiders surged, their fist-sized chitinous bodies flowing between collapsing metal plates as the level above collapsed down on top of the corridor.

The destruction completely blocked the hallway, though a few spiders still slipped through. I aimed the pistol and fired a fan of flame that cooked the few stragglers.

The collapse stopped no less than three meters from me, blocked by the bulkhead we were standing next to. I'd love to take credit and say I'd planned it that way, but the truth is that I'd expected us to die in the collapse...I just hadn't seen any other way.

My heart thundered, and my hands shook with the adrenaline. "How much longer, Kurz?"

"Finished!" Kurz rose to his feet. He'd left a ring of powder around the urn. Sand maybe? Or salt? "We must be swift. We don't want to be in this part of the ship in five minutes, much less an hour. The dead will come, and the urn will corrupt them into wights. The resulting ghosts will be hungry, and they will never stop killing the living."

I didn't need convincing. I scooped Kurz up and threw him over my shoulder in a fireman's carry, then used an infuse strength spell to increase my running speed. I dashed down the corridor, and sprinted back into the cargo hold where we'd crashed the *Remora*.

I skidded to a halt when I found a forest of spellrifles and staves pointed in my direction. A cloud of hatchlings, led by Cinaka, and arachnidrakes, led by no one I recognized, stood ready for combat. Briff and Rava stood with them.

"We need to get out of here. Swiftly. The swarm is still coming, and there will be worse than that soon enough." I pushed past the rifles, and made for the *Remora*.

The ship stopped me in my tracks. She was magnificent. Her hull was the same, but the dents and discolorations and patches were all gone, just as I'd seen in the vision. She was clean and unbroken, her lines long and lean.

A vicious-looking spellcannon was slung along her underside, which told me that there must be a spell matrix inside. For the first time I'd have a chance to magically pilot a real ship.

"Sccrreeeeeeeee!" A sudden tide of spiders burst from the corridor at the far side of the cargo hold, then from a corridor on the opposite side. The room began filling with spiders, all of whom seemed to be scuttling in my direction.

Rifles and staves came up, and about forty defenders stood against uncountable spiders. Every last one of us was armed with *fire* magic, and overlapping spells filled the hold.

The hot scent of ozone billowed out around me as I added my own spells to the mix. Every spell killed hundreds or even thousands of spiders, but still they continued to advance, continued to force their way closer to the *Remora*.

Our lines tightened, and we fell back until our backs were pressed against the ship's hull. The flurry of spells from our ranks never slackened, and fireballs or jets of voidflame carved rents in the enemies' living skin.

And then, just like that, the spiders receded. They pulled back into the corridors, and the screeching ceased.

"They let us live," I muttered, utterly perplexed. "Why? It makes no sense."

"Maybe we finally killed enough of them?" Rava asked.

"No," Kurz supplied. A grim, cruel smile dominated his features, and he'd focused it on the retreating spiders. "They sense the arrival of their destruction, and are fleeing to avoid it. Every soul on this level has come to the urn, and they are hungry. We would do well to flee. Quickly. We have bare minutes before the wights begin to explore. When they do...we are not far from the urn."

"Briff," I called as I scanned the crowd in search of him. There he was. "Take Cinaka and her hatchlings, and watch the corridor where the urn is. Be ready to fall back if you have to."

I spun and glanced at the dozen or so arachnidrakes clustered near the *Remora*'s now ivory hull. They were all staring back. I strode over, and tried to figure out which was in charge. "Kek gave me this staff. Kithik, its name is. Which of you will take it up, and speak for your comrade?"

One of the drakes scuttled forward, a female who was smaller than the rest, but that the others gave a healthy berth to. She dipped her many-eyed face down, and extended two clawed hands to take the eight-eyed staff.

"I am called Lawl," she chittered as she took up the staff. "I will speak for Kek, and will honor his memory by wielding the great Kithik."

I handed the staff across. The relic hunting scavenger in me screamed that I should keep or sell it, but Kek had literally given his life to save us. The staff belonged with someone who would honor his legacy and speak for his people.

"Thank you, Lawl." I turned back to the *Remora*. "I'm going to find my way inside. I'd like you and your people with me when I do."

"Of course, friend Jerek." She delivered a surprisingly

graceful standing bow. "We stand ready in case the vessel contains a threat."

I moved to the *Remora*'s airlock, and noted that the placement of the ramp was identical, though the alloy differed. It exuded a faint magic, as did the entire vessel.

I marched up the ramp and studied the keypad next to the door. It was nearly identical to the one outside the weapons locker where I'd obtained the Heka Aten armor what seemed a lifetime ago, but the sigils were all fresh and pristine.

Did I have time to flame read before the wights arrived?

My hand came up of its own accord, and began tapping sigils. There were five, and I tried to memorize the sequence. Part of the prophecy spell maybe? I couldn't begin to understand everything at play here, which I found maddening.

Everything had a reason. Everything. Someone had constructed that spell, and obviously had thought to impart the door code.

The airlock door hissed open, and revealed the very same cargo hold where I'd first shot Vee with a dream bolt, back when she'd been lurker girl.

This time a single figure in gleaming golden spellarmor stood in the center of the room. He held a massive spellshield in one hand, and a wicked chopping blade in the other.

He did not seem happy to see me.

INTERLUDE V

F ield Marshal Bortel had mortgaged his soul, and it wasn't even clear what he'd really received in the deal, other than that fancy title.

He rolled his vape pen between his fingers, and watched as his carrier approached the *Word of Xal*. This would be the deed history remembered him for, if it remembered him at all. They'd damn him for this, yet there wasn't any way clear of it.

If he betrayed the Inurans, then his breach of contract would ensure he never worked again, and that he was stripped of all assets, and likely jailed or executed. It wouldn't be pretty, and the worst part? It wouldn't save even a single one of those damned kids.

Jolene had already bought out his underlings. His officers belonged to her, and if he wouldn't obey she'd simply remove him and give someone else the command. That's what he kept telling himself anyway.

It was still his mouth giving voice to the orders.

"Take us in slow," he ordered the black-robed mage in the spell matrix that piloted his ship. She wasn't enlisted in the traditional sense, but the monastic *void* mage was the best pilot he'd found. He turned to his comm officer, who possessed *fire* magic, but also a degree in engineering. She was proficient with it all. "Deploy screens of fighters around the ship, just in case. I want two legions to head for the *Word*'s bridge. The other eight will fan out through the ship, and isolate the target area. No one gets in or out of the cargo hold containing Highspire. Once it is isolated they are to await further orders."

He leaned back in his chair and enjoyed a long draw from the vape pen. He held the vapor in his lungs, and then exhaled a cloud of sweet swelling mist. Brief euphoria raced through him, and for a fraction of a second he forgot who and what he'd allowed himself to become.

Then it all came rushing back. He sat there, powerless, as the scry-screen displaying a cutaway of *Word*'s interior began to update. They were using the very maps the students themselves had created, which still only covered about forty percent of the ship. The parts closest to cargo bays or to the bridge.

Smart kids would take their chances that the parts of the ship that hadn't been explored. The rest, the vast majority, would flee back to a place where they felt safe. Officers would make for the bridge.

The rest would head to Highspire, which had somehow been saved and placed in a massive cargo hold. Bortel silently thanked whoever had been responsible for that bit, the saving of these kids.

It was a pity that the move had only bought them an extra few days of life. More a pity that he was the one bringing about their deaths. Yet he didn't see any way out of the mess he'd landed himself in.

As if on schedule the scry-screen chimed with an incoming missive. There was only one person who would call him moments after an operation had begun. One person who thought distracting a commander during the battle a fine idea.

"Matron Jolene." Bortel inclined his head in a polite nod, then savored another pull on his pen. Gods, but he hated this monster of a woman. How he wished someone would bring her to justice. Someone would eventually, and he just wished he was there to see it when it happened. "Combat has begun. Splitting my attention may be counterproductive. How may I help you?"

"You can deliver me the *Word of Xal*," Jolene snapped. Her eyes flashed in anger, and her nostrils flared. It was like dealing with a toddler just before nap time. "I want no dithering. I want no backsliding. Kill them, Bortel. Kill them all. No witnesses. It's more than my neck on the line here."

Defiance swelled in his chest, and pride, because her words proved that she knew nothing about him. She believed fear of legal reprisal to be what motivated him. She knew nothing of duty, or honor, or a lord's responsibility to their vassals.

"Of course, Matron." He bowed his head deferentially. "I'll follow your orders to the letter. Not a single occupant of the *Word of Xal* will survive."

Was it wishful thinking to hope that the Inuran Trade Moon, or the confederacy, or someone was monitoring this? That they were hearing the matron issue the order that would damn her career? Fantasy or not, he gave it fuel and used it for warmth.

"Excellent." Her eyes narrowed. "Get it done quickly. My flame readers tell me that they cannot accurately predict the outcome of today's events, and that shouldn't be possible. Your victory should be swift and total. The only possibility I can think of is your disloyalty."

"Ah hah." He drew on the pen again, and this time really took his time before finally exhaling. "So in all your years in a position of power, with all the enemies you've made, with all the people and gods who want these ships...my disloyalty is the only possibility you can think of?"

Her face drained of blood, and Bortel knew he'd signed his own death warrant. That was the last time she'd allow him to embarrass her, and they both knew it. She needed him exactly as long as it took to finish the op, and then whatever contingency she had to tie up his loose end would be utilized.

"I will leave you to your operation, Field Marshal." She inclined her head in the barest of nods. "No, on second thought, I don't believe I will. What kind of commander leads from the rear? I want you on that ship, Bortel. Get onto the *Word* and take the bridge."

He raised an eyebrow, but managed to stow what he'd been about to say. "You want me to leave a tactically secure command post so that I can observe combat directly?"

"You heard me." The missive went dark, and Bortel gave a bitter laugh. He noted the covert glance from his pilot, but ignored her. She could think what she wanted, and her judgement was nowhere near as harsh as his own.

"Let the boarding commander know that I'll be joining him shortly." Bortel enjoyed a final draw from his pen, then placed it in his breast pocket. He considered donning his armor, but why? The best possible scenario was that some enemy sniper found a way to end him. He could die in the line of duty never having broken faith with an employer.

It wasn't much. But it was the only currency hope came in right now.

21

What do you say to a man who has, theoretically, just been yanked ten millennia through time? Did he know? Did he think he was still in the past? Had his master prepared him?

I stepped into the hold, and noted how similar it appeared to the ship I knew, though this reflection hadn't been ravaged by time.

"I'm Jerek," I explained. My hand rested on my sidearm, but I didn't draw. "I'm going to explain the situation as—"

"You are going to get off my ship, you mean." The deck rang as the paladin took a step forward, and his chopping blade began to radiate a brilliance that would have blinded me if not for my helmet. His shield blazed in an identical fashion, adding to the radiance. "I don't know how you got the door open, or even how I ended up back on this ship, but I do know I'm not letting some random pirates claim my vessel. Last chance. Leave, or die."

"That's not really an option right—"

The paladin glided across the deck like a master duelist. His sword came down in a tight arc that would have bisected me had I still been standing there.

I may not have been the sector's best fighter, but I was quick, and if I excelled at anything it was running away. I blinked behind the paladin. Up came my pistol, and I shot him in the back of the helmet with a dream bolt. He started to turn, so I did it again.

He did not seem impressed.

The paladin lunged with his shield, which I hadn't expected to be used as a weapon. It knocked my pistol out of my hand, and sent me tumbling across the deck into the wall. Several yellow spots flared on the armor's paper doll, and of course my new paladin buddy was now standing defiantly between me and my pistol.

That left his back to the ramp, though. Rava sprinted silently up to the paladin's rear with vibroclaws extended from both wrists. Somehow, at the last possible moment, the paladin's boot came up and caught Rava in the gut. The kick arrested her momentum, hurled her to the deck, and sent her sliding into the opposite wall with an audible crack of bone.

Rava cried out, then lay crumpled where she'd fallen.

"You hurt Rava!" Briff bellowed as the enraged hatchling entered the cargo bay. He charged the paladin, who set to receive it with his shield.

Briff is canny, though, and the dragon's tail lashed around one of the paladin's ankles. He yanked the armored opponent into the air, then dashed him helmet first against the wall. The armor crunched, and the paladin grunted, but seemed otherwise unharmed.

The paladin's blade came around, almost too fast to track, and sheared through Briff's tail. My friend loosed an agonized shriek, just in time for Cinaka to crest the ramp and see the deed.

The cinder-hatchling's spellcannon came up, and she lobbed a ball of superheated rock into the paladin's back. The spell slammed him into the wall with an explosion of flaming magma that coated the rear of his armor, but he rebounded off and quickly recovered his footing, apparently no worse for the wear despite the sizzling tendrils clogging the hold with smoke.

"Are there more of you? This isn't a proper party yet." He twirled his blade and backed slowly up against a wall. "Who's next?"

"I am. " Kurz strode up the ramp and into the hold, holding no weapon and apparently unconcerned about the combat. "You are one of the Maker's paladins?"

The paladin hesitated, and studied the soulcatcher as if he recognized him for what he was. His entire demeanor shifted.

"I am sorry. I did not know." The paladin sheathed his blade, then dropped to one knee before Kurz. "Honor to serve, soulcatcher. I don't recognize your garb. Which vessel do you hail from? Can you tell me how I arrived here, and why? Last I remember...Soulcatcher Patra and I were in the core of the *Word of Xal.*"

Kurz raised an eyebrow in my direction, as if seeking direction. The implication was clear. If we deceived him he'd be pliant and easy to manipulate. But was that really how I wanted to start off this relationship?

"Tell him the truth," I ordered. I holstered my weapon. "He deserves to know where and when he is, and how he got here. If we play straight with him, hopefully he'll do the same with us. I want to know why he speaks modern galactic common if he's stepping out of the distant past. And I have a bunch of other questions. He's not going to answer them unless we start with his."

"Very well." Kurz licked his lips, and glanced back at the ramp. "In about ninety seconds a tide of wights will find us, enter the hold, and kill us all, so excuse me for being brief. You are ten millennia in the future. The world you know is gone. We came to this place in the *Remora*, but our version of it. Old and decrepit. While on this ship we were given a prophecy scale, which told us how to retrieve this ship from the past. We were meant to find you. Now, can we go? Captain Jerek will be happy to answer any questions once we are safely away."

"Ten millennia in the future?" The paladin rose

instantly to his feet, and his blade flicked out like a viper until the very tip rested against Kurz's throat. "Are you really a soulcatcher? Do you even know what that means? Inura's blood flows in my veins, human. Show me that it flows in yours as well."

Kurz paled. At first I thought the paladin was going to cut him, and literally check his blood. Then I realized he must mean some sort of magic that made soulcatchers what they are.

"I do not carry the Maker's blood. Not directly. That has been lost to all but a few." He slowly raised a hand, palm out, and pressed the paladin's blade away from his throat. "My sister does, however. Vee, show him your magic."

Vee blinked, obviously surprised to find herself the object of everyone's attention. She moved slowly to the paladin, and raised one trembling hand to her brother's neck, which glistened with a thin line of blood where the blade had grazed the skin.

Vee's bracelet flared and soft golden light washed over the wound. The flesh knit shut and Kurz gave a relieved exhalation of breath as the magic washed through him.

The paladin relaxed, then re-sheathed his blade.

An awful keening came from the hangar outside the ship, and it was closing quickly. The paladin gave a joyous laugh. "You were not lying. You used an urn. You called down wights on this place. What could you possibly have faced to justify such a thing? Well, so be it. I will trust you until we are away. If you have a pilot, and if you really know this ship, then you will have no trouble taking us out. I will deal with the wights."

"Okay, I'm on it. Vee, can you see to Rava? She's in bad shape. Oh, and one more thing. Do you have a name?" I paused long enough for the paladin to give it.

"Seket," he said, though his attention was already on the ramp as he once more drew his blade.

The name started a couple wheels turning in my head. The minister's ship was called the *Lance of Seket*. Was there a connection, and if so how? He'd been trapped in the past. Had someone else passed the name on somehow? Gah, so many questions I didn't have time to answer.

I turned from the paladin and sprinted for the bridge. Either Seket could do what he said he could, and keep those wights at bay, or he couldn't.

And, just as critically, either I could figure out how to pilot this ship using a matrix, or we were about to join the wights. That's the best part of being killed by them...if they slay you, then you rise as one. The death that keeps on giving.

The original *Remora* wasn't much different from my version, though everything was newer and nicer...and there were a lot more rooms. How extra quarters and cargo holds fit in the same space could only be explained through a sizable void pocket. Or several. They must have been ripped out of the *Remora* long before I'd inherited her.

I sprinted onto a totally alien bridge. Not a single part of it was the same as my ship. Gone were the navcom station and the pilot's seat. Gone were most of the instruments.

In their place lay two identical consoles, each facing an enormous scry-screen. Between them stood a spell matrix not unlike the one I'd seen on the bridge of both the *Flame of Knowledge* and the *Word of Xal*.

It was already active, with all three rings slowly spinning around the area I was meant to stand in. A glowing ring stood at waist height...the stabilizing ring, in case the ship took a hit and I took a tumble.

"Well, here goes." I ducked between the silver and gold rings as they hummed past, and then stepped onto the slightly raised silver disk anchoring the matrix to the deck.

I tapped the *void* sigil on all three rings in rapid succession. Theoretically I could have done *fire*, and some ships could even accept *dream*, but *void* was the undisputed master of travel. Especially in space.

The ship rumbled as a chunk of negative light rolled out of my chest. Wave after wave fell onto the disk below me, which drank it greedily. The flow stopped, and my connection to the ship finalized.

It was...the experience defied description. I was still me, but I was also the ship. I could feel every part of her, including her spellcannon, which I could use if I needed. I wiggled her sensors like fingers, her diagnostics like toes. And I could will her to fly.

Before lifting off I took a moment to size up the situation outside the ship. A sea of spectral figures from many different races and eras all surged toward the *Remora*. I'd never seen wights, and was unprepared for the malevolence rolling off them like a cloud of exhaust from some old combustion vehicle. They hated the living. Hated us.

Cinaka and her hatchlings had retreated into the ship, and Seket stood at the doorway blocking the wights as they climbed the ramp.

"Inura, protect me!" he bellowed and a wave of golden energy sprang out around him, identical to the one I'd seen Vee use.

Where she prayed to the Maker, though, he prayed to the god I assumed had given birth to the Inurans.

The wights met the edge of his ward, and stopped with a screech, unable to advance. Vee raised a hand behind him and launched a beam of pure white light into the closest wight. The creature flickered into a negative image for a single instant, and then faded to memory, as if erased from existence by a disintegrate.

I remembered that I was supposed to be piloting, and guided the *Remora* off the deck and toward the shimmering blue membrane separating us from space.

"Buckle up, everyone. We're entering a vacuum." We rippled through the membrane, wights spilling off the ramp like the last leaves of autumn, and then we were into the black, lost in the shadow of a Great Ship.

I could still see the ship, which included the cargo hold. Seket dispelled his aura, whatever it had been, and then yanked off his helmet with a hiss. Vee stood next to him panting, but she straightened, her eyes slightly widened and her cheeks flushed when she glimpsed the paladin's face.

Golden hair spilled down well muscled shoulders, and they framed a man so handsome that it made me believe that the blood of Inura flowed in his veins. He was, quite literally, perfect.

Envy surged up like bile. I'd have given a great deal to earn even a single glance like that from Vee. I didn't like the anger or resentment toward Seket, even as I recognized that they were unfounded. So I jettisoned them, or pretended to at least.

I had a job to do and focused on that. I pushed my consciousness into the *Remora*'s senses, and focused on flying. A heady rush washed through me, salving my ego.

Flying was amazing.

22

I guided the *Remora* away from the *Flame*, and toward a derelict carrier missing half its hull. We sheltered in the shadow, while I tried to get my bearings. Flying the ship was far easier than I'd feared it would be. I'd had no trouble bonding it, and thus far I simply willed it where I wanted to go.

I hadn't been trained though, and if we got jumped I did not want to be the guy standing in those rings. I'd do it if we had no better option, but I already knew that Captain Perfect was probably the most amazing lover—I mean pilot—that had ever lived.

That didn't mean I couldn't catch up. I was a fast learner. That began with magical communications. I concentrated on the vessel, and realized I could activate ship wide simply by thinking about it. "Everyone, this is your captain speaking. We're going dark while we get our bearings. Cinaka, Lawl, please get your people situated, then meet me in the mess. Kurz and the rest of my squad, please escort Seket to the mess as well. It's time we compared notes."

I tapped the *void* sigil on all three rings to disengage, then ducked through the rings. It wasn't as hard as I'd expected, as they moved slowly and intuitively. Such an odd piloting system. I wished I understood why they'd been built this way.

I left the bridge and headed back to the mess, and was mildly surprised to find a completely different room. I mean, I knew logically where I was, but my brain kept supplying info from my version of the *Remora*.

The new version was way better.

A pair of familiar black boxes, both with the dragon logo, had been built along one wall. The rest of the wall was devoted to the control panel, and to many, many vials of materials. Tables hovered throughout the room, each surrounded by hoverchairs.

The room looked like it could comfortably accommodate a good thirty people, and even had a sign with refuse on it pointing toward the foundry, which would reclaim the molecules for reuse.

"Hey, Vee," I said into the comm, certain she could hear the grin in my voice. "You're going to love what you find in the mess."

I heard approaching footsteps, and Cinaka stepped into the room, followed by Briff. The hatchlings took one of the far tables, and sat together, where they conversed in low tones. I hadn't been wrong about the chemistry there.

Next came Seket, followed closely by Kurz and Vee. Seket blazed an aggressive path in my direction, and stopped well within what I considered my personal space. He was just as handsome in person. His breath even smelled like mint.

"We have a problem." Seket fixed me with those icy eyes, and his grip tightened on the hilt of his spellblade. "You introduced yourself as captain. Well, I don't recognize you as captain. I let you aboard, and I saved you and your crew from wights, but I have not ceded command."

"All by yourself?" I snapped. My eyes narrowed, and a hot flush rolled through my entire body. "I piloted the ship. Vee helped you take down wights, and while you might feel like you're hot shit, everything you did she can do too. Vee has exactly the same miracle you used to keep the wights at bay."

That brought Vee's attention to our conversation. She'd been inspecting the forge's control panel, and I could hardly blame her for that. She said nothing.

"The fact remains." Seket's perfect eyes narrowed into twin chips of ice. "This is my ship. It belonged to Patra, my soulcatcher. With her death it belongs to me."

How could I be so blind? I suppose it was fair to forget about it during all the turmoil, but I realized I was holding the key to Seket's cooperation in my pocket. So I produced it.

I opened my palm and showed him the prophecy scale. "Activate it."

He eyed me suspiciously. "Why?"

"Because it will prove we're telling the truth." I offered it to him again, and he raised a hand to accept it. "You can study it at your leisure, but you're going to want to meet the scale's archivist."

"Fine." Seket rubbed his suit's thumb along the scale, and it activated as it had for me.

As before, Patra's flowing blond hair and easy smile appeared in the illusion over the scale. She took one look at Seket, and that smile evaporated. "Oh, you poor boy. I am so sorry. This is more than any paladin should have to deal with, especially one who was an apprentice just days ago."

Seket's rocky exterior finally cracked, and he stumbled a step back, dropping the scale to the deck. It winked out as it left his hand, though the tremor it left remained. The paladin was clearly shaken.

"I'm sorry," I said, and scooped up the scale from the deck. I'd give it back to him when he was ready. In the meantime I could probably study it again. "What did she mean by apprentice?"

"I was a paladin elect as recently as last week," Seket snapped. His gaze shot up to meet mine, and I could feel the anger at me. All of it was focused on me.

"You didn't fight like an anything-elect," Rava said from behind him. She kept a wary distance, and one hand rested casually on her spellpistol. "You could solo most Arena teams, in that armor."

"I did fight like an elect." He barked a derisive laugh that made him ugly for only a moment. "You're just bad. All of you. A faded shadow of the world my people built."

"Maybe." My voice was ice now, and in that moment my dislike solidified. "As I understand it, your people are why it all came apart. My people, your ancestors, survived by finding our way down to the planet in this system. You know, after that war that you lost."

Vee appeared as if she wanted to say something, but gave a disgusted sigh and returned to the forge.

"You are not my descendants, nor my people." Seket's hand tightened around his blade to match mine.

"If you draw that blade we're going to have a problem." I forced a deep breath, and released my sidearm. "My squad can and will take you down, but I'd much rather work together. You're right. I'm not your descendant. But I can tell you about them, if you'd like. They just blew up my planet, and killed billions of people."

Seket's hand left his blade, even as the anger drained from his expression. "You've lost your world? I—mine was destroyed just days ago, from my perspective. I am sorry."

"And so am I." I offered a hand in friendship, and he shook it. Apparently that custom was older than either of our cultures. "The Inuran Consortium is led by a woman named Jolene. They've got a trade moon in the system, and are here to steal the Great Ships. They want the *Flame of Knowledge*. They also want the *Word of Xal*. They blew up my planet to get them."

The righteous anger returned to the paladin's expression, though it no longer appeared directed at me. He folded heavily muscled arms, made even more attractive in that golden armor.

"The Consortium was new in our day. I am...unsurprised to learn of their treachery." Seket shook his head sadly. "They worked with Nefarius, who tore apart the dragonflights. Our whole galaxy burned. I wonder if there are even embers left after so long?"

Something clicked in my head.

"You're one of the embers," I realized aloud, suddenly excited. "Patra sent you! You're a paladin, with all the knowledge of the dragonflights."

"He can teach us," Kurz added quietly from where he'd been sitting. I hadn't even been aware he was listening, as he was staring at his lap. "He can restore the knowledge of our religion as it was, and help us understand who we are meant to be."

"Why send me? Why not someone with more wisdom, or experience?" Seket licked his lips and cocked his head as if tasting the answer to his own question, and not enjoying it. "Maybe I was all she had."

"Regardless of why you're here," I interjected. We had

problems, and were on the clock. "I'm hoping we can ask your help in dealing with the Inurans. They're going to try to take these ships. If we can get you back to the *Word of Xal* we can see if they've made their move yet, and maybe even stop them."

Seket turned back to me, and his expression hardened into an alloy of resolve and dedication. "I will help you, Captain Jerek, until you give me cause to do otherwise. Lead us into battle."

23

A mixture of relief and frustration washed through me as Seket stepped into the matrix to pilot the *Remora*.

"You're sure you want to let him do this?" Rava asked quietly as she folded her arms and stared hard at the paladin. "Pretty boy can't be good at everything, and I'd trust you to fly us before I'd trust him."

That got a laugh out of me, which I didn't realize I'd needed so badly.

"If he's flown even once he has more experience than I do." I shook my head and gave a self-deprecating laugh. "I do plan to master flying, but maybe when we're not charging into potential combat."

"Are missives still jammed in this system?" Vee asked from the corner of the room where she'd been standing with Kurz. They'd been chatting in low urgent tones, but I was trying to honor their privacy.

I sketched a *fire* sigil, then a *dream*, then a *fire*. The spell resolved, but didn't zip off as a missive normally would. It simply hovered there, as if confused.

"Looks like it. We're going to have to make contact manually." Even as I said it I knew that was wrong though. There was another way I could communicate with the minister.

The Web of Divinity.

I was linked to it now, and as long as I didn't mind a face full of mind-melting insanity, then that was an option. I'd bet scales to rocks that I could use the Web to brute force my way through whatever the Inurans had set up. I was half tempted to do it right now, just because I knew it would piss off the Inurans.

"Seket, can you take us to the *Word of Xal*?" I nodded at the scry-screen, which showed my ship in the distance. It was a damned sight for sore eyes. "Odds are good the minister will be close by."

Seket tapped the *life* sigil on all three rings, and the *Remora* hummed to life. "I see him, and will get us there. I also see a gigantic sphere nearly as large as a Great Ship. Is that the Consortium's monstrosity?"

"That's the trade moon," I confirmed, though I'd never seen it in person. I'd heard of them, and they featured in a number of holos, usually as the antagonist.

The *Remora* leapt into motion, and accelerated an

order of magnitude faster than we'd have managed with conventional engines.

We spun past the destroyer where Visala had ambushed us, and then past the cruiser where we'd sheltered on our approach. Seket zipped across the vast gulf between the hulks around the *Flame*, and those orbiting around the *Word of Xal*.

"What's that?" Vee asked. I followed her gaze and realized she was focused on a ship on the far side of the *Word*.

"I recognize that ship," I realized aloud. "Briff, is that Bortel's new carrier? The one the Inurans gave him to get those ten legions off planet?"

"They've deployed fighter screens," Rava pointed out. She nodded at the area around the *Word*. "That's a pretty clear perimeter too. They've staked out the *Word*. They're isolating her from people like us."

"Their comms are still working, too," I growled. I needed to find us an advantage. "That means they'll all know we're here any moment now. Anyone have eyes on the minster's ship?"

Seket cracked his knuckles, then rolled his neck as if enacting a familiar pre-Arena ritual. He finished by resting on the balls of his feet, and enacting a series of rapid breaths.

"That wing of fighters is headed our direction." Rava pointed at the closest group, who'd left their flight pattern around the *Word* and were now headed in our direction.

"Seket, is there anything we can do?" I felt greedy, but suddenly I wished we had more than one matrix. Even a single one was a luxury, but if we'd had two I could handle offense while Seket flew.

"Watch," Seket crooned, "and be amazed."

The *Remora* accelerated again, and we hurled through space at our opponents. It would be a jousting match. They'd get one volley, and so would we, then we'd be past each other and they'd have to circle around for another pass.

All three spellfighters were Mk. VII, which wasn't top of the line, but was better than average. Each discharged a life bolt as we approached, but at the last possible instant Seket stabbed the *life* sigil on the gold ring, then the bronze, then the silver.

A cocoon of wards wove themselves over the hull just before the spells hit, and all three did nothing but discolor it.

"My turn." Seket's eyes narrowed, and he tapped *life* on gold, then poured a thick wave of *life* magic from his chest into the deck.

The whole ship rumbled as the spellcannon discharged the spell. I could feel the magic beneath my feet, feel it streak out of the ship, and then saw it on the scry-screen as it streaked into the fighter on the left.

Everything from the nose to the canopy simply ceased to exist. The fighter's remains cartwheeled for a few moments, then detonated spectacularly.

"Yes!" Vee yelled and pumped a fist. "It should take the remaining two a few minutes to reach us." She gave Seket a grin, which he returned.

"Do you have a destination, Captain?" Seket demanded. "Other patrols are starting to head in our direction."

"Use the *Word* as cover," I instructed. "Follow the hull onto the underbelly, then latch onto the deck near the center."

Seket gave me a look that suggested my mind was gone. "You realize that's suicide, right? We'd be a stationary target."

"Do it!" I roared. "Or get out of the matrix and let me do it."

My heart thundered as the next wave of fighters approached. I wasn't certain my plan would work, but I had to try.

I ordered my helmet to slither over my face, and spoke the very instant the HUD had lit. "Guardian, can you hear me?"

We were flying fast and low along the hull, and I figured whatever the Inurans were doing, it couldn't be that bad with us being so close.

"I can hear you, Captain." Kemet didn't appear, which suggested the Guardian was still limited. "I am pleased you live. The vessel is under full assault. Two full legions have taken the bridge, while the others are moving against the cargo hold containing Highspire."

"Not now," I snapped. "Do we have enough magic to activate the point defense cannons on this side of the ship, the ones closest to this transmission?"

"We do," Kemet confirmed. "They are now active."

I exhaled in relief, and shifted my attention to the scry-screen. Seket did as I'd ordered, and guided the *Remora* to a stop against the *Word*'s hull. Our magnets engaged, and we locked into place. A sitting duck, whatever a duck was.

A trio of fighters swung into view and flashed toward us so quickly I could barely track them. Fortunately, the automated defenses were much more accurate than I was.

The *Word of Xal*'s defense cannons came online, and took aim at the approaching fighters. The first two died long before reaching us, but the third was an incredibly skilled pilot.

They flipped up and away, and zipped back toward their carrier. Crap. I'd given away more than I intended. The idea that the *Word* had defended us would be of extreme interest to Bortel, or whoever was running the op. They'd be after us soon.

I needed to be one step ahead of them.

"Maybe you primitives aren't so useless after all." Seket offered a goodnatured smile, and his tone was friendly. "Nice work, Captain. We're safe for the time being."

"Now what?" Vee asked. She approached the scry-screen, and touched the image of the carrier. "There's no way we can handle the number of troops this thing can hold. Even with Cinaka's people, and the arachnidrakes, there's no way we can make a meaningful difference."

"You're not wrong." I suppressed a sigh, and considered our options. "Seket, move us four hundred meters, then shut down the ship. We're going dark, and keeping the cannons active. That will buy us a little time."

"Aren't you going to make a run for the minister?" Briff asked. He fluffed his wings behind him, and peered at the scry-screen. "It feels like we're out of our depths. I don't know how we can help."

"I'm still the captain of the *Word*." I shook my head slowly. "We can't just abandon her. We could go to the minister, but beyond protecting my mom I don't see how that helps. Visala needs us more. It doesn't matter if we can win. We can help. I just need to think about the best way to do that. We can't take out ten legions, but if we can find a way to deal with their command structure, maybe we don't have to. Guardian, are the internal defenses active and helping?"

"They are online," Kemet confirmed, though the Guardian had a hesitant note in his voice. "They are not functioning well, though. We lack the magic to power them. The ship is, in Terran parlance, running on fumes. Whatever solution you enact will rely on your wits and whatever magic you possess."

24

Silence reigned on the bridge for a good thirty seconds as everyone waited for me to come up with a plan. How did I do that with no external help?

I ordered my helmet to slither off. "All right, guys, I need your help with a plan."

Once I'd gathered their attention I put the beginnings of my plan into words. It sounded exactly as vague as I feared it would. "We need to hit their command structure as hard as possible. That may not win us this battle, but maybe we can delay them, and who knows? Maybe removing Bortel will be enough."

"How do we find him?" Briff asked. He fluffed his wings and walked over to the scry-screen, which still showed Bortel's carrier. "If it were me, I'd be on the bridge surrounded by troops and automated defenses. How do we get him off the ship?"

"Good question." I moved to join Briff. "If he's on his carrier, then we'd need to teleport in somehow, or land as close to the bridge as we could manage."

"Casualties would be high," Rava pointed out. "Those carriers are designed for exactly that sort of defense"

"Let's hope it doesn't come to that." I prayed to the Maker for a bit of luck. "It's possible Bortel is leading the assault. If he's on the *Word*, then I can probably use the Guardian to track him."

"You can track a specific person?" Kurz raised an eyebrow.

"Can I, Guardian?" I asked, and paused until he responded into my suit's comm, this time loud enough for the squad to hear.

"Negative, Captain. Not without some sort of magical link, or genetic sample."

"Hmm." There had to be a way, and I was determined to find it. My eyes widened, and I turned excitedly to Briff. "Bortel always has that vape pen, right? We even saw it in the recruitment video he sent to Kemet at the end. That pen was solid gold. There's no way he leaves that lying around."

"Gold is too common to track, I'm afraid," Guardian lamented over my comm. Faces fell all around me.

"What about the tobacco?" That was it! I was almost positive I had him. "Bortel owned a plantation on the southern continent. There aren't many left. Vaping isn't as popular as it used to be. There can't be that many on board."

"There probably are," Briff corrected, then gave his toothy grin. "They're probably not filled with tobacco though. There were much more popular herbs in our neighborhood, at least. And at academy."

I knew exactly which herb he was talking about, and he was right. Most people who did vape would be using it for marijuana or some other substance, not tobacco.

"I have located four separate instances with a passenger having tobacco on their person," Guardian offered. "Two of them are within the cargo hold where Highspire currently resides, and are therefore unlikely to be your target. The other two might be. One is on the bridge. The other just arrived in a docking bay."

"Blast it," Seket cursed. "That only gives us a fifty-fifty chance. There aren't enough of us to send multiple teams."

"Good thing I'm a flame reader." I raised a palm, and blocked out the *Word*. Fire flowed down my arm, and pooled into my hand. I studied the flames carefully, and willed them to show me the bridge.

The *Word of Xal* was warded, but as the captain, I was exempted from the wards. The bridge leapt into clarity in the palm of my hand. Two dozen Inuran mages stood clustered around the room.

"The substance is on the one in the white armor, over there by the matrix."

I immediately saw which one he'd indicated. A guard in ivory armor stood at attention near the matrix.

"That can't be Bortel." I shook my head. "Guardian, I've never been to the cargo hold where the substance was found. Can you give me an active camera in that room, or internal scrying?"

"There is a camera in that hold, yes. Shall I put it through to your armor?"

"Do that," I confirmed, then willed the helmet to slither back into place. When the HUD lit, it already had a small window with the requested feed.

It showed a man leaning against a railing, which I realized overlooked the cargo hold containing Highspire. In his right hand he held a familiar ornate vape pen, the gold glinting in the light. Bortel's beard was unmistakable, as was his fleet marshal's uniform.

"It worked?" Rava wore her incredulity openly. Her jacket creaked as she shifted back and forth, ready for action. "Can you teleport us there? Or are we going to sneak in? I'd recommend a small team, rather than bringing everyone. We'll move faster and more quietly on our own."

"She's right," Briff agreed. His tail curled around his feet, and he squatted down to examine the flame. "If we take our squad in, bring maybe Cinaka and Lawl, then we could probably take him down. You can see where guards are and stuff, right? Like you did before, when we took the ship."

"I can see guards," I allowed, then grinned inside my helmet. "I'm not sure why we should risk going to him, though. I have a much, much better idea."

"Oh?" Vee raised an eyebrow. Seket and Kurz flanked her, all three peering intently at the flame.

"I'd much rather bring him to us." I closed my hand and banished the flame. "Guardian, you're too low on magic to perform spells, right? Without a source of magic?"

"Indeed," Kemet confirmed, his tone a mixture of embarrassment and shame. "It has come to this."

"Can I provide that magic?"

"In theory," Kemet allowed, this time with a healthy dose of skepticism. "The loss of efficiency in the transference is...immense."

I cocked my head and ran the numbers again. It seemed to line up. "So, what? Three to one? Four to one? How much magic do I need to give you to handle a single teleport for a Bortel-shaped target?"

"To be safe I would call it five to one, Captain."

"All right, then." I knelt and placed my hand against the deck. "Drink up."

A torrent of dark magic rolled from my palm into the deck, which drank it eagerly. On and on it went, until pushing more magic from my chest became painful. I began to pant, but pushed again, hard.

"How's that?" I managed through gritted teeth.

"That is sufficient. Where would you like me to teleport your target?" Kemet sounded impressed.

"Into the brig below, one of the ones that is sealed." My knees were shaking, and the nausea began to grow. "I think I'm just going to lay down for a minute."

I slithered off the helmet, and lay down right in the middle of the corridor. The deck was blessedly cool against my cheek, though it did nothing for the nausea.

"It is done," Kemet's voice came over the suit's speakers. "The target is now confined in your cell. Well done, Captain."

"Hey, Briff, buddy, can I ask you a huge favor?" My whole body shook, and my teeth began to chatter.

"Sure, Jer." He knelt next to me.

"Can you get me a buck—". My body convulsed. Too late. "Never mind. Now I need a toothbrush."

"You're going to interrogate this Bortel?" Seket asked. He leaned down and offered me a hand. I took it, and he hauled me back to my feet.

The nausea had eased, though I was coated in sweat now. Guess I may have overdone it with the magic. Time to see what it had bought me. "Seket, Kurz, Vee, you're with me. Briff and Rava, go set up your Arena station, and see if you can make us some pizzas."

"Oh, thank the Maker." Briff perked up immediately. "I thought you were going to make us go do stuff."

"We'll let you know what Bortel has to say, and I'll

record it just in case, but I figured you two could use the R&R instead."

"You think he'll talk?" Rava asked as she followed Briff up the corridor toward the crew quarters.

"He'll talk. I can use my breath to torture him." I smacked my lips and wished I had a clean mouth spell. "Let's go."

I strode down the ramp toward the Brig, with Seket, Vee, and Kurz in tow.

25

B y the time we reached the brig Bortel had already made himself comfortable. He sat on the bench with his back against the wall, and one leg propped up. He twirled his vape pen absently in one hand.

"Now that," he drawled, "was a very impressive use of magic, as well as being a near instant display of karma. Well done, son."

Bortel rose and straightened his uniform, then moved to stand near the crackling energy field that separated us.

"Thank you." I stepped up to the field and let him look me in the eye. "Do you recognize this armor?"

"Of course I do." He gave a harsh, self-deprecating laugh. "It's at the heart of this whole mess, and I watched four people get eaten by that reactor. Or rather, I heard Jolene scream about it. The Heka Aten spellarmor. Absolutely priceless. Made for a king, or a hero. The only way you could have pulled off that teleport was being captain of this ship. Am I right?"

I nodded, then folded my arms and allowed my condemnation to leak into my gaze. "You're unlawfully assaulting children, Bortel. Why?"

"Contract." He shrugged, and returned to his bench with an exaggerated sigh. "It's my own damned fault. The money was too good. She gave me a carrier and a command. I knew she was going to blow our planet up, but she'd have killed me and done it anyway. I didn't protest and now my soul is blacker than the void. You'd be right to execute me, though if you're going to do that I have a favor to ask first."

"Oh?" I raised an eyebrow. Did he really believe he was in a position to bargain?

"I have enough evidence to take down Jolene with a Confederate court." He licked his lips, and was suddenly unable to hold my gaze. "I don't need a deal. You can have the evidence, and then do whatever you need to with me. Lady knows I deserve it. I wish I could have stopped today. If I'd had any idea when I signed on what she'd ask me to do..."

Sympathy extinguished my anger, and I relaxed the fists I'd balled. He was a man out of his depth, from the sound of it. He'd done some terrible things, but at least he felt remorse.

"Can you call it off?" I demanded.

"No." Bortel sighed again. "Jolene bought all my officers, and no doubt their officers too. If we object...she'll off us. They know that, and they aren't going to follow me. They're going to turn me in and claim the reward, and probably my rank."

"All right, is there any weakness in your troops we can exploit?" I wrapped a hand around my pistol, and forced my breathing to slow. I knew a lot of the kids involved in the combat, and considered myself responsible for the rest.

He shook his head. "I'm sorry. Truly. I trained them as best I could, and they'll do what they were paid to do. If they refuse...it's not like there's a planet to go back to."

Something buzzed in my head; that was the best way I could describe it. Like a swarm of wasps had taken nest there, and they were pissed. There were words hidden in the buzzing. *He lies...*

In that moment I knew the voice was right. There was magic in me now that hadn't been there before. *Fire* magic. It must have happened when I'd lost control of the temporal matrix. That was the new enchantment I'd felt afterwards, but hadn't really had time to investigate.

"Tell me the sky is red," I ordered.

Bortel gave me the oddest stare. "Okay, son, but that don't make it so. The sky is red."

The buzzing came back, and again I knew he was lying. I could test it more later. At least I knew he'd be truthful for the rest of the interrogation.

"You said you didn't know of a weakness." I shook my head, and offered a knowing smile. "That isn't true. Let's try again. How do we stop your men?"

"I won't sell them out." Bortel savored a long draw from his vape pen, and filled the cell with a greenish cloud. "You can't get tactical data from me. Not without torture, and you ain't gonna do that, son. Here's what you can get. I can tell you how to hit Matron Jolene. You want to end this? You cut the head off the Wyrm. Once she's dead my men have no reason to be here. She blew up our planet, son. Someone has to make her pay. It can't be me, but maybe it can be you...assuming you've got the manpower."

"All right." I forced myself to relax. "Tell me how to hit her. I've got a full platoon to work with."

"That ain't gonna get it done." Bortel took another pull, then made a production of exhaling a ring. "Not unless they're the finest soldiers who ever lived. You're gonna be hitting an Inuran cruiser. Fast, stealth enabled, and packed with automated defenses and well trained defenders. They've got thick bulkheads and strong wards, and every last defender is either mind controlled or brainwashed. They will fight to the death."

"So let's say," I drawled in my best Bortel imitation, "that the great fleet marshal had to plan an assault and he had twenty cinder hatchlings with spellrifles, and a cadre of well armed *fire* mages. How would you get it done?"

"You got a ship?" Bortel gave me a half smile that suggested he was enjoying the exchange.

"We do. She's got a spellcannon and a teleportation disk. She's fast, and our pilot is...enthusiastic."

Seket laughed at that, the first change in his expression. He'd been glowering at Bortel quite effectively, and returned to it.

"Then I'd attach to the very center of the upper side of the ship." Bortel rose and approached the energy field again. "If you've got the mages I'd dispel the wards. If not, then you'll have to light up the hull on your approach. Best bring some serious juice if you want to take those out. If you can, though? Then you attach like I said, and start teleporting in. You're three levels above the bridge. You cut through the deck, and tunnel right down into her fortified position."

I turned to Vee, who'd been listening silently, as she often did.

"Are you any good with explosives?" I raised my hand and mimed a bomb dropping. "We cut through the first two decks, then I teleport an explosive directly onto the bridge. We let it detonate, then cut through the last deck and start dropping in."

"I can rig up something." Vee started up the stairs, then stopped and turned back. "Oh...I'll be needing the forge. Keep people away from me. I don't like distractions when making explosives."

I nodded to Seket. "Go with her, please. Make sure no one bothers her."

"Yes, Captain." Seket offered a short bow, then headed up the ramp. I didn't like putting him with Vee, but I had to think like an officer, and not some love-struck kid.

That left Kurz and I facing Bortel. Kurz hadn't said anything.

"I don't suppose you have another urn?" The words were out before I even realized what I was asking.

"I do," Kurz said quietly, "and it will not be affected by the explosion. In fact, if you murder half the bridge crew with a bomb, then they'll rise as wights and aid in the slaughter. However, I would get off the ship quickly as it's likely to be overrun."

"Are you sure you want to cross this line, boy?" Bortel demanded. "Using wights on living foes...that's some dark magic."

"Not as dark as blowing up a planet for profit," I snapped, and fixed him with a glare. "It's just being pragmatic. We use one urn and one bomb, and then we pick up the pieces. She murdered billions, and now she's trying to exterminate the survivors. This is war, and she's about to learn exactly what that means."

INTERLUDE VI

Visala stood atop Highspire and surveyed the legions of students who'd gathered to make their final stand. Most hadn't yet met the enemy, but they stood resolutely nonetheless.

It was a sight any Wyrm would be proud of, her Outriders gathered and ready for war. Few suspected her true nature, but they were about to find out, as were the Inurans.

They were expecting frightened children. The Inurans quite rightly had no fear of the weapons in the armory, most of which barely functioned anymore. Those they would fear would also destroy Highspire, and possibly this entire section of the *Word of Xal*, and the Inurans knew it.

That meant that an army of students with their frightened headmistress was all that stood between them and victory. She looked forward to instructing them on the folly of rushing an elder Wyrm in an enclosed space.

She would need help, though. A lot of it.

Visala raised her shriveled human hand, still alien after all this time, and began sketching. She wove *fire* and *dream* sigils into a tight ring, then erected a second ring, and a third. The Inurans' wards were powerful, and they would not allow her missive through, unless she made it so powerful it could pierce their wards.

Their fire dreamers could counter it nearly instantly, but she might get a three-minute conversation out of it if they were sloppy. They probably thought their wards impenetrable, and Inurans were known for nothing if not hubris.

The final sigil flared and the spell coalesced into an illusionary mirror. Smoke played across the surface for long seconds, but eventually resolved into minister Ramachan's surprised face.

"How did you break the Inurans' wards?" The minster's exhaustion was clear. A human failing. They were only animals, after all.

"No time. The Inurans have taken the bridge. They'll be on to us soon." She glanced down at the hangar, at her Outriders. "We won't be able to hold them for long. We need you to relieve us with anything you can bring."

"You have my deepest apologies, Headmistress." Ramachan shook her head, and loosed genuine tears. "We cannot save you. Our only hope is Confederate intervention. We're taking the fleet and making a run for Shaya in the hopes that we can present evidence of what happened here."

"By that time every student on this ship will be dead." Visala's mouth firmed into the tight line normally reserved for malcontents like Jerek. "Either you get us some help, right now, or you accept that you signed the death warrants of these kids. We need you, Minister. Do your job."

"I am." The minster's face went stony.

"Where did you get a *void* mage?" Visala's eyes narrowed. "You can't get into the depths without one."

"Irala survived her bonding with the ship," the minister explained. "She'll open the Fissure for us. I'm sorry, Visala. Die well."

"What will the boy think of you and his mother when he finds out? He is still captain."

The connection ended.

The minister had been broken. The cowardly human was running, and abandoning her culture. She had to know what would happen. Their offspring would die, and even if they succeeded in winning Confederate support it would still bring about their doom. The Confederacy would prosecute the troops who'd killed the children. Those troops were the last living Kemetians, which was precisely why the Inurans had allowed them to survive the destruction of their planet in the first place.

Once the dust settled, their culture would be gone,

and the Inurans would be there to claim salvage on the
Great Ships. If only Visala had known the truth sooner,
that the ships lived. Now the thing she most needed was
time, yet she had none.

Her place was here, defending the spire. She'd do
exactly that, at any cost. At least she would die well,
protecting her Outriders.

It appeared her opportunity to do exactly that had
arrived.

A line of ragged students sprinted into the hold, and
explosions echoed from the corridor behind them.

A dozen blue-scaled hatchlings sprinted after them
into the hold, each holding a metal shield twice as wide
as they were. They planted the barricades, then ducked
behind them as a withering volley of spells and rifle
rounds came from her students.

Rank after rank of tech mages in spellarmor charged
out of the corridor, each returning fire as they used the
barricades for cover. More hatchlings emerged, and the
barricade expanded until dozens of enemy troops had
perfect cover, while being able to return fire with
impunity.

Visala considered her options. Saving her appearance
for a critical moment would be the most effective strategy.
But morale was low, and for good reason. They were
being pushed back all over the ship. Everyone knew
they'd lost the bridge.

She had to rally them, and that started with their

hearts, then their minds. She needed to give them reason to fight.

Visala leapt into the air and began to transform. It took three precise heartbeats to go from shriveled woman to a two-hundred-meter Wyrm. Her snowy scales glistened under the cargo hold's soft magical lighting as she swooped down on the barricades.

She landed with a tremendous crash, and simply crushed them all under her bulk. Visala stuck her mouth into the corridor and breathed.

A river of white-gold plasma jetted into the ship, cooking everything it touched. There were brief screams, and then nothing but ash left in the corridor. By her estimation she'd just wiped out an entire reinforced platoon. Not bad as a start.

She pivoted, and turned to face the students. It was difficult as her head brushed the ceiling, and her wings threatened to crush unwary students.

"Children," she growled, her voice low, but probably still recognizable, "I have heard the rumors. Some of you call me the dragon lady. Well, you're more right than you know. I fought in Planetfall. And I remember when rocks were invented, too. And I tell you now that these bastards will not have you. I will defend you until my dying breath. But I cannot do it alone. Stand fast, my Outriders. Stand fast, and we will prevail!"

She reared up on her hind legs and leapt into the air as deafening applause echoed through the hold like thunder. Visala basked in it, even as she shifted back to human form and landed atop the pyramid.

Her move would buy time. Any sane commander would pull back and formulate a plan that involved dealing with her before advancing. She didn't doubt they had an answer, and would employ it.

Odds were good it would involve an elite unit, or ten, all adept at Wyrm slaying. They'd likely never seen a dragon as large as her, but that wouldn't deter them for long.

Visala once again cursed the minister and the boy's mother. They could have turned the tide, maybe. Not definitely, but it would have been a real roll of the dice. Instead they'd panicked and run, ensuring defeat.

Where was the boy? Trapped aboard the *Flame of Knowledge*, and jammed by the Inurans most likely. Was it worth expending the magic to contact him? No, probably not. He was too far away to help, and even if he were here, what could he really do? This ship was dying, even if its owners didn't know it.

There was almost no magic to begin with, and the sudden addition of a massive crew was stressing the core. If they didn't acquire it soon, none of this would matter anyway, and that lack of magic meant having the ship's captain counted for almost nothing.

At best, Jerek could alter gravity, but every one of their *void*, *life*, and *spirit* mages could counter that. He could remove the atmosphere, but that too they were ready for. The internal defenses all required magic.

No, there was little point in contacting the boy. It wasn't as if he could defeat the Inurans, no matter what he'd accomplished recently. She was willing to admit to the occasional mistake, and Jerek was one of them. The boy had more potential than she'd recognized.

But potential was not skill, nor experience. Potential didn't win battles. In a way, the boy was better off where he was. Hopefully he'd managed to find some wealth and abscond with it.

If he did, she prayed to the Maker that he learned what his mother, and her twice-damned lover, had done. If he lived—if she lived—she would make certain he knew, if it was her last act.

26

I rose to my full height, and tried to look impressive as I faced my people. The armor helped a great deal, or so I hoped anyway. I channeled my dad's confidence when I finally spoke.

"Let's go over this one more time," I said as I surveyed my assembled troops. There were thirty-nine in total, from at least four species, all united by one common goal. I pointed at the holographic model we were studying. "This is the target."

The holo in the corner of the cargo hold displayed the enemy cruiser, which was roughly five times larger than the *Remora*. That was smaller than I'd expected, and I was glad we didn't have to hit the trade moon instead.

"We're going to dock along the upper hull. Seket will be piloting." I nodded at the paladin, who'd once again donned his full golden armor, though there was no sign of his weapon or shield. Why did everyone but me own a void pocket? "Cinaka will lead the first team through, and her hatchlings will focus on the initial strike. That's where resistance will be fiercest."

The ship grew larger on the holo, and a cutaway exposed its various levels, all the way to our destination on the bridge near the center of the ship, which bore a blinking red light.

"Once Cinaka has secured our drop point," I continued, "then Lawl and her mages will use their ritual of flame to melt the hull, which will expose the second level. Lawl's mages will rush the defenders and secure the area. We expect lighter resistance."

The cutaway zoomed in to show the bridge and the level above it, where the next part of the plan would play out.

"I'll teleport the bomb and the urn onto the level below us, while—"

I trailed off because every face had gone slackjawed. They were all staring at a point behind me. I turned and nearly jumped out of my skin when I found the demon goddess Nara in all her terrible beauty standing directly behind me.

Her helmet was tucked under one arm, and her girlish grin, complete with dimples, was fixed on me. "Hey, there, Captain. Sorry to interrupt your briefing. Can we talk for a minute?"

"Sure." I turned back to the platoon. "Take five, everyone, then get ready to move out. Now's a great time for one last bio break."

Nara raised a hand and a wall of silence cut us off from the rest of the hold, the same I'd seen her use with Frit. "I really am sorry, Jerek. You're enacting justice in going after Jolene, but...killing her changes nothing. The Inurans will still take the Great Ships. There are a thousand more Jolenes waiting to take her place, and they'll use the contract she convinced your minister to sign to do it."

"True, but only this specific Inuran asshole blew up my planet," I protested. "I'm not even sure I can take her down. What do you suggest I do to stop the rest of them?"

"You can't do it on your own. You need the Confederacy." Nara raised a gloved hand, and sketched a dizzying array of sigils, their bright light filling the air around her. *Spirit* and *water* mostly, from what I could see. Some sort of ward. "No one can see us now. No scrying. No eavesdropping. I must keep this brief, because my enemies will use this to claim I interfered in local system events. You must contact Voria aboard the *First Spellship*. If you can't reach her, then your people are doomed. She can save you. Contacting her is more important than punishing Jolene. You need to take your ship, and make a run for the Umbral Depths. You can be in Shaya in four days, and contact Voria well before that. You can ensure the Inurans can't take your ships."

"My people will be dead by then." I shook my head

vehemently. "We need to end this now, or none of the rest of it matters. I can't just run."

"If you don't contact Voria none of it matters anyway." Nara eyed me with pity. "You need to find a way to reach her. Right now. Yesterday."

I closed my eyes and sought the strength to do what I knew I'd have to. "What if there was a way to contact her via missive, right now?"

"That would require bypassing the Inuran's magical jamming." She raised an eyebrow and offered a skeptical smile. "Even I can't do that."

"Not bypass. Counterspell. I can end it entirely," I said. I opened my eyes. "There's a cost, of course."

"There always is." Nara rested a hand on my shoulder. "Pay it, and pay it gladly. We do what we must because no one else can. You're a leader, Jerek, and your people badly need that. I shouldn't be telling you this, but the final assault on Highspire is about to begin. Visala is there. She'll delay it for awhile, but someone will take her down, and those kids will be overwhelmed. You saved them once. Can you do it again?"

She was right. I had to. No one else could, or would. I was the captain not just of the *Remora*, but of the *Word of Xal*, at least until my mother stepped up. I needed to save those kids, and from the sound of it, Voria would be able to do that.

I knew little of the Lady of Light, a brand new goddess that had apparently stood against Krox in the skies over Shaya, and had saved their world. As I under-stood it the year before she'd been a mortal commander in the confederate fleet, fighting very much as I needed to now.

Hopefully she'd empathize and understand what I needed, and how quickly I needed it.

"I need to go. Good luck, Captain." And just like that the demon goddess was gone. The ability to teleport with no magical signature terrified me. You could go anywhere, including inside wards from the look of it. But then Nara was a literal goddess.

That left nothing between me and the awful task I knew needed to be done. I reached inside myself, inside the buzzing, where my link to the Web of Divinity lay. I thought about the Web, and about using it.

A vast tapestry of silvery strands stretched out before me, all bounding out from the Web back on the *Flame of Knowledge*. I could feel them all at once, even if I couldn't consciously separate them.

I could also feel the shadows, lurking at the edges of my vision. The longer I studied the tapestry, the more shadows accumulated. They were heavy, and cold some-how. I needed to be swift.

I focused on the Web itself, and all the strands between it and the Inuran trade moon. The jamming spell had its own visible signature, and it wove through the entire system. Millions of strands pierced that signa-ture to the point where they couldn't really be separated.

How did I interact with the Web though? A growing apprehension broke my concentration. Something was watching me. Something vaguely familiar.

"Kek?" I whispered into my helmet. "Can you feel me?"

I am here, friend Jerek. You should not be. My control is tenuous at best, and that is of the ship. I have no providence over the Web. The shadows are thick here. You must flee. The voice echoed in my head, though I couldn't find a source. Maybe everywhere.

"I can't yet." I paused as pain built behind my eyes. "I have to break the trade moon's jamming, and I know the Web can do it. It's supposed to be one of the most powerful divination artifacts in creation."

It can be done, theoretically at least. I will aid you, friend Jerek. Let us be swift. You must vibrate as many strands as possible. They will shatter the sigils, and weaken the enemy spell. Once enough are broken it will cease to function.

I did as he asked and moved around the strange mental landscape strumming strands like chords on a guitar. Cracks began to appear in the enemy spell, small at first, but wider as I worked.

The opposite side of the spell was crumbling as well, I noted. Kek's handiwork.

Both the pain and the shadows grew as I worked, but I focused on execution. Long minutes passed, and the pain lengthened, and doubled, and grew. The shadowed thickened, gathering in the edges of my vision like scav-

engers waiting for a dying animal, their greedy fingers
already pawing at my mind.

We finally hit some sort of critical mass, and the
Inuran spell simply dissolved into fragments of magic. It
was rather anticlimactic, given the extreme effort.

I ran like an army of tech demons were after me,
mentally speaking, and slammed shut my connection to
the buzzing.

"Thank you, Kek," I whispered, and then immediately
opened my eyes. Was it me or was the *Remora*'s cargo hold
darker than it had been a moment ago? My overactive
imagination, I prayed, and not a sign that I'd brought
something back with me.

I used my suit's HUD to trigger a missive, and
directed it to Voria. I knew her signature from my time in
the temporal matrix, enough to reach her, anyway.
Finding a goddess of light who took no pains to hide
herself was much easier than locating a normal person.

A moment later a video feed opened in my HUD. It
showed a statuesque woman, beautiful and regal, but not
intimidatingly so. She wore a simple blue jacket with
gold trim, and cradled a golden staff in one hand. That
staff immediately reminded me of Ardaki, though I
couldn't say why.

The weapons couldn't have been more different in
appearance, beyond both being staves. This one was
golden, with a stylized head meant for stabbing, dominated by a gigantic sapphire in the middle. The other,

Ardaki, was silver with a head meant to mimic a dragon in flight.

"Are you going to explain," the woman began dryly, "why you've missived me? I don't know you, and it's rare for someone to contact me out of the black. Who are you?"

"My name is Jerek," I explained, my words tripping over themselves. "I'm contacting you from the Kemet system, where the remains of the Vagrant Fleet still rest. Your, ah, mother is here. She blew up our planet, and is now trying to wipe out thousands of children in order to steal the ship the last of the survivors are sheltering on."

"Oh, mother." Voria rubbed her temple with her free hand.

Are you going to lay the smack down, Voria? The sapphire in the side of the staff suddenly pulsed. *Can we go? We should bring the Spellship and be all like PEW PEW PEW, that's what you get, Inurans. Galactic justice!*

"Ikadra." There was a warning in Voria's tone, and the staff fell silent. "Is this assault transpiring currently?"

"Yes, they're closing in on Highspire, our last fallback position, in one of the cargo holds aboard a Great Ship called the *Word of Xal*." I licked my lips, and tried to think of what else she needed to know. "Can you send troops? I've, ah, met a goddess who can teleport instantly. Translocation, I believe it's called. If you can do that...we need it."

"You can rest easy, young man." Voria inclined her head respectfully. "I'm sending Crewes to deal with it."

"Crewes? Is that a regiment or a ship?" I asked.

"It's a man." Voria smiled at me. There was an amused wickedness to it.

"One man?" I raised an eyebrow, and looked askance at a goddess. "You can only spare one man?"

"The right man." Her smile added a layer of satisfaction. "Were I you, I'd focus on stopping my mother. Jolene will find a way to slip away, I assure you, and I cannot stop her. That is up to you."

"Yes," I growled. "Yes it is."

"Use terminal force if need be, and beware her magic. She is powerful beyond knowing, and cunning enough to use that power." Voria released Ikadra. "Goddess-speed, Captain."

"Thank you, ma'am."

I released the missive and turned back to my platoon. I'd done all I could for Highspire. It was time to end this. "Break time is over people. It's time for some payback. Get your gear ready, and seal your tethers. We're moving out."

27

Waiting in the cargo hold as Seket piloted the *Remora* was both a blessing and a curse. A blessing in that I didn't have to see the Inuran response fighters, or if the trade moon was sending aid. If combat went south I'd be dead before I knew anything was wrong.

A curse in that how did you think about anything else?

I knew at least some of my people would be stewing. I glanced around the cargo hold through the anonymity the helmet provided. Cinaka's hatchlings were stoic to a dragon, while Lawl's arachnidrakes were too alien to read. How did a spider express nervousness?

My squad was much easier. Briff and Rava were whispering in low tones. Briff had apparently heard about an

Arena league. That was his way...distract himself until he had to think about combat.

Kurz had both hands wrapped around his bandolier, which sported replacement vials for those lost on the *Flame*. A new urn was tucked into the bottom, sheltered in a padded pouch. His expression said resolute, but the quaver in his hands spoke volumes.

Vee stood in her dull grey environmental armor, but with no obvious armament. That was one advantage an eldimagus like the bracelet provided. Almost everyone would underestimate her. She wore a helmet, but I could see her eyes inside, specks of emerald kissed by the sun, and she seemed ready.

I envied her faith, both in me and in whatever deity she believed in. Vee had confidence woven into her core, and never seemed to worry about anything, even life-threatening circumstances.

Seket's voice suddenly rang over the cargo hold speakers. "Captain, we may experience a bit of turbulence. Please secure yourselves."

The entire *Remora* shook from external detonations, but either they were stopped by Seket's wards or were too far away to harm us. Either way it was the paladin keeping us alive, and I needed to trust him to do that.

"Screw it," I muttered into the helmet.

I could trust him, and still watch. I opened a feed to the *Remora*'s external sensors, and saw what we were up against. A trio of fighters were still on approach from our destination, an ivory cruiser that hovered in space as if unperturbed by our arrival. *I know you're coming, and I'm ready.* It didn't exactly fill me with confidence.

The shots that had rattled us came from a second trio of fighters, which had flown right by us and were now coming around for another pass. Seket was good, but six fighters were going to toast us if we parked alongside the cruiser.

We didn't have enough firepower, and we didn't even have the rear cannon that my version of the *Remora* had possessed. I'd have killed for a rear-facing gauss cannon. Then it hit me.

Rear facing.

"Seket, we're going to open the cargo bay doors," I said into the general comm, and heard it echo through the ship. "We'll lose atmo down here, so everyone seal up. Secure yourselves, and get a firing lane on the back door. Fighters are fragile. Seket, you're going to have to let them get in close, but if they do we might be able to take them out."

The *Remora*'s momentum evened out as Seket chose a course, and I glanced at the feed on my HUD. One fighter trio was pursuing...which put them behind us.

"Everyone get ready," I roared into the mic. "Going in 5, 4, 3, 2, 1." I punched the airlock button, and the siren next to it began. I punched it again, and the membrane disappeared.

I snapped against my tether as the atmo was sucked out

of the cargo hold. For a terrified instant I worried that we'd lose someone to explosive decompression, but it appeared everyone had secured themselves, and their gear, well.

"Wait until I give the word," I ordered as I tightened my tether and set up a firing lane out the airlock door.

"You're sure the enemy vessel is vulnerable to our spells?" Lawl chittered into her com. She cradled Kek's eight-eyed staff in three clawed limbs.

"We're about to find out." I drew my new pistol and took aim. More and more she felt right in my hands. "We'll wait until they're right up on us. It will be real easy. When I yell fire...launch your strongest spell. Hopefully at least a few of us hit."

No one replied, but I did see almost everyone get a rifle, staff, or, in Vee's case, a bracelet into a firing position.

"Brace yourselves," Seket's voice echoed over the comm. "They're coming in for the next pass. I'm not erecting wards, so this might hurt."

A pristine fighter in the form of a stylized dragon appeared directly behind us, but too far out. There was no way my pistol could hit at that distance. So I waited. I watched as the fighter swam up in our wake, eager to devour us.

The fighter's spellcannon flashed, and a bright beam of white light lanced out at the *Remora*.

Kurz's hand shot up, and he sketched a *spirit* sigil,

then a *water*, then another *spirit*. A blue ball streaked from his hand into the light bolt, and both spells shattered.

"Fire!" I roared, and unloaded the highest magnitude void bolt I could manage.

A barrage of fire bolts rained from the hold, and they streaked into the fighter in waves. I think my void bolt did some damage, but when fourteen other spells hit roughly the same area, it's kind of hard to know what caused the final detonation.

"Yes! Nice work, people. Two more times." I turned to Kurz. "Did you just counterspell a fighter?" I blinked at the soulcatcher. "That has got to be a first. Nice job."

"It seemed the appropriate response. The cost is requisite to the spell countered, and so I avoid doing it unless I must. I cannot counter many more." He leaned against the wall and closed his eyes, though I noticed the tremor in his hands had eased now that combat had begun.

The next fighter drifted into our wake, and loosed another light bolt. This one slammed into the *Remora's* left fin, which detonated in a shower of debris. That caused the fighter to position itself directly in front of the airlock door.

We lit it up like it was our job, and the fighter paid for its temerity. The final fighter reversed course and began circling back to the cruiser.

"Hey, Seket," I panted. "Has the trade moon done anything since we stopped the jamming?"

"Negative, Captain. It appears they are allowing the cruiser to determine its own fate. I am envious."

The *Remora* jerked hard to starboard, and my tether snapped me back into the wall. I kept my grip on my pistol, but a few hatchlings lost theirs. Spellrifles spun slowly in the zero G, their owners swimming out to recover them.

I watched the feed on my HUD to see what had prompted the maneuver. Seket brought us into alignment with the fleeing fighter, then activated the spellcannon.

A life bolt lanced into the fighter's wing, and that side of the ship sheered off, causing the rest to go into an uncontrolled spin. The pilot might live, but the craft had been disabled and they were no longer in the fight.

The second trio of fighters was close enough to begin their attack run. They came at us head on, but as they approached, a cocoon of white sigils enveloped the *Remora*.

All three enemy fighters connected with their spells. The first discolored the wards. The second tore a hole and the vessel rumbled. The third hit the nose of the ship, and something exploded in the distance near the bridge.

"Seket?" I called into the comm.

"I live, Captain." Despite the words, I detected a note of pain in his voice. "The bridge took the brunt of it. We will need repairs, though the matrix functions. The scryscreen does not. I have patched my armor into the ship, and am using my helmet to guide us."

"Good thinking." I maneuvered the feed until I spotted the fighters, which were coming around into our backfield. I noted that they were keeping their distance. "Looks like they're wise to our little trick. What can we do to help you deal with the last three?"

"Pray for their souls."

The fighters streaked toward us and unleashed their hail of death. Seket's wards enveloped the ship once more, but as before, the last shot got through and tore off the remaining fin.

Seket flipped the *Remora* using the attitude thrusters. Our momentum meant we were essentially flying backward, which allowed him to line up the main spellcannon. It was a clever move.

A life bolt shot from the cannon and obliterated the closest fighter. The last two veered off, but Seket pivoted and took out another one. The last fighter maneuvered into our backfield, but got a little too close.

"Fire!" I roared. We did. It ended poorly for the fighter, and I smiled grimly at the expanding debris cloud we'd created. "All right, Seket, get us bolted onto the hull. It's game time."

My stomach lurched as the vessel wildly altered course, the severity overpowering the inertial dampeners, which sometimes happened on smaller ships.

I watched the feed in my HUD, and tensed as the *Remora* closed the distance to the Inuran cruiser. We came in above her, and as before she didn't run. She didn't even launch a spell.

"They're definitely waiting for us. Cinaka, are your people ready?" I glanced over at the hatchling, Briff's new lady friend, who was standing atop the silver teleportation disk in the rear of the hold along with two of her companions.

She wore dark armor over dusky scales, which elicited a sort of grim reaper vibe. Pretty cool, and backed up by the menacing spellrifle she cradled in both arms.

"Begin when you're ready. Once you and your people are through, my squad will back you up." I turned to Lawl and her arachnidrakes, who also stood ready. She held the staff Kithik in two clawed appendages.

"Kek will be protected this day," she chittered. "He sacrificed himself to the ship, and we will not let these tomb robbers pillage our vessel. We will see Kek's dream a reality. The ship will fly once more, as a part of the Vagrant Fleet."

"Let's hope so." I didn't mention the madness Kek contended with.

The hold rumbled as we connected to the Inuran ship. It was time for the end game.

28

I'd never seen a teleportation disk used, though it had happened once or twice in a holo. The concept was pure insanity, and offered such a massive tactical advantage. The ship supplied most of the magic, with the balance drawn from a pilot.

What made the magitech special was that somehow they'd built it to accept any aspect of magic. It didn't matter if your pilot had *void* or not; you could activate a teleportation disk and it would send you up to about forty meters.

The more wards and matter between you and the target, the less likely it would work though, so it wasn't without risks. That seemed a good enough reason to keep the teleports as short as possible. Also keep in mind everything I knew came from an episode of the show *Relic Hunter*.

Cinaka and her two companions disappeared in a silvery flash as she began the assault. Three more hatchlings stepped atop the disk and disappeared in a similar flash. That kept going on, every three seconds, until we were running low on hatchlings.

The last group went.

It took me about a thousand years to realize I was supposed to be next. I stepped up, and Briff and Rava joined me. Briff leaned down and whispered to me, off comm. "Stay close, Jer. I'll keep you safe."

"Thanks, bud."

Silver flashed, then we stepped into Hel.

Dozens of combatants littered the corridor, but I only had a vague impression of hatchlings battling smaller figures in white armor. They vastly outnumbered us, and were attacking from both directions.

One of the lights above had gone out, and another had started to flicker, which added to the madness. Thankfully, my helmet filtered out most of the light and some of the sound.

That was all the time I had before I heard a *tink, tink, tink*, as a fat black grenade with an angry red light rolled by my feet. There wasn't time to dive onto it, or away from it, or even to decide which was the right action.

The grenade exploded, and I found myself riding a wave of flame that hit me so hard it knocked me into slow motion. The world crawled around me as I sailed over the hatchlings and deep into the Inuran ranks.

My flight abruptly terminated when I slammed into a pair of white-armored mages carrying rifles, and all three of us were knocked to the deck. One of the pair didn't rise, but the other leapt to his feet even as I did the same.

I'd never been involved in a quick draw before. The idea of gunslingers, or spellslingers as some of them called themselves, had always intrigued me. I'd very intentionally avoided it outside of video games, though, because the idea of racing someone for my survival wasn't the kind of thrill I was seeking.

The Inuran's hand reached his pistol at the same instant mine wrapped around my sidearm. I yanked her from her holster, and almost got her up. The Inuran was faster.

"Pathetic." I could hear the sneer in his voice. The spellpistol discharged and a life bolt hit me in the helmet. My HUD flickered, and then thrust me into sudden darkness as the plasma bolt knocked me into the wall. Sounds were muffled, but I could still hear the Inuran taunting me. "I'll enjoy taking that armor from your body."

I pulled at the *fire* and *void* inside of me, and fired blind as I unleashed my spell. Just after I completed the spell, light suddenly returned. I could see! My HUD was still dark, and I could still hear my breath panting in my helmet. Yet somehow I could see.

A faint buzzing hummed in the back of my head. That had to be the magic I'd gained from the *Flame of Knowledge*. Maybe I could see not only through lies, but through illusions and barriers. I wished I understood the limits.

Talk about a clutch last minute power to suddenly discover that you have. Bet you didn't see that coming, random Inuran goon.

I adjusted my aim to point my pistol directly at the Inuran's chest, then thumbed the selector to explosive rounds and shot that prick right in middle of his monologue. The impact blasted him into the corridor wall with bone-cracking force, and his armor did little to protect him.

"You know," I pointed out, as my opponent crumpled to the deck, tendrils of smoke rising from the hole in his chest. "If you win the draw maybe shoot twice instead of running your mouth."

"Jer!" Briff roared from down the corridor, where most of our forces were holding. "Get back to the line!"

A trio of Inurans stood between me and our ranks. They were advancing on Briff and Rava, even as Vee, Kurz, and Seket teleported in to support them.

All three Inurans were raising their rifles, and my friends were going to get the brunt of it. And it hadn't even gotten complicated yet. Behind me I could hear many sets of booted feet. Like...easily a thousand. Or, like, twelve, if I was being real, but if I somehow lived and got to tell this in a bar...a thousand.

The subconscious is a funny thing, and in this

instance it saved my life. Maybe the lives of my squad too. It had figured out the following.

All the Inurans appeared to be using identical gear.

The Inurans were using grenades.

I'd just killed an Inuran.

That Inuran hadn't yet used his grenades.

I dropped to my knees and pawed at the dead man's belt. Sure enough, there were three angry black spheres. Thankfully, my plan only called for one, and I didn't even need to take it off his belt. I just pressed the red button.

A thin red line sprang up around the grenade, indicating it was armed. A second line appeared exactly a second later. You could see where this was going. I didn't stick around.

I reached for the *void* in me, and blinked. The last thing I saw as the frost covered me was a third red line. Then I appeared behind Briff, still in a kneeling position. Rava had taken cover on the other side, and had her pistol drawn in one hand.

Briff grunted as he took a life bolt to the wing. "There's no way we can—"

By the time my little present detonated, the Inurans trotting right by it, and the ensuing wave of death rocked up the corridor in both directions. They didn't even have time to scream. The flames faded to a faint whiff of heat by the time they washed over Briff's wings, which sheltered both me and Rava from the blast.

Shrapnel pinged off his scales, and I'm glad none hit

me. My HUD was still down, which meant I couldn't see the paper doll to know how much damage I'd suffered. It could be gone in places for all I knew.

Since the grenade had dealt with our immediate problem on that flank, and we had Briff and Rava on overwatch, I turned to survey the other direction. Vee knelt next to a hatchling who was clutching at a nasty hole in her gut.

The familiar golden glow surrounded Vee's wrist, and the dragon's flesh began to knit back together. Even the scales grew back, though their dusky hue was slightly off from their neighbors.

"Thank you," she rumbled, then picked up her rifle and dove back into the fray on that flank.

Kurz knelt behind Vee, with a scarlet vial clutched in one hand. His face was obscured behind his environmental armor. "I have a river of flame I can use. It is the soul of a powerful Ifrit, but it will only obey a single command. Shall I save it, or use it to relieve the hatchlings, Captain?"

"Save it unless we're getting overrun," I gave back immediately. "We've got two more decks to get through."

I glanced behind me to see how Rava and Briff were doing. A new wave of Inurans were approaching, though they were obscured by the heavy smoke that the scrubbers were working overtime to deal with.

Something flashed in the darkness, and a grenade

sailed into our ranks. I didn't even have time to panic, though.

Because my sister caught it.

Rava leapt up into the air, snatched the grenade in her free hand, and then whipped it back up the corridor at the sender. It bounced three times, then there was another explosion and then no more Inurans on that side.

"Yeah, you're definitely getting a raise." I clapped my sister on her heavily armored back. "I wish Dad had seen that. He'd have loved it."

She glanced back at me with a threadbare smile, and clapped me on the forearm. "With an op like this, I might get to tell him myself by the end of the day."

"Just hold the corridor. I'm going to check in with Cinaka." I rose and trotted back toward Vee and Kurz. They'd hold position at the rear of the hatchlings, where Vee was still patching wounds.

It worried me that Inurans were willing to toss grenades in their own ship. You didn't do that if you worried about it puncturing the hull, and while the deck had been damaged, the wiring underneath was still intact. How tough was this ship?

Not my problem yet. I needed to secure our drop point first.

I realized there was no sign of Seket, and glanced up the corridor to see where he'd gotten to. "Oh, you have got to be kidding me."

The paladin had charged past the hatchlings, and engaged a trio of white-armored figures in melee. A grenade landed at his feet, but instead of running, Seket snapped down his spellshield and used it to direct the blast.

Fire and shrapnel enveloped his opponents, and flung all three into the bulkhead like discarded cans. None rose.

Cinaka and several other hatchlings fired over Seket's head, and took down the next wave of Inurans that were on approach. I glanced behind them, but it looked like there were no more enemies. The last few stragglers were running.

"I think we did it," I called into the comm. "Let's get sentries up. Lawl, your people can come in and start working on the deck. We're going to need to be quick. They probably have teams on the next level that they'll dispatch to our location."

This hadn't been "easy", but it was still too easy for my liking. The hard part was yet to come. Right now this was the Inurans bleeding our mages of spells so we would be dry for the final fight.

They, on the other hand, probably had mana beer, so they could keep fighting long after our side ran dry.

I only hoped that the deck would be easy to cut through.

Spoilers, it wasn't.

29

A dozen arachnidrakes cradled their staves in scaly hands as they moved into a tight circle behind the protective eye of our hatchlings. I studied their ritual, which I understood in theory, but had never seen cast. There'd been a rituals class back at the academy, but I think I'd taken a music class instead, because that's how I thought you impressed merc women.

Ah, younger Jerek. Even more naive and inexperienced than current Jerek.

The drakes raised their staves and all began chanting. I expected sigils, as I used when hardcasting a spell, but there was none of that. Just a low sonorous chant, with a single word that went on and on, "*Ohhhmmmmmmmmmm.*"

I'd been taught that magic can come in virtually any form, but this was the first time I'd encountered a style so different from that used at the academy. A ritual is the intertwining of multiple casters performing the same spell. That much was the same. How they added magic, though, I didn't even recognize.

The effects were immediate. Each arachnidrake raised a staff, and those staves had a gem set near the tip, which began to glow a bright crimson as the chant deepened.

A beam radiated from each, stabbing down into the deck like the wrath of eight angry stars. Those beams converged on a single point near the center, and the heat rolled off, so hot that it raised the ambient temperature twenty degrees almost instantly.

I expected the deck to redden and melt under the weight of that magical onslaught. The strength of it was immense, and all focused on a tiny section of the deck.

After several seconds, and another fifty degrees, enough to cook an unarmored person, the deck finally reddened. Slightly.

My grip tightened on my pistol, and I wished I knew enough about the metal we were melting to understand how long it would take. Ten seconds passed. Twenty. There was still no real change in the deck, though a meter of it now glowed a faint orange.

"This isn't feasible," I decided over the comm. "They're going to get reinforcements up here long before we get through that deck."

"A tactical withdrawal then?" Kurz's voice came back, flat and emotionless.

"No." I paced back and forth like a caged animal. There had to be an answer. "Seket, you're familiar with teleportation disks, right?"

"I am." Even the bastard's voice was beautiful. "What do you wish to know, Captain?"

"What is the maximum range of the teleport?" I called up a cutaway of the Inuran ship and glanced at our target.

"I wouldn't push it beyond thirty meters," the paladin cautioned. I glanced down the corridor and spotted him standing near Cinaka and her hatchings, his blade still glowing with magic. "You're considering porting down another level?"

"That's the idea, yeah." I wished I had some way to see how many defenders....

The deck dissolved, in my vision at least. I was staring down at the next level, and the half dozen Inuran defenders divided into two groups of three. Both had set up overwatch positions, and were ready to hit anyone coming through the deck above them.

I wasn't a fan of the madness, but I had to admit the new magic was pretty over-powered. There were so many uses.

"Looks like they're waiting for us." I drew my pistol again and cradled it in both hands. "There are six defenders, two squads, thirty meters apart. Seket, Cinaka, and Briff, you're up first. Rava, myself, and Vee next. Vee, get up a ward as soon as you arrive. Then Kurz and Cinaka's people. Let's move. We need to get everyone out of here before the Inuran reinforcements arrive."

"Concentrate on the disk," Seket instructed. "It will remember you from the first teleport."

For a moment I worried if I'd be ready at the right time. How would I know when the first wave had arrived? But my new ability, which needed a name, allowed me to see them appear below.

Even as I willed the teleportation disk to move me down to join them, I saw combat begin. All six Inurans were waiting, and launched a withering barrage of death. Now, I know I've been rather disparaging of Seket, but that paladin is damned useful in a firefight.

A beautiful golden ward spun up around Cinaka and Briff, and blunted the Inuran offensive. Briff breathed on one Inuran, and caught the mage in the chest with a wave of plasma that carried into into the wall and set him aflame. Nuclear flame.

Cinaka raised her rifle and calmly headshot her first target, then blew off the last one's knee.

Vertigo seized me as the disk moved me down to join my team, and as I arrived I spun to face the remaining trio. My pistol snapped up almost of her own accord, but I didn't aim her at any of the three armored mages.

Instead, I focused on the deck in front of them. Magic is malleable, and smart mages can invent spells on the fly, provided we understand the magical theory behind them. You're kind of like a chef with a set of ingredients, and you can cook dishes with whatever proportions you want.

Void is great for teleportation, disintegrating things, and influencing gravity. I'd used gravity to make things heavier. Why not make things lighter? Why not remove gravity entirely?

Magic surged in my chest, and flowed down my arms into the pistol. The barrel filled with a glow that could have been mistaken for a void bolt. Even the spell I fired looked like a poorly aimed attack, as the cracking purple ball splashed into the deck at the foot of the central target.

One of them barked a harsh mocking laugh. The karma was instant. All three armored figures abruptly floated into the air, their arms windmilling as they sought to control their movements.

Rava appeared in my peripheral vision, and my sister snapped her rifle to her shoulder, the stock set against a pad sewn into her leather jacket. "You shouldn't have, little brother." She walked her rifle down all three Inurans, and fired three precise shots at each. One in the head, two in the chest.

The explosive rounds shattered the armor, and sent a wave of shrapnel into the pilots. All three stopped moving, and a few seconds later my spell ended.

Kurz and a pair of hatchlings appeared behind me, then another wave a few seconds later. The process would take several agonizing minutes, and I had no idea when the response team would arrive on the deck we were abandoning.

I glanced down a level, through the deck, and saw no defenders waiting on the level above the bridge. I tried peering further, but a spike of pain shot between my temples when I attempted to see the bridge itself. Some sort of ward, I guessed.

"We are under assault," a coarse hatchling voice hissed over the comm. "The Inurans have arrived on the first level. We cannot endure."

I glanced up through the deck with my fire sight and the blood drained from my face. Inuran assault squads were hitting both flanks, and there were only a few hatchling defenders left. The arachidrakes had abandoned their ritual, and were joining the assault, but it wasn't enough.

A wave of grenades detonated, then a hail of life bolts followed. My people were getting cut down, and the problem grew even worse as another wave teleported out, weakening the defenders.

Lawl raised her staff and lobbed a blue fireball into one Inuran flank, and the resulting explosion killed a dozen opponents. The remaining Inurans unleashed their assault from the opposite flank, and Lawl went down with a pained shriek as a half dozen life bolts sizzled into her back.

More grenades landed, and I forced myself to look

away as the deck above us rumbled. "This is everyone who made it."

A ragged score of survivors stared back at me. Their armor was blackened and damaged, though thanks to Vee, everyone was still on their feet.

"Captain," Cinaka called as she approached. "I recommend a tactical withdrawal. If we couldn't get through the deck above with the drakes, then there is no way we can do it without them."

"I agree." I suppressed a sigh that I hoped no one heard. "We can't proceed with this few people. Reverse order. If you just arrived, you're the first out. Get back to the *Remora*. We're getting out of here."

"War-leader," one of the hatchlings called. The nervousness in his voice added to the bile in my gut. "We are unable to teleport for some reason."

"We've been cut off," Kurz said, his voice just as emotionless. "The Inurans have erected wards on the outer hull to stop us. They let us inside. It was a trap."

30

I don't know how long I stood there frozen. My hands shook, and every bit of moisture in my mouth deserted along with my courage. We were cut off, outnumbered, and most definitely outgunned. I'd led my team into a slaughter, just like my father had once done. Overconfidence ran in the family.

"Does anyone have any ideas?" I managed. I cleared my throat, and spoke again with more strength. "We need a plan."

"Maybe we make for a shuttle?" Vee suggested. She rose from tending to a wound on a hatchling's thick leg. "If we can steal one, then maybe we can get back aboard the *Remora*, and try to get out of here."

"Can't, church girl," my sister countered. I was surprised by the vehemence. She and Vee weren't close, but I couldn't think of a reason for any hostility between them. I chalked it up to stress. "We wouldn't survive getting to the pods, but even if we did...this cruiser is five times our size. They'll blow us out of the sky long before we can make it back to the *Word of Xal*, and as I understand it that ship's being taken by them too. Face it. We lost."

I tried blinking down a level, but of course the deck below us was warded as well. Nothing. We'd have to move on foot, and the Inurans no doubt had both routes covered. We were herded into one of two deathtraps, our choice. It was a nonstarter.

"Seket," I called, and strode over to the paladin. "You prayed to Inura before. Your god granted you a miracle, right? Can you pray for help?"

"It doesn't work that way." Seket removed his helmet, then flicked sweat from his brow. "Inura is no doubt inundated with prayers, and cannot aid any one worshipper. I am granted specific power, and I have used that power for the day."

"Vee? Kurz?" I asked. If they didn't have an idea I wasn't sure where to look next.

"I'm sorry, Captain." Kurz heaved a resigned sigh. "We are unlikely to survive. It is an ignoble end after we have come so far."

Briff straightened and flared his wings. "At least we can make them pay for it. Let's try to kill as many as we can."

"He's right," I decided. "Let's get whatever defenses we

can set up. Strip the dead, and pile the bodies as cover. Kurz, if it looks like we're going to be overrun, then break the urn. We may not survive, but we're taking these bastards with us."

Despite my bravado, my stomach was a war zone, and my mouth was a desert. I didn't want to die. I didn't want my people to die. What choice was there? Would a run to the escape pods be the best choice? They had to expect that, and have contingencies in place as they had for everything else.

How did you teleport past wards? Only...a goddess... could do that.

I blinked a few times and a desperate plan began to come together. My knowledge of religion was iffy, but as I understood it, intent mattered. If I prayed to a god or goddess, then they should hear it. I hoped. Normally they might be too busy to answer, but the goddess I had in mind had just spoken to me twenty minutes ago.

"Xal'Nara, demon princess," I intoned, my hands clasped together. "I call upon you to save my ass in a godlike fashion. Please, save us—"

"I told you I couldn't intervene." And there she was, Nara in all her glory and beauty, though there was no sign of her rifle. She hadn't come to fight. She wore no helmet. "I'm sorry, Jerek. I wish I could do something. I do. I'd love to see Jolene punished, and it kills me that she might acquire the *Word of Xal*. I can think of few things worse. But my hands are tied. I cannot help you without triggering a sector-wide war."

"You're a goddess," I plowed on as if she hadn't spoken. "Can't you grant miracles? I've seen both Vee and Seket use them. They pray to Inura. If I pray to you will you disintegrate the levels between us and the bridge?"

"Jerek!" Vee stalked up to me, her face a twisted caricature of itself as she glared hatefully at Nara. The words were directed at me. "You don't know what you're asking. If you make a deal with a demon she'll forever own a piece of your soul. When you die...you will go to her."

"That's not necessarily true," Kurz countered quietly. "If it were, there would be no reason for soulcatchers. There's a chance, especially for strong souls, that you will journey to a god you pray to when you die."

"That isn't how it works anyway." Nara's tone was laced with annoyance. "You'd have to take a covenant. A magical bargain. If you adhered to my dictates, then I would grant you a miracle. If you proved yourself I might grant more, over time."

"Okay." I folded my arms, and asked the hard question. "Exactly what does this covenant entail?"

"I ask two things. Deny either, and our covenant is broken." She folded her arms to mirror me. "First, I require that you preserve knowledge. If you discover it, and it is in your power to do so, then you must bring that knowledge back to the sector rather than allowing it to be destroyed."

I blinked at her. She was asking me to do something I already did. "And the second dictate?"

"I'm getting there." She uncrossed her arms, and her eyes hardened. "When your power increases to a point where you are no longer mortal you must make a pilgrimage to Xal to meet with me."

"She's asking you to go to the heart of demon power." Vee stepped protectively up next to me. "If you make this deal, then what comes back won't be Jerek."

"Maybe," I allowed, "but if I don't take this deal, then none of us live to find out anyway. Nara, if I take this covenant can you grant me a miracle that will allow me to get through the deck?"

"I can." She nodded. "The miracle is called weaken. If used on the deck it will make it brittle enough to break through. If used against an armored opponent it will dramatically lower their defenses."

I considered what she was asking of me. The first dictate was effectively meaningless, no ask at all. The second was a bit of a mystery. If I survived long enough to become a demigod, then I'd be asked to journey to the stronghold of demonkind.

Every myth and holo said that I wouldn't return, and I wondered if Nara harvested the people who came to her. It didn't seem to fit her, though what did I really know about her beyond a few conversations?

I hated that I had to make this decision without all the facts. If I accepted I had no doubt there'd be consequences, but I couldn't see any compelling reason not to take the deal.

"I accept your covenant," I decided, and felt right about the decision. "Tell me what I must do."

"Put your hand up, palm outward." Nara raised her own hand, and I pressed my palm against hers. "Do you swear to protect and defend knowledge, and to undertake a pilgrimage to Xal when your divinity exceeds your mortality?"

"I do." I nodded. Vee sobbed beside me.

"In exchange for this covenant," Nara intoned, "thrice per day you may call upon me, and I will provide you with the miracle weaken. Prove yourself in my service, and more miracles will follow."

Electric power flowed from Nara's hand into me, and the fibers ran up my arm and into my chest, until they wrapped around the heart. There was a smothering moment when I couldn't breathe, then the effect passed, and Nara lowered her hand.

"It is done." She gestured at the deck. "Go ahead. See what you've purchased."

"What have you done?" Vee whispered, tears running from both eyes. "I respected you...and now..."

"And now nothing," Kurz snapped. The soulcatcher grabbed his sister by the shoulder and spun her to face him. "What better choice can the captain make? If he does nothing we all die. All of us. He is doing this for you. For me. For hatchlings he doesn't know."

"It's a fair bargain." Seket nodded in what I took for approval. "I don't know who this goddess is, but if she's delivered the power to save us, then I laud her."

I ignored the squabbling and knelt in the center of the deck. There just wasn't enough time. I placed one gloved hand against the deck. "How do I activate it?"

"That's up to you." Nara opened her void pocket and withdrew her helmet, which she sealed over her face with a hiss. "Some people add a phrase, and always use it. Some people merely think about it. I'm not picky. Whatever works for you. I'm going to Highspire. I may not be able to help, but at least I can observe."

"Thank you, Nara." I bowed in what I hoped was an appropriate way, and since I was already kneeling it looked like I was genuflecting. You can imagine how much Vee loved that.

I straightened, then placed my hand against the deck again. "Weaken."

Entropy, raw entropy, rolled out of my chest and into my hand. It leaked into the deck and everywhere it touched, lines of corrosive rust appeared. They ate through the deck as if centuries in the rain were passing, and not a few seconds.

After a few more moments the deck collapsed under my weight, and I plummeted to the next level.

INTERLUDE VII

Crewes inspected the action on his new spellcannon, and smiled at the satisfying *kthunk* as the heavy weapon chambered an explosive shell. The cannon used the exact same rounds as a hovertank, and was far too massive for any mortal, even the ones who didn't skip leg day.

But then he wasn't mortal anymore.

It was hard to accept the changes, even months after the fact. His whole body had been replaced with magma, basically, making him more like Frit than a normal human. Just the thought of her drew a scowl, though time had stolen too much of the anger. Now he was just angry out of habit.

The *Talon*'s scry-screen flashed with an incoming missive, and he nodded to accept it. The screen filled with a familiar freckled face, topped by a mop of red hair. Pickus blinked owlishly, and Crewes couldn't help but chuckle.

"What's up, Pickus? You only call when Voria needs something crisped." He slung his cannon over one shoulder, and glanced down when Neeko's furry form pressed up against his leg.

He dropped his free hand to pet the ghost leopard. She was the only creature whose poop he'd ever clean up, but since she was also a set of living armor it was totally worth it. Plus she kept his feet warm at night, something a normal cat wouldn't survive.

"We need something crisped. Or rather, we need to prevent some people from getting crisped." Pickus pushed his glasses up the bridge of his nose. That could have been fixed with either cyberware or magic, but the kid had never done so for some reason. "Jolene's found a new way to cause trouble. The government of Kemet contacted us asking for aid. They claim she blew up their planet, and are trying to steal ancient ships that rival the *First Spellship*. Some kids are pinned in a cargo hold. I'm sending a scrying now. You have permission to use terminal force, though if you can capture or route the Inurans that's fine too."

"I can arrange that, but Rhea's visiting her father on Virkon." Crewes face split into a gigantic grin. "You know, I probably shouldn't go alone. This is official confederate business, right? So it would be okay for me to invite another government to send a representative?"

The blood drained from Pickus's face. "Fine. Please don't blow up the ship. That's all I ask. Keep the kids alive."

"Oh, please." Crewes waved dismissively at the screen. "I'm great with kids. Kids love me. Look what happened to the last kids I fostered."

"They're demons now," Pickus pointed out.

Crewes glared hard at the mousy man, though Pickus was one of the few who didn't find him intimidating. "That don't make 'em bad people. You gotta get over this racism, man. It's the post-godswar era."

"Did you not catch the part where they were demons?" Pickus rolled his eyes.

"We'll work on it. I'll let you know when it's done, Administrator." Crewes didn't even have to tell the *Talon*. The ship knew to kill the missive, and did. "Okay, Neeko. I'm gonna need you to turn into armor. We've got a lunch date."

The cat purred as she slithered around his legs, then disappeared in an explosion of manly-magenta light, which spun around Crewes's body in a method that in no way resembled the magical girl transformation from those blasted holos.

"*Talon*, I got something you'll like." Crewes patted the ship's shiny black wall, and smiled up at him. "I want you to get me Aran on missive."

The ship's walls pulsed with *fire* magic, which Crewes had decided meant the ship was smiling.

Crewes dropped his spellcannon off his shoulder and into both hands so he could be properly menacing, but as the screen lit to show his old friend, Crewes ruined it with a big stupid grin. Damn it.

"Hey, man, whatcha got going on today?" Crewes approached the screen, and slung the barrel back up on his shoulder.

"You know, demon things." Aran smiled, and despite the midnight skin, his friend and former commander hadn't changed from the wipe he'd first shepherded through his first battle back on Marid. "Why? What do you have going on?"

Aran rose from a throne cut from bone, and rested a hand on the hilt of Narlifex, a sword that had saved Crewes more than once. The demon prince moved with deadly grace, though his face was all smiles. He wore no spellarmor, and instead had some sort of stupid black tunic and trousers with purple trim. It was like the uniform for some kid gang back in the gutters on Yanthara.

"Listen, man, what you should be doing is shopping, because that getup is embarrassing." Crewes waved his hand at the screen. "Did I interrupt you from your ballet class and eating yogurt? Come on, man, you're supposed to be menacing."

"You're right." Aran gave a serious nod, and for once

seemed to be listening. "I should totally replace it with a set of *pink* armor. Then they'll be terrified. No offense, Neeko."

A faint mew rolled across the bridge.

"My armor is *magenta*." Crewes raised an eyebrow. "I didn't realize being a demon made you color blind."

They both started to laugh, and it went on longer than any self-respecting Marine should allow.

"Pickus just called," Crewes explained in a serious tone. "Jolene's causing trouble, and some kids are about to get fried. I figured you're in need of some good PR, being a demon and all. These kids just lost everything. Their whole world. We can't let 'em die too. I ain't never gonna have another day like Starn or Marid."

"Done. Can you send me the coordinates?" Aran slowly drew Narlifex, and his eyes pulsed with a purple-black energy that terrified Crewes. Now he looked like a proper demon.

Crewes waved at the *Talon*, who transmitted the destination.

"Meet you there?" Crewes asked.

Aran nodded.

Crewes closed his eyes and focused on the scrying that Pickus had sent. It showed a hangar bay inside a massive ship, dominated by an ancient stepped pyramid that had no right to be there.

Thousands of kids were clustered around the pyramid, and were being pushed back by divisions of hovertanks backed by adult Wyrms. The defenders had a Wyrm too, but the mighty white creature was favoring her right rear leg, and hanging back behind wards.

Crewes envisioned the hangar bay and the *Talon*'s bridge being the same place. It didn't make no kinda sense, but that was how it worked anyway. You imagined two places as one, and when you were a god you just magicked yourself there. Nara probably had some charts she could show about it, but Crewes didn't pay it too much thought.

He appeared in the hangar bay with his helmet already on, and ready to party. First, he needed targets. The kids were being pressed back to the base of the pyramid, which meant that the entire right flank belonged to the enemy.

It was filled with hovertanks, dragons, and other tasty targets. Time for lunch. He wondered how much it would take to break them.

Crewes gathered his legs under him, then leapt over the kids he'd come to save, and kept himself aloft on a plume of superheated flame.

"I am authorized by the confederacy," he blasted out over the battlefield, loud enough to draw blood for anyone not wearing head protection, "to stomp the crap out of any mercs stupid enough to be attacking kids. Your action has been declared unlawful, and you got about three seconds to retreat. If you're not familiar...my name is Crewes. I'm the god who's about to put a foot up your ass."

The enemy ranks didn't seem to pay him much attention. Guess they hadn't heard of him. Awesome.

"Oh, man," he purred. "I've been waiting to try this."

Crewes drew on the magic infusing every fiber of his body and mind, and poured in as much as the new cannon would hold. The XalTech Mark XI was a prototype Kazon had sent, bless his rich demonic ass.

Once the barrel began to steam and hiss, and the runes on the sides flared an angry orange, Crewes flung his spell at the nearest platoon of enemy soldiers. They were tech mages. Mercs who should have known better than to assault teenage kids. No sympathy.

The flame cooked them all where they stood, and when it washed away, their blackened armor ran in rivulets along the warped floor...oops. He hadn't met to harm the ship.

"Nice cannon." Aran winked into existence next to him in his jogging outfit, or whatever it was war mages wore. He already held Narlifex in one hand, but there was no sign of his spellrifle. "I remember when I still needed guns."

The demon prince raised a hand, and the division of hovertanks that had been firing at the white Wyrm were all yanked into the air. Aran made a fist, and eight titanic machines crumpled together into a ball of metal that would have fit in his pocket.

"See, now I feel like you're just showing off." Crewes turned toward a cluster of black-clad cybered-up mercs that were charging in his direction. "Heh, mage killers. Cute. Got something for ya, boys."

A river of white flame flowed out of his mouth like the Winds of Hel, and showed the mercs exactly how little their "magic resistant" bones mattered. Mage killers were terrifying back when he was Sergeant Crewes, what felt a lifetime and a half ago.

The air shivered above him and to his delight, which Crewes would never admit publicly, Nara appeared. The demon princess cradled that long-barreled artifact rifle, and grinned down at Crewes. She looked a little odd with horns, which he could glimpse through her armor's face-plate, but then Crewes wasn't the one who had to sleep with her. Those things looked awkward. "Hey, Sarge. It's been a while. Aran's just too cool to use guns because he's never landed a headshot. But if we're going to have a contest I'd be happy to join in. You're here on confederate business, right? The kid got through?"

"I don't know about no kid, but yeah someone got through. I gotta invite you to make it official." Crewes lobbed a conventional tank shell from his rifle just to see what it would do. It detonated over a squad of hatchlings, and ended poorly for three out of the four. "I'm here as a duly appointed representative of the Confederacy. As an agent of a member government, will you assist me in this task?"

"On behalf of Xal, and my pompous boyfriend, Xal'Aran, I accept," Nara raised Shakti, the rifle, and fired. A tiny marble of black zipped into the midst of the last remaining division of hovertanks. The marble grew slightly, then shrank.

The tanks, Marines near the tanks, the floor panels, and everything else near them was sucked into the micro-singularity that Nara had cast.

That broke them. The enemy started to run, and a rousing cheer went up from the kids around the pyramid.

"Man," Crewes muttered, a bit dejectedly. "That was over quicker than I thought. Should we go after Jolene?"

"Nah." Nara deposited her rifle into her void pocket. "The kid who called us in, Jerek, is dealing with the problem. Young, but he's got a good head on his shoulders. He's who we'll have to deal with if we want to acquire this ship, but I have an in with him now."

"Do we? Want this ship I mean." Crewes's former CO peered around him in that distant way he sometimes got that said he was feeling things he could neither sense nor understand. "I can feel this ship's power, but he doesn't belong to us. He already serves another. Maybe we can acquire one of the others."

"You can do your politics crap later." Crewes gave them a smile, and nodded at the throng of kids that were nervously approaching. "Hey, you wanna go play hero? You guys should do some selfies or something. Gotta work on that PR, I'm telling you."

"Maybe I need a social media page. Hey, I'm Aran," the god whispered mockingly. "Former war hero, currently demon prince. I love long walks in space, translocating, and showing off my hot girlfriend."

Crewes chuckled as he followed Aran toward the kids. Saving the day never got old.

31

I landed on my feet if you can believe that. Rust rained around me, the last remains of the incredibly resistant deck that had stopped the arachnidrakes and their ritual. It hadn't stood up to the power of a god, thank...well, thank Nara, I guess.

"Jer, you okay?" Briff called as he leapt into the hole and spread his wings to slow his fall.

The deck shook when he landed, enough that people on the bridge below us might have heard. Hopefully they chalked it up to combat.

"Fine. Better than fine." I glanced back up at the hole I'd made, and saw my crew clustered around it. "Let's get everyone down, starting with Kurz. I want to get that Urn in position as soon as possible. Cinaka, do you have any illusionists among your people? Anyone who can make the deck look intact?"

Cinaka leapt gracefully into the hole, and landed nearly soundlessly next to Briff. She fluffed her wings once, then checked the action on her spellrifle. "We're warriors, not scholars. There are no true mages among my ranks. What of your soulcatcher? Can he not summon some *spirit* to fulfill this task?"

Kurz dropped down the hole, and I moved instinctively to catch him. It shocked me how light he was, and I set him gently on the deck and waited for Vee.

She allowed me to catch her, though she wouldn't look me in the face. I guess that was progress. I didn't know why she feared demons so much, but I was hoping she'd be willing to talk about it...if we lived.

Seket landed in a crouch that sent a boom rolling across the deck, easily louder than Briff's had been. He rose, and flicked a bit of remaining blood from his blade. "They will respond quickly, I'm sure. How long until the urn is ready, Soulcatcher?"

"Longer if I'm interrupted," Kurz snapped as he knelt and withdrew the small clay urn from his bandolier. "This must be done precisely, or we will not have enough time to get away."

"We'll leave you be. Briff, make sure he isn't bothered." I flipped on the unit-wide channel. "Everyone get down to the bottom level and into position. We're changing the plan on the fly. Originally I wanted to teleport a bomb onto their bridge, but the bridge is warded. That means we have to cut through the deck, just like I did on the last level. Seket will drop the bomb, and everyone else will lob grenades. We want as much collateral damage as possible. Then we'll roll the urn into the room and bug out. We want to be back on our ship before the wights overwhelm the Inurans."

There were nods all around, and since no one seemed to have any questions I just went with it. I moved to the deck, and placed a palm against it. Before using the ability I peered at Kurz, and figured since my helmet was on, it wouldn't disrupt his concentration.

He carefully dribbled salt in a precise runic pattern until he'd created a perfect ritual circle around the clay urn, so deceptively innocent for a weapon of mass destruction.

I longed to ask him what the salt was for, but interrupting him could have catastrophic results. I focused instead on my task. My fingers were still splayed across the deck, and most of my people were down.

"Weaken," I murmured, and as before, the deck began to corrode. This time I ran a chronometer in my HUD...five seconds to corrode a two-meter-by-two-meter area.

The power of it was heady, far stronger than any spell I could cast. I just hoped the price wasn't half as large.

"I am ready, Captain." Kurz rose from the urn, and slowly removed the cork. "You may consider the urn primed. When I kick it from the ring of salt the spirits will be able to reach it, and it will instantly transform them into wights. All we need do is knock it through the hole after the explosion."

"Rava." I nodded to my sister. "She'll handle it. I want that urn planted up their tailpipe as soon as the flames die down."

"On it, little bro." She slung her rifle over her shoulder and took up a position behind Kurz so she could scoop the urn up when needed.

I was about to kick the deck I'd weakened, but hesitated when I saw what was happening around the urn. Two spirits, blue-white wisps, had already found it and were prowling around the edge of the salt ring trying to get inside and reach the urn. How many ghosts were on this ship? Everyone ever killed here, I guess.

"On three." I stepped back and drew my pistol, then aimed it at the floor. "Three. Two. One." I lined up the pistol and fired an explosive round. The floor shattered into rusty fragments, which rained onto two techs standing at a console. They appeared utterly unprepared for our assault.

All around me hatchlings were tossing grenades through the hole I'd made. A cascading detonation rolled by below, and abruptly silenced several screams.

"Now, Rava!" I shouted. The adrenaline raced through me, and my whole body shook as I waited for the Inuran response. What kind of forces would they have on the bridge? What if they survived this?

My sister's ponytail bobbed as she scooped up the

urn, and threw it in a low underhanded toss that carried it through the hole at an angle that took it out of sight... well, everyone else's sight.

I could see through the deck, and watched as the urn rolled into the middle of a trio of bodies. Wisps were rising from each, and they were joined by those who'd been following the urn, and those of the other corpses we'd just created.

About a dozen wights sprang into existence, and rushed the defenders, who were more numerous than I'd expected. Ten squads of crack Inuran mages were waiting, and our little ship-warming gift had only wiped out a single squad.

The wights glided into their ranks, and the closest Inurans died. The wights swelled, and surged forward...at first.

Several Inurans in heavier spellarmor charged forward, and as they ignited heavy spellshields, their blue and white runes swirling protectively around them, I realized I was looking at the modern equivalent of Seket.

Each paladin performed the same miracle, and a golden halo sprang up around them. Their collective brilliance pushed the wights back, and the spectral undead were unable to approach.

That made them easy targets for the remaining mages. Spellrifles began to fire, and the life bolts they discharged acted as disintegrate might when it hit one of the black ghosts. They simply burst into a cloud of golden motes, and then were gone.

A few more defenders at the fringes died, but a solid dozen remained, and in their rear I spotted a hawk-faced Inuran woman shouting orders while she cowered behind a console.

"The target is here," I spoke into the comm, "but it looks like they're dealing with the wights. We're going to have to finish this the old fashioned way. I'm going to tag your HUDs with the defenders' location. Let's get in there and make them dead."

Rava leapt through the hole without further prodding, and landed in a catlike crouch, then went to one knee and lined up a shot with her automatic rifle. She had *fire* now, but hadn't picked up or been trained with a spellrifle. If we lived, I'd have to remedy that. She'd be even more lethal.

As if contradicting her need for more lethality, her rifle bucked and an explosive round ended the first paladin. She pivoted fifteen degrees to the right, and the rifle bucked again. A second paladin dropped, also from a headshot.

The golden auras in those parts of the defending lines suddenly winked out, and the last few wights were able to get in close. Two more defenders went down with screams as the wights touched them, then the ragged black souls rose from their bodies in a shimmering wave.

It took only seconds before the new wights were also

seeking the living. The Inurans were trained to deal with just such an attack, but that was hard to do when my sister was shattering skulls like overripe fruit.

I landed next and launched my brand new zero G spell. It landed at the feet of the third paladin, and he, plus all his buddies on that side, floated into the air. It didn't harm them, but it did prevent them from finishing the wights, or dealing with the rest of our forces as they came tumbling into the fight.

Cinaka and Briff led the hatchlings into combat, automatic rifles chattering their deafening cry as Briff's cannon added a deeper thump every few seconds. They concentrated their fire on the targets in zero G, and five Inurans I'd trapped died in seconds.

That left only one paladin remaining, which Seket seemed to take personally. He ignited his spellshield, then bellowed a war cry as he sprinted toward his opposite.

The last paladin spotted him, and raised a longsword in salute. The spellblade dripped with magical gems, indicating its worth and magical potential. Its slender blade flared to brilliant life as he strode out to meet Seket in single combat.

"Focus on the other targets," I instructed over the comm. "Let Seket handle this one."

I circled wide around the room and focused my attention on Jolene's position. I couldn't see her directly, but I spotted her shadow on the console next to her hiding

spot. She was still back there, and not actively partici-
pating in the combat.

That made me hesitate. Nara had adamantly maintained that Jolene was powerful. Voria had repeated that
warning. Jolene was an archmage, with access to every
greater path of magic. That kind of versatility should
have let her wreck my forces, pretty much on her own.

At the very least she'd be able to counter our most
powerful spells, or erect a ward, or disintegrate some of
us. But she was cowering behind a console, and letting
her forces be slaughtered.

Why? It made no sense.

Oh, well. I withdrew a grenade from my belt—thanks,
Inurans—and teleported it into the corner where Jolene
was hiding. I expected a ward. I expected a defense.

What I did not expect was a detonation that launched
Jolene's body spinning into the air, then slammed her
into the ceiling hard enough that her back snapped.

The matron's battered form crumpled to the deck,
and didn't rise. She wasn't even wearing spellarmor.

I slowed as I approached. The last defenders were
going down now under the relentless pressure from the
hatchlings. As I watched, six of them cascaded their
breath weapons, and roasted one of the last surviving
Inuran squads alive in their armor.

By the time I reached Jolene's body all the Inurans
were down.

Vee approached me with a hesitant smile, which was

welcome. She cleared her throat, then spoke in a low tone. "Have you gotten the justice you were after? I think you've made the sector a better place."

"It was too easy," I muttered. I rose a trembling hand. "I'm going to verify a hunch."

The rest of the squad gathered, along with Cinaka, but I paid them no mind as I summoned a blue flame over my palm. I envisioning the bridge before we'd arrived, and began rolling back minute by minute.

I didn't know precisely what I was looking for, but watched Jolene carefully as the flames rolled back time. I froze the image when I spotted something that made my heart shudder.

"She's not dead." Two Jolenes stood in the flames. "She cast a simulacrum. A dummy. Then abandoned that creature to die in her place."

"Where did she go, though?" Kurz asked. I noted the tremor in his hands, and the fact that he was swaying on his feet. I moved to assist him, and wrapped an arm around his waist.

"Does it matter?" The flames vanished as I supported Kurz. A few months ago someone would have been supporting me. "She got away."

I thought I'd feel angry. Mostly I was just relieved. She'd run, and we were still alive. If Nara was right, the Inurans might keep coming, but at least there was no one left giving them orders.

My magic was almost entirely spent, but I couldn't

rest yet. This had been a raid, which it seemed the trade moon was allowing. If I tried to keep the ship their neutrality would come to a swift and decisive end.

I needed to get back to the *Word of Xal*, and see if the fight was still raging.

32

The trip back to the *Word of Xal* was made largely in silence, and I stared back at the Inuran cruiser we'd raided. A cloud of ships rose from the trade moon like a swarm of flesh-wasps, and they were closing fast with the cruiser.

How would they react to what they found? Would they take revenge? I couldn't even worry about that right now. I needed to get back to Highspire, and ensure that it still stood.

I closed my eyes and counted three deep breaths. It fortified me, enough that I could open my eyes at least. I cleared my throat, then whispered into my suit, "Guardian, can you display the tactical situation in the Highspire cargo bay?"

The mental image of a sea of dead students wouldn't be banished, not until footage appeared on my HUD.

"The battle is over, Captain," Kemet said, his tone more jovial than usual. "We received aid from an organization that identified itself as the Confederacy. They declared the attack unlawful, and routed the Inuran forces. The survivors are currently boarding their carrier, and have abandoned control of the bridge since they lacked a suit of Heka Aten armor."

"Any word from the minister or my mother?" I struggled vainly to keep the hope from my voice.

"Negative, Captain. I believe they are still in the umbral depths."

"Where is Visala?"

The footage shifted to show the top of Highspire, where Visala stood in human form. There were controls to rewind and replay, so I wound back through the battle and watched it in reverse.

"Maker's wrath…" I muttered.

"Are you going to share with the rest of us?" Rava's voice was punctuated by a light shove.

I willed my helmet to slither back into the armor, and eyed her soberly. "The students were going to be wiped out. They were losing. Then a couple gods showed up. One of them was a demon lord, and the other some sort of fire god. Nara joined them, and the three of them wiped out a pair of legions before the rest of the Inuran forces could retreat. The fight is over."

Vee shook her head sadly. "I understand why you

made the deal you did, and how attractive demonic help looks. There is always a price."

"Maybe," I allowed. "In this case I'm glad I paid it. We're alive. Those kids are alive. The assault has been foiled."

"Not everybody lived," Briff pointed out forlornly. He nodded at Cinaka, who stood huddled with her surviving hatchlings on the far side of the cargo bay. Less than half had survived, and none of the arachnidrakes.

"The cost was high," I admitted. "Not paying it would have been higher."

"Captain," Seket's voice crackled over the cargo bay's speakers. "We're docking with the *Word of Xal* now. The Inurans have made no move to pursue."

"They'd do it through diplomatic channels, I bet. They'll want to speak to the minister, not us." I rubbed my temples and wished I had time to sleep. At least the fighting was over. "I'm going to meet with Visala and see what she makes of everything. Briff, I'm putting you in charge of the *Remora* while I'm gone. Guardian, can you teleport me to Highspire near the headmistress?"

"Jer, are you sure that's a good idea?" Briff's expression shifted to comically horrified.

"You can handle it." I nodded confidently in his direction, and meant every word. "Work with Cinaka to get her people into quarters, and see that everyone has access to the forge if they need food or munitions. We've earned some R&R, and once you have everyone settled if you

want to put together a tourney I bet that would lift everyone's spirits."

"An Arena tourney?" Briff's tail rose cautiously. He
fluffed his wings, and rose a little taller. "I can do that. I'll
start setting up the brackets right now. Do you think we
should give out some sort of prize?"

The hatchling was already off and running, and my
sister trailed after him as they approached the rest of the
dragons. Hopefully that would keep them busy.

That left me standing with Vee and Kurz. Vee
wouldn't meet my gaze, and I didn't want to press it. Kurz
looked as if he were awaiting orders.

"Kurz, when Seket has us docked, will you take the
time to start interviewing him? I want to know more
about his time and the events that led to him being here."
I scratched my chin, and realized that I'd accumulated
enough scruff to almost have a beard. "I've got the feeling
that we haven't found out why he was sent here yet, and
now that we have him I want to see if we can get ahead of
this."

"Of course, Captain." Kurz inclined his head deferentially. "I'll report my findings when I have something to
share."

Vee turned without a word and headed up the ramp
toward the bridge. I let her go. We'd have time to work it
out, but for now space was probably best.

"She will come around, Captain." Kurz rested a hand
on my shoulder, just for an instant, but it still meant the

world. "I know my sister. She is rigid in her beliefs, and our scriptures are quite clear about the void. In time she will accept that they are merely old words in a book, as I have. Your actions scream your intent, Captain. You are a good man."

"Thank you, Kurz." I clapped him on the shoulder. "Guardian, will you teleport me now?"

There was a flash of light and a moment of vertigo, then I was standing on Highspire's top step, the same place I'd been the day we'd saved the pyramid from planetary destruction.

"You live." Visala's skepticism was so ingrained that even though her words were surprised, her face remained a glower. "I must admit I am impressed. As you can see we drove back the enemy. I called for confederate aid, and—"

"*I* called for confederate aid," I interrupted. "I also broke the jamming preventing us from calling for that help. Nice try though."

Visala offered a smirk. "Can't blame a Wyrm for trying now, can you? Very well, thank you for saving us. I acknowledge the debt, much as I hate to. What comes next?"

"What do you mean?" I glanced down at the recovering students, who were still cleaning up and hauling bodies away. "We recover, and deal with the Inurans. Their trade moon is still here, and they are still going to want to get paid for the deal the minister inked."

"Haven't you asked yourself where the minister is? She ran, Jerek, with your mother, and their ragged little fleet. They abandoned us." Visala's glower deepened, and the tone matched. "You are in charge, like it or not. You are this vessel's captain, and I will back you in negotiations. The Inurans are likely to want arbitration, rather than to deal with the Confederacy directly. They'll be willing to deal."

I rubbed my temples again. The need for sleep was becoming paramount. "I have proof that Jolene attacked illegally, and the testimony of Bortel to back it up. They'll deal, but they are still going to want to get paid, and we still have nothing to sell. I am not cut out for this. We need the minister back to represent our people. I don't know why she ran, but I want to hear it from her before I make decisions."

"Jerek, listen to me." Visala stretched out a hand and took mine in both of hers. "I have opposed you, it's true. I have tried to take the armor. You resisted me. You retained your power. You have proven you have the strength. If you give up that power, then you will never be able to reclaim it."

"I know." I squeezed her hand gratefully, then released it. How odd that we were no longer enemies, just like that. Dragons were strange. "If I turn over the captaincy to my mother then I'm giving up a lot of power. But surviving encounters with you isn't the same thing as administrating a ship this size. I'm not qualified. My mother is. I can barely run the *Remora*. And whatever we think about the minister I trust my mother."

"Do you?" Visala snapped, a low inhuman growl rumbling from her chest. "Love blinds, child. Your mother is in love. Take great care in what decisions you make."

"I understand the severity, trust me." I folded my arms and watched the kids below. My classmates not very long ago. "The minister bailed. Sure she was doing the right thing in bringing the Inurans to justice, but doing it posthumously, after writing us off? It doesn't sit well with me. And I'll have words with her before I agree to anything."

Being out of my depth had become the new normal, and it never stopped being terrifying. Exhaustion kept turning the gravity up, notch by notch. I needed sleep.

"I'm going to get some rest. If any new emergencies crop up I'll be on the *Remora*."

33

An insistent chiming penetrated the nightmares. Dark, smothering things fled from me as the lights came on in my quarters aboard the *Remora*. I could feel them lurking there, at the edge of my vision, even when the buzzing was silent.

"On screen," I slurred as I forced myself into a sitting position atop my bed. Unlike the cot I'd had before, I now had a luxury hovercouch, absolutely the most comfortable thing I'd ever slept in.

The scry-screen covering one full wall of the captain's quarters flared to life, and showed a photorealistic view of the minister's desk, with her seated behind it. It was as if I were suddenly standing in her office.

"Morning." I stifled a yawn as I rose to my feet. "Looks like you finally left the Umbral Depths. Where did you run to? Shaya?" I scrubbed fingers through my hair, and moved to stand before the screen, reveling in my silken pajamas.

My armor hovered in the corner, and I saw Ramachan's gaze flick over to it. Not covetously so much as cataloguing. Always cataloguing.

"You are angry." There was no emotion in the minister's tone. Even her bun was restrained, and her suit a dark muted blue. "Do you take issue with my decision to flee to the Confederacy for help? Do you believe staying would have made a difference?"

"Let me think about that." I peered up at the ceiling as if thinking. "Hmm. I stayed. I made a difference." I speared her with my eyes, and let her see how upset I was. "You ran. Had you stayed you could have helped me take down Jolene. We might have gotten there in time. As it stands she got away, and we lost lives we didn't need to lose."

"She got away?" Ramachan cocked her head to the side and I read genuine confusion there. "That makes no sense. You have no idea what you have achieved, young man. The Inurans are policing their own. They claim that Matron Jolene is dead, and that her shares reverted to her daughter, Voria. She's lost all power, and the Inurans are taking responsibility for the attack. They've issued a formal apology."

I forced a calming breath, and clasped my hands behind my back in what I hoped was a regal way. My bed-head hair probably wrecked that image.

"Where does that leave us? Do we still owe the Inurans?"

Ramachan rose from her desk and began to pace. Her hands shook, and her agitation was palpable.

"They've asked for arbitration," the minster said. She stopped her pacing, and her face hardened even further, almost brittle now. "They admit that Jolene attacked unlawfully, but not that she is responsible for the destruction of our planet."

"Bortel will testify that she is." I folded my arms and ignored the gurgling from my stomach. "Scrying will provide any evidence we don't have."

"Maybe." The minster finally dropped into her chair again, as if she lacked the strength to stand. "But the Inurans claim we still need to provide the commerce we promised or the cancellation fee. They may be willing to negotiate the price, but that hardly matters. We don't have the money to buy them off."

"Then we play for time." Now it was my turn to pace. "We call in the Confederacy officially. That buys us time to try to find something valuable enough to sell."

"And there was nothing aboard the *Flame of Knowledge*?" Her hope rose, and it killed me to dash it. There was no way I was telling her about the Web of Divinity.

"Nothing." I shook my head sadly. "We found knowledge scales, but nothing close to the amount of money you'd need. The ship is overrun with monsters, and not suitable to be sold. We might be able to investigate one of the others, though. If you can keep the Inurans busy, then I might be able to find something. There are five more ships out there. One of them has to have something to sell."

"I can buy you time." She leaned back in her chair, and eyed my shrewdly. "In the meantime I think it's time for you to pay us a visit. As I understand it your mother needs you here in person in order for you to turn over command."

And there it was...the entire purpose for the call. She wanted this dealt with, before I found a way to wiggle out of it. Did I want to do that? Did I still trust my mother? I noticed she was nowhere to be seen, which suggested the minister wanted us kept apart. That seemed odd.

Last time she'd included my mother as extra leverage. What had changed?

"I can be there for breakfast," I allowed. "Where is my mother?"

"She, ah..." the minister glanced off screen, and her mask finally cracked, revealing the scared person underneath. "The truth is I'm a bit worried about her. She took leaving the system hard, especially since she feared the worst for you. She believed you lived, because if you died she'd have become captain, but she didn't know if you'd been captured by the Inurans. I'm glad I can reassure her now."

The minister left out that my mother had served a term as the headmistress of the academy. She loved the school, and Highspire, but mostly she loved the students. It must have killed her to run away, and I wondered what kind of scars that had left.

"I'll get cleaned up and head over to your ship."

"Of course. See you soon." She inclined her head, and the missive dissolved back into a blank wall.

Now what? Did I turn over the captaincy? And what did I do about Vee? There were so many questions. So much to think about. I still hadn't had time to properly honor my father, or to even think about where I stood in regards to his death.

I sat on my bed again.

The entryway chimed.

"Come in," I called. I'm not going to lie. I hoped it was Vee.

Briff's scaly head poked through the doorway. "Hey, we ran a tourney yesterday and had a great time. We're about to start another one since we have the day off and all. You want to join in? I figured you could use some downtime."

I thought about that. The responsible thing to do was go to the minster's ship, and turn over the captaincy.

But you know what? I'd earned a day off.

"Yeah, man, I'm in." I stifled a yawn. "Just let me get some breakfast."

"Awesome! You're gonna have so much fun." Briff charged off, the deck shaking as he ran.

I considered changing, or putting on my armor, but

instead padded barefoot out of my quarters. I was among friends, and besides, in that moment I was far too lazy to try putting on gear.

The mess was mostly empty by the time I arrived. Vee sat by herself, and glanced up as I came in. Her auburn hair shone under the soft lights, and the way they caught her eyes made it tough to look away.

I led with the smoothest thing I could think of. "Hey, I worked all night on this hair. The least you could do is compliment me."

She rolled her eyes, but patted the chair next to her. "You know we have a forge now. I can make you a brush."

"I just need eggs. And maybe some ham." I headed to the console of my foundry, on my ship, and ordered eggs, which I took to sit with the woman I very much hoped would one day be my lady. "I have a feeling the hardest stuff is behind us."

You can already guess how that turned out.

INTERLUDE VIII

Every molecule of Inura's body, his magic, and his very soul screamed out that the ship was *wrong* the instant he translocated into a remote corner of a trivial cargo bay aboard the *Inura's Grace*.

The Great Ship had been his crowning achievement during the final age of the dragonflights, during the last epoch when they'd worked together, all eight of them.

Setting aside their bickering had allowed them to conquer a galaxy, and to shape the destiny of thousands of worlds. There had been power and plenty for all, and this vessel had been built by the version of Inura who knew only blind optimism.

It had been a refuge for his children, an ark capable of carrying them to distant stars, where they could spread his light and improve the lives of all they touched. It had been a vessel of knowledge. Of invention. The *Inura's*

Grace had spearheaded magical development for centuries, and many of their most impressive relics had been created here.

But the ship had changed.

Those changes weren't yet visible to the naked eye, at least not in this part of the ship. A glance at the cargo bay showed that while it was not in use that it had been maintained and kept in good repair. There were no spots of rust, and the magical lighting had been freshly enchanted no more than a decade ago.

No, the changes were subtler than that. The energy that hummed through the ship, that animated it and made it the forge that it was, had changed. The song of *life* had been replaced with its mournful cousin...*spirit*.

That made no sense. One did not simply reshape a vessel as large or potent as this, and even if so, his children were of *life*. Even the metal that comprised the bulkheads and corridors was infused with *life*.

Yet the wrongness persisted. It defied his disbelief, flaunting the twisted nature of his crowning achievement. Somehow the ten millennia of isolation had murdered the soul of his vessel. That terrified him. Such sacrifices were not accidental. Someone had willfully killed the ship and transmuted the magic.

It was the only possibility that made any sense.

Inura found the strength to leave the corner where he'd been hiding, though he'd wrapped himself in layers of cloaked spells that rendered him undetectable on every possible level. He was invisible, inaudible, and immune to attention. Eyes would slide past him without seeing anything.

He glided up the corridor, and made his way toward the heart of the ship. During his journey he encountered no one, which disturbed him further. Who'd been caring for the ship? Where had they gone?

The answer came near the ship's heart.

All corridors led toward the center of the primary level, just as he'd intended. Inura drifted up the golden corridors, where the first clue presented itself. Golden walls gave way to an unwholesome silver in the process of losing its luster.

Inura fluffed his wings behind him in agitation. Corrupting the heart of a Great Ship was no simple feat, nor one that could be accomplished quickly. Whatever had been happening here had been going on for centuries, or longer.

As he approached, silver gave way to a sickly white, the worst of the corruption. He followed it down a corridor, and finally reached the outer ring of the amphitheater itself.

Unlike the other Great Ships, the *Inura's Grace* had been designed to welcome and embrace. The heart of the ship was a giant floating sun, but one that shed clean, wholesome light that did not harm the eyes or skin as a star would.

For many millennia scholars had filled the rings of

seats ascending up from the center of the amphitheater. A stage had been built precisely at the center, a silver disk that moved as the bearer wished, and ensured that their voice was heard by all.

All that had changed.

The seats near the center were occupied by bipedal figures, but the wrongness emanated from each and every one. They basked in the glow of an unholy sun, the clean *life* energy somehow replaced by wretched *spirit*, the insidious corruption that allowed corpses to continue on past their allotted life span, and that shackled souls for their twisted uses.

Inura froze. He'd seen this before. The mages on the lowest level were the most powerful, so powerful that he could parse each individual aura in spite of the density of the cluster.

Their auras made it clear that they were unliving. Their bodies were ancient husks, but their magics had shackled their own souls to that desiccated flesh. They would do anything to prevent being woven back into the Great Cycle.

He'd seen power mad necromancers before, and had eradicated many sects in his time. This was different. These were his children, yet somehow they'd abandoned their reverence for *life*. It made no sense. How had they fallen? Why mortgage away their immortality for this unnatural imprisonment?

Many of the mages in the back rows still drew breath,

though their flesh was sickly and pallid. Necromancers, every one, drawing upon the souls of others to fuel themselves. The dark reflection of his own soulcatchers.

A procession of white-robed figures began marching into the heart from a corridor opposite his location. In their center floated a shackled woman, who thrashed wildly at her bonds.

Another procession came from a second corridor, then a third, and so on, until twenty groups of robed figures brought their prisoners down to the light.

Inura had often longed for his draconic form since his...lessening. Never so much as now. He was not a war god, but his dragon form could have laid waste to everyone in the amphitheater with a single breath. Now though? It would be a magical battle, and those rarely ended well for a lone caster, god or no.

The procession finally halted when it reached the sickly sun, the perversion of life that had somehow overcome one of his most beloved creations.

One of the figures in the lowest row floated into the air over the processions, up near the wan sun. She stretched both hands high into the air over her, and bathed in the glow of that unwholesome star. When she spoke the words were crisp, but the accent was strange.

"The cycle has turned again, and once more we honor the Maker's memory. His death cries out for vengeance." The high priestess, a soulcatcher he would guess, extended a hand toward the score of prisoners, and in that moment dread gripped Inura's very core. A faint light pulsed in her hand, then in the sun above. "We offer these souls to strengthen the *Maker's Wrath*. Once, you were our father's grace. Now, you are the terrible instrument of his vengeance. Our father is gone, but his memory remains."

A sickly wisp of smoke puffed up from the priestess's palm, and flowed rapidly toward the first victim. Inura forced his wings erect, and stood tall. He would witness their deaths, even if he couldn't prevent them.

Inura knew the greater paths of magic better than all but a few gods, and an understanding of what he was about to witness was already growing. Necrotech had been banned during the reign of the dragonflights, thrown aside in favor of magitech.

At the time Inura had opposed the move. It made little sense to ignore so potent a weapon. Spirit and bone had intrigued the artificer in him, though even as a youth the idea of using souls to power tech had been disquieting.

Never more so than now.

The smoke emanating from the priestess's palm divided into twenty flows, which each stalked a victim. They flowed through the air like snakes, then pounced on their helpless prey, flowing up noses and through mouths opened to scream.

The flesh paled immediately, the victims a mix of drifters and humans, and a lone Inuran. The life left their eyes, and their chests ceased to rise, but the spell was only half done.

The smoke burst out of its victims, and flowed back to the priestess's outstretched palm. She raised her other hand, and an ivory ceramic urn floated up to meet her. The smoke flowed into the urn's mouth, and Inura knew he wasn't imagining the screams as the priestess corked the vessel.

"The bodies of the defilers are yours to do with as you wish, our gift to you." She waved at the processions, who offered a single unified bow, as if they'd been practicing together for a lifetime. Each began marching back the way they'd come, and the woman didn't speak again until the last had exited to the room.

She set the urn next to the bench where she'd been sitting, but remained hovering in the air, clearly ready to address her flock once those she deemed unworthy had departed.

"Lesser business is concluded," she intoned. All eyes were fixed upon her, and Inura could feel the strength in her, enhanced as it was by ingesting some of the spiritual energy she'd just taken. "Now to the greater. Kemet is no more. The lurker sheep are few in number, but they will heed our war cry. The time has come to take revenge on our enemies. The Inurans have revealed themselves, and they have no idea that the *Maker's Wrath* is active. The time has come—"

Inura's attention was diverted by a tug on his soul.

The kind of tug that hadn't occurred in ten millennia. One of his faithful had just prayed for, and received, a miracle.

How? Who?

Everyone with that kind of connection had been exterminated millennia ago, hunted down systematically by Nefarius's agents. They'd been wiped out, because she knew it would hurt him. Had she missed one somehow?

He retreated into the corridor, and sketched a scrying spell. As the opaque surface of his magical mirror liquified into the paladin's location a subtle numbness crept through him.

The vision showed a paladin in the old style. One using armor and shield that had not been worn since the dragonflights had been unified. One that he'd not seen since the world that had borne his name had been obliterated by Nefarius.

Beside the paladin stood a figure in Heka Aten armor. Fully bonded Heka Aten armor. It could only be the captain of the *Word of Xal*.

What did it mean? It couldn't be coincidence that he'd discovered these necromancers at the precise moment where awarding his faithful with that knowledge might save countless lives.

Someone had manipulated events. A god, or a powerful mage, but someone. The question was...who? And when? Was this some prophecy orchestrated by a long dead deity as a last gasp of their power? Or was someone manipulating him into revealing himself?

Inura glanced back into the heart chamber at the unholy sun. This ship had become a threat to every living being in the sector, and it sounded as if they were ready to start taking action.

They had to be stopped. That was his responsibility. They were his children. The time for running had ended.

It was time to warn this paladin and the captain of the *Word of Xal*.

NOTE TO THE READER

If you enjoyed *Hatchling*, we have a complete seven-book prequel series with an ending already available, and it leads seamlessly into the book you just read.

We're also working on a pen & paper RPG and the Kickstarter went live right around the same time this book came out. You can learn more by signing up to the mailing list, or visit magitechchronicles.com and our Magitech Chronicles World Anvil page.

We've got maps, lore, character sheets, and a free set of rules you can use to generate your own character, plus a **Facebook group** where we geek out about this stuff.

I hope you enjoy and we can't wait to meet you!

-Chris

Printed in Great Britain
by Amazon

25280623R00178